RUINED CITY

RUINED CITY

by

NEVIL SHUTE Norway

HEINEMANN : LONDON

William Heinemann Ltd

LONDON MELBOURNE TORONTO

CAPE TOWN AUCKLAND

First published 1938 (Cassell)
New Edition 1951 (Heinemann)
Reprinted 1952, 1954, 1956, 1958, 1960
Reset 1965, Reprinted 1968

434 69904 7

Filmset, Printed and Bound in Great Britain by
Bookprint Limited, Crawley, Sussex

CHAPTER I

DURING the winter the pace accelerated tremendously for Mr. Henry Warren. In spite of the depression the banking house of Warren Sons and Mortimer had never had so much to do; as his marriage slid away to nothing the work piled heavily upon him.

The last fortnight was a bad one. Monday began with two conferences in the morning on the Moresley Corporation (1933) Development Loan, followed by lunch at the Savoy with Plumberg to discuss the Silver Conservation Pact. From Mr. Plumberg he went to call on Mr. Heinroth in Copthall Avenue to enlist his aid in the matter of the Finnish Equalisation Account; he found Mr. Heinroth difficult and it was not until after six o'clock that some measure of agreement was attained. He reached his office at about six-thirty and telephoned his house in Grosvenor Square about dinner; his butler told him that Mrs. Warren would be dining out.

He worked till half-past eight and dined, alone and rather extravagantly, at his club.

Tuesday continued the business of the Moresley Corporation and the Finnish Equalisation Account; the latter robbed him of his lunch. From twelve till four he was speaking on the telephone or waiting irritably for calls, calls from Helsingfors, from Stockholm, from Berlin. At four o'clock he spoke to Heinroth on the telephone, and then settled down to earnest work with all his staff to clear himself of business for the next two days. He left his office at ten minutes to nine; by ten o'clock he was at Croydon boarding the night plane for Stockholm.

He slept fitfully in the plane during the long crossing to Amsterdam in spite of the rainy, squally night. In the early hours he was awake from Amsterdam to Malmo, but in the cold grey dawn he got a little sleep between Malmo and Barkaby, the airport of Stockholm. By half-past nine he had had a cup of coffee and a shave and was in conference in a banking house in Stockholm; by one o'clock he was in the air again and on his way to Helsingfors.

He was in conference in Helsingfors from five o'clock till midnight. All the negotiations took place in German; he spoke the language competently but not fluently, and by midnight he was very tired. He rested for a few hours then, but by eight o'clock he was in the air again on the short sea crossing to Tallin, on his way down to Berlin.

He met his agent on the aerodrome at Tallin and made him travel with him on the next stage; they talked in German for an hour down to Riga. Then he went on alone, through Kaunas and Königsberg on to Berlin. He managed to sleep a little on the latter stage, and got out of the machine at Templehof dazed and unwell.

An hour later, spruce and neat, he was in conference again with his associates in Berlin; by nine o'clock he was back at the Templehof to catch the night mail plane for England. He dozed fitfully to Amsterdam, where he drank a cup of coffee with a cognac in the middle of the night; then he slept soundly, if uneasily, to Croydon. He reached his house in Grosvenor Square before the milk, before his servants were awake, slept for an hour, had a bath and dressed, and went down to his office in the City.

He did not see Elise. She did not normally appear before he left the house.

That day, Friday, was an easy day. He had a talk with Heinroth in the morning; the Finnish business moved another step upon its way. His secretary told him the result of the Council meeting of the Moresley Corporation—not so good. The secretary had made an appointment for him to meet them that afternoon, at four o'clock.

Moody and depressed, he lunched alone. If they didn't want the money, they needn't have it. Corporations had to cut their coat according to their cloth, like other people.

They came to him in the afternoon, a deputation of three. He knew them well, these members of the Finance Committee—Sir Thomas Lambe, the chairman, whose grocer's shops extended all around the city, Mr. Tom Bullock, who had been a petty officer in the Navy and now drove a tram, and the other one whose name he never managed to remember—Mr. Bung the Brewer. He greeted them courteously and settled them with cigarettes before his massive desk. The meeting was on.

A quarter of an hour later they had reached a deadlock.

'Taking it your way, Mr. Warren,' said the chairman, pink-cheeked and ruddy, 'it'd mean another fourpence on the rates—after allowing for the Park receipts. The Council won't like that.'

'Ratepayers won't like it, neither,' said Mr. Bullock. 'Not next November.'

Warren said quietly, 'I'm sorry, gentlemen.'

There was silence.

Mr. Bung the Brewer said wheezily, 'But there's the bottle factory waiting to come to Moresley, soon as we get these sites opened up with the Western Road. There's seventy employed, right from the start.'

'That's our point, Mr. Warren,' said the chairman. 'The development of these roads, opening up these sites,

3

will make this productive money. We shall be paying less in outdoor relief. We shall be getting an income from the factory sites. I cannot see that there will be any need for the special fund you have in mind.'

Warren said, 'I appreciate all that, Sir Thomas. But if, in fact, this scheme can pay its way, I see no objection to making the interest chargeable upon the general rate.'

'We don't get nowhere, way you look at it,' said Mr. Bullock. 'To develop the factory sites we've got to put up the rates, and if we put up the rates nobody won't come to take up factory sites, and money's gone for nowt.'

'That is a risk, of course,' said Warren. 'But that's your speculation.'

'Aye,' said Mr. Bullock, 'I noticed that. You get your money any road, even if whole of Moresley's on the dole.'

Warren bent forward, leaning both his elbows on the desk. 'This is a bank,' he said. 'I think I may say, a bank of good repute, Mr. Bullock.' A wintry smile moved across his face. 'Otherwise, I am sure you gentlemen would not be here this afternoon. We take in money on deposit, and it is my business to keep that money safe. We lend it out again at small interest on good security. It is no part of our business to take risks, or to make speculations with the money deposited with us. That is not our understanding with our depositors, and that is not our policy.'

Mr. Bullock drew himself up with a certain dignity. 'That's right, Mr. Warren,' he said. 'You're a bank, and you don't take no risk. We've come to you rather than to one of them fly-by-night financial houses because we're prudent business folk in Moresley, and we knew you did the loan in Staventon. But I want you to see it as we see it in the Council chamber.'

He paused for a moment, and considered. 'Three years ago we hadn't more than fifteen hundred unemployed in all Moresley,' he said. 'Last year we had seven thousand. This year, nine thousand five hundred. That's over twelve per cent of the people of Moresley on the dole, Mr. Warren—and still going up.' He stared at him earnestly. 'Moresley's a working town—always has been. We've never been what they call a depressed area, or anything of that. And Moresley's not going to become a depressed area, neither. We're out to fight that on the Council—we won't let that happen. But we want some help from the Bank to tide us over, help us get these sites attractive for new factories. In Moresley we don't call that speculation. Normal development, that's what we call it. In Moresley we reckon it's the job of everyone to do what he can to get the lads back to work. Banks, and all.'

There was a pause.

Warren leaned back in his arm-chair and said, 'I'm sorry.'

Sir Thomas said, 'Um—I am afraid the Council will have difficulty in proceeding on these lines. Let me be quite clear upon the matter. You require that provision should be made for the interest to be guaranteed from the general rate, in preference to all other payments. And that a resolution should be passed by the Council to that effect before the matter can proceed further.'

Warren inclined his head. 'That is so, Sir Thomas. Given that resolution we can at once proceed to the details of the finance you will require.'

Mr. Tom Bullock got up from his chair and stood erect. 'My bloody oath,' he said quietly, but firmly.

5

'And then they write this stuff about the banks helping industry. All the bloody banks do is to help themselves.'

The chairman was distressed and fluttered. 'Councillor Bullock—please . . .' he said. The deputation rose to take their leave.

Mr. Warren showed them courteously to the door. 'You may be right,' he said to the tram driver. 'But I think the business of helping the distressed areas lies more with the Government than with the banks.'

He turned back into his room alone, tired and stale. He wondered what would happen at their Council meeting; he did not greatly care. He would proceed with the matter if they wished; old Mortimer, moribund in his house at Godalming, liked Corporation loans and would be pleased. Warren himself had no objection to them provided that the money were very safe; that was the main thing in these times. But he could use the money better on the Continent.

His mind dwelt with pleasure on the Visgrad Waterworks, in Laevatia. Better than all the Corporation loans put together.

The buzzer on his desk sounded a low note. He pressed a switch, and the voice of his secretary spoke from the instrument.

'Mrs. Warren was on the telephone, sir. I told her you were in conference. Shall I get her now?'

'Please.' He was desperately tired. While he was waiting for his call he felt for a cigarette in the silver box upon his desk, fumbled a little, and dropped one upon the floor. He left it there, too tired to pick it up, took and lit another, and sank into his chair. The telephone bell rang.

His wife's voice spoke to him. 'Oh, Henry—is that you? It would be nicer if you answered me when I

6

rang up, dear. I rang you up over half an hour ago.'

He said patiently, 'I'm sorry, but I was in conference. Didn't Miss Stephens tell you?'

'She may have done—I'm afraid I don't pay much attention to Miss Stephens, dear. Henry, wherever have you been all this time? I haven't seen you for eight days.'

He thought for a moment. 'So long as that? Well, you were in Scotland last week, weren't you? I was at home Monday and Tuesday nights. Then I had to go to the Continent. I'll be dining in to-night.'

'To the Continent? Was it amusing?'

He said, 'Not very. I had to go to Helsingfors—and to Berlin.'

'Oh. Such a tiresome place, Helsingfors. All trees and water, and all those Finnish people so dull. I didn't bother to go on shore—they told me it simply wasn't worth it. I remember we played contract all afternoon. Tommy Samson won fifteen pounds off Violet. She was furious.'

He said patiently, 'I'll be dining in to-night, dear. I'll tell you all about it at dinner.'

She said, 'Oh yes. I've asked one or two people in to dinner, so you can tell us all about your trip.'

His face fell. 'Who's coming?'

'Only Violet and Mary, and Sir John and Lady Cohen, and Pamela Allnut. And Jerry Shaw and Lord Cheriton.'

His brows contracted in a frown. 'What do you want young Cheriton for? I didn't know you knew him.'

'Oh, don't be silly. Violet says he's terribly fun-making. And besides, Sir John wants to meet him.'

It had been in Warren's mind to tell his wife that he was dropping with fatigue, that he would dine quietly at his club, perhaps sleep there. He changed his mind. If Cohen had chickens to pluck, let him pluck them in his own house.

'All right,' he said. 'I'll be home about half-past six. Who's the other man?'

'What other man, dear?'

His face hardened. 'You've told me four women, and three men. You're not having an odd number?'

'Why, no, dear. There's Lord Cheriton, Sir John, Prince Ali, and Jerry Shaw.'

'Prince Ali Said is coming?'

'Yes, dear. I asked him.'

His face was very hard. 'All right. I'll be home at half-past six.'

He laid down the receiver and pressed the button for his confidential secretary, Mr. Thomas Morgan. 'I've got to go over and see Heinroth, Morgan,' he said. 'I shan't be back to-day.'

He went walking down Throgmorton Street towards Heinroth's office, tired and depressed. Two young jobbers on the steps of the exchange stopped tossing for half-crowns to watch him as he made his way through the crowd.

'Who's that?' said one.

'That's Henry Warren—Warren Sons and Mortimer. One of the soundest little houses in the City. He runs the business now. Don't you know him?'

The other shook his head. 'Looks as if he'd swallowed a bad oyster,' he remarked.

The other spun a coin into the air, and smiled. 'So would you,' he said, 'if your wife was sleeping with a black man every other night.'

His dinner party passed before Warren in a blur of fatigue. With Lady Cohen on the one hand and Pamela Allnut on the other he talked mechanically, alternately, and competently about hunting and glass furniture, about schools and ski-ing. At the far end of the table

8

his wife sat facing him, fair, slender and vivacious, between the subaltern callowness of young Lord Cheriton and the grave dignity of the Arab in tails and white waistcoat. Both of them, he reflected, worth half a million—more perhaps. Lord Cheriton he could tolerate, but he disliked the Arab very much indeed.

He roused himself a little with the brandy, when the ladies had left the room. Cohen had moved up to Cheriton and was talking about industry. 'Wonderful opportunities just now,' he was saying. 'In almost every line. Every day. One can't take all of them.'

'That's very interesting,' said Cheriton. 'You think this is the time to buy.'

'I do, most certainly. With discretion—of course.'

Warren set his glass down carefully. 'You may be right,' he said carefully. 'But it seems to me that you want the discretion of a nun and the vision of an archangel to buy these days.'

'I don't agree at all,' said Cohen. 'Look at gold.'

'No good looking at gold now,' said Warren. 'Tell me what to look at now—not what I might have looked at six months ago.'

A shadow passed quickly across Cohen's face. Warren thought. That got him. He's got those Bulongo mines on his hands. I wonder if he wanted to shove those off on Cheriton? He might be able to. That boy is fool enough for anything.

Prince Ali Said coughed delicately. 'For myself,' he said, 'I do not understand the Stock Exchange. I prefer to play with horses. I find that I can make money more certainly in that manner.'

Warren nodded. He could respect competence in all forms. 'That is because you act upon your own knowledge. It's when you start taking tips that the trouble starts.'

Cheriton laughed. 'Either on horses or the Stock Exchange,' he said fatuously.

Warren nodded. 'I'm a banker, of course. I don't take tips, and I don't make any great killings, but in my quiet way I get along all right—even in these times. But I wouldn't say this was the time to buy.'

'What would you do?' asked Cohen sullenly.

Warren smiled. 'I'd get a very big safe, and put it all in that—in gold—and sit on it,' he said. 'But real gold, I mean—none of this paper stuff.'

In the dim light beyond the shaded candles, at the back of the room, Evans his butler laid silver noiselessly upon a tray, covered it with green baize, and moved silently, unnoticed, from the room. He took the tray down to his pantry, transferred it to the silver cupboard, locked it up and pocketed the key. Then he went to the housekeeper's room.

Elsie, the housemaid, was sewing by the fire. 'Where's Mrs. Higgins?' he asked.

'Gone out to the pictures. Did you want her?'

He took down his pipe from the mantelpiece. 'I want a box of matches.'

'I've got some, Mr. Evans.' She watched him while he lit his pipe. 'Get any tit-bits?'

'They're trying to swindle that young Cheriton again.'

'Not Mr. Warren?'

'No, Cohen.'

She dropped her sewing on her lap. 'What did they want him to do?'

'Buy some dud mining shares, I think. Warren was trying to stall them off.'

'I'd believe anything you told me of that Cohen,'

she said. 'I think he's horrible.'

He nodded slowly. 'They're a useless crowd,' he said. 'I've been in service nearly forty years, ever since I was a little nipper in the stables. But I've never been in such a place as this.'

There was a little silence.

'That black man,' she said presently. 'He was up there again this afternoon. With the door open, too. I do think it's beastly.'

'It won't last for long,' said the butler. 'I reckon I know when a place is cracking up.'

He finished his pipe in silence, glanced at his watch, and went upstairs again to carry a tray of glasses, syphons, and decanters in to the big white drawing-room. Two tables of bridge were in progress, but Cohen and Cheriton were both dummy, and were talking earnestly aside, before the fire.

The evening passed for Warren in a blur of fatigue. He played efficiently and lost a little money to his guests by courtesy; one had to do that with Pamela Allnut in the game. Presently the rubbers came to an end; the final drinks, and then his guests were ready to depart.

He helped Cheriton into his coat. 'It's been pleasant meeting you again,' he said.

'A most delightful evening,' said the young man formally.

A thin smile curled round Warren's lips. 'You've enjoyed yourself?'

'Why—certainly.'

'I'm sorry to hear it.'

There was a momentary pause. 'Well, I don't quite know what to say to that,' said Cheriton.

'I'm sorry you came here to-night,' said Warren. 'It's been my pleasure. I hope it won't be your loss.'

The young man stared at him reflectively. 'You mean Cohen,' he said at last. 'Thanks for the tip.'

'I'm afraid my guests aren't quite your sort,' said Warren pleasantly. 'I wouldn't come again, if I were you.'

He saw the young man to the door, and turned back into the house. His wife was talking quietly to their last guest, the Arab, in the hall. They broke the talk off as he turned towards them.

'It's been a great pleasure to have had you here this evening, Prince Ali,' he said formally. 'I hope you'll come again.' He stared reflectively at the aquiline features, the fine olive texture of the skin. 'But there— I know you will.'

The olive darkened into brown. 'I have never enjoyed myself so much,' said the Prince. 'It was so kind of you . . .' He took his leave.

Warren turned to his wife. 'Did you enjoy your party?' he enquired.

She yawned, a little sullenly. 'Not a bit. I think that young Cheriton's a crashing bore. I wouldn't have had him, but for Violet Cohen. Said the old man wanted to meet him, or something. Why people can't manage for themselves . . .'

Warren glanced at the petulant features of his wife. He smiled a little. 'If that's the sort of entertainment they want,' he said, 'I suppose that's what you've got to give them.'

They went upstairs together. 'Did you meet anyone interesting in Berlin?' she asked idly.

'I was only there four or five hours. I met Heinroth's cousin with a couple of Finns.'

'Oh. That must have been terribly fun-making for you.'

Warren went to his own room. The firelight flickered on the walls and ceiling; on a chair before the glow his pyjamas were laid out to warm. He sat down to unlace his shoes, desperately tired. As he leaned forward the stiff collar of his evening shirt cut deep into his throat; his vision blurred, and a pressure grew upon his temples. He leaned back in his chair; the pressure eased and he began to feel more normal, but now there came a persistent drumming in his ears that would not stop.

'Christ,' he said half aloud. 'A ruddy nigger . . .' In that he was unjust, and he knew it; among the six or seven strains that went to make Prince Ali there was no negro blood.

He got up and loosed the collar at his throat, and undressed slowly. His business worries and responsibilities surged in his mind to the surging of the blood that thundered in his ears, Heinroth and Plumberg, the Moresley Corporation and the Finnish Equalisation Account. And Ali Said leering at him down the dinner table . . . in his own house.

He must sleep. He crossed to his dressing-table and took up a small white box, opened it and took out the little vial. It was empty. He threw it in the grate and took a fresh packet from a drawer, shook out three tablets of allonal, and swallowed them.

'Sleep,' he said, half aloud.

He got into his bed. Already he could feel his mind at ease; his worries were no longer the sharp torments they had been, but had become mere incidents of the day. Even Prince Ali was—an incident. He thought drowsily, as he settled in his bed, that cuckold was the word. It seemed to be the right word. He was not quite sure what a cuckold was, but it seemed probable

13

that he was one. Even that had now no power to worry him. It was an incident, merely an incident of the day.

He did not see his wife before he went down to the office in the morning, went in the car with Donaghue, his chauffeur, as was his habit. It was a Saturday but in the years of depression that meant little to him; he had been absent from his office for two days during the week, and might have to go away again. He settled down to clear up his arrears of work with Morgan, his girl secretary, his chief accountant, and three clerks. In the middle of the afternoon he ate a sandwich, drank a whisky and soda, and went on.

Hours later he stopped, suddenly, irrationally, in the middle of a sentence as it were. 'That's enough,' he said to Morgan. 'We'll go home now.'

'As you like, sir,' said his secretary. 'There are only the Czech payments to transfer. We can do those on Monday.'

'When do they fall due?'

'Not till the fourteenth.'

'Let me have them on Wednesday morning. I shan't be here on Monday. I'm going to Hull to-morrow night with Collins—the East Yorkshire thing. Ring me ten-thirty Monday morning at the Paragon, and give me the post.'

'Very good, sir.'

Warren glanced at his watch; the winter dusk had fallen long ago; it was half-past seven. 'I had no idea it was so late,' he said. On his way out he passed through the outer office; his three clerks and the girl were putting on their coats. He stopped and spoke to them. 'I'm sorry I've been so long,' he said with formal courtesy, 'and on a Saturday. Thank you for staying.' He passed on, out through the swing doors into the deserted City street.

'That's all right, far as it goes,' said one of the clerks. 'But look what time it is! Seven-thirty!'

'More hours, more money,' said another. He was a married man, and Warren paid his office overtime.

The girl pulled on her little hat.'I think he's looking terribly tired,' she said. 'Do you think all this they say about his wife is true?'

Warren went home and dined alone. His wife, he learned, was dining out, the butler did not know with whom.

He left for Hull after lunch next day, Sunday. As the train swept northwards Warren dozed uneasily in his empty compartment, twitching in his sleep from time to time and becoming suddenly awake. He reached Hull in the evening and dined alone in the hotel. Because he wished to form his own impression of the city he had not told his business associates of his arrival. He wished to be alone that night.

It was part of his routine. He liked to be alone for his first night in a new town, especially a town where he was to do business. He walked out in the wind-swept, empty streets after dinner, savouring the place, the broad streets, thin alleys; the gaunt factories and the mud-filled docks. He was not pleased with what he found. After an hour's walk he returned to the hotel having followed no conscious train of reasoning but entirely resolved that he must be careful; this was no place in which to take a chance. He felt the dominant psychology to be that of the town at the end of the road, stagnant and insular; the through traffic of the shipping, he felt, had not enlivened the place.

He went to his bed and lay restlessly awake till the

small hours. Then he got up and took an allonal.

All the next day he was in conference in Hull, a difficult, unsatisfactory day spent upon a difficult and unsatisfactory business. Towards evening he delivered an ultimatum which he knew would stay the wheels of progress for six months, and left on the night train for London, tired and depressed. His car met him at King's Cross in the winter dawn, and he went home to bathe and change, and drink a cup of coffee. Then he went down to the office.

In India, a few hours previously, a small brown man had stood in Congress for two hours and said his piece. That morning the Silver Conservation Pact lay in ruins; by eleven o'clock Warren had Plumberg in his office, a Plumberg who talked eloquently about adjustments of a minor nature to the scheme, and whose thin hands twitched nervously as he was talking. Warren spent the day in a welter of Indian politics broken by distracting snatches of his other work; in the afternoon he went with Plumberg to the India Office and sat in conference for two hours. In the evening he got rid of Plumberg and dined with the Secretary of State for India, quietly at a club. They talked far on into the night.

Wednesday was an easy day. He spent it largely with Heinroth; the Finnish business was going smoothly to a sound conclusion. He felt that he had done a good job of work in that quarter; his visit of the previous week had facilitated matters very much. In the afternoon he rang his house, meaning to speak to Elise, to ask her to dine with him that night and do a theatre. His butler told him she had gone to Paris, with Lady Cohen.

Warren dined alone that night.

Plumberg was with him most of the next day upon his Indo-Mexican agreement, schemed to save something from the silver wreckage that lay strewn about their feet. The Moresley Corporation met, and turned down his proposals. In the evening Heinroth rang him up; his cousin was in Paris with the Finns and would appreciate a further talk. Warren decided to go there next day.

He crossed by the earliest air service, and motored into Paris from Le Bourget before ten o'clock. He sat in conference for an hour with the Finns, then left to lunch with Heinroth's cousin, and to walk for an hour in the Bois. By four o'clock he was in conference again in the Hotel Splendide; by eight their business was concluded for the day.

'Kom,' said the leading Finn genially. 'We will now eat dinner after our great labours.'

They washed and went downstairs to the public rooms. The lounge was thronged with people; in the great dining-room the tables clustered thickly round a small bald patch of dancing-floor. They were in morning clothes, but the head waiter met them obsequiously and bowed them to a table reserved for them in an alcove, a quiet table where they could talk undisturbed. They settled to their meal, commenting now and then upon the dancers or the cabaret.

Presently Warren called the head waiter to him. 'The gentleman of colour at the table over on the other side,' he said. 'Prince Ali Said.'

'But certainly,' said the man. 'He is a friend of monsieur?'

'An acquaintance,' said Warren carelessly. 'He stays in the hotel?'

'But yes, monsieur.'

'And the lady?'

The man smiled gently. 'Monsieur . . .'

'I think I have met her in England,' said Warren quietly. 'If you could ascertain her name for me?'

'But certainly.'

He moved away among the crowd. In a few minutes he was back again. 'Monsieur,' he said. 'Her name is Miss Naughton. She is registered as British.'

'Ah, yes,' said Warren carelessly. 'She stays in the same suite?'

'But certainly.'

'I am infinitely obliged.'

The man bowed himself away, and Warren turned again to his companions. 'One meets so many people,' he said apologetically.

He stayed with them through a long dinner, to the coffee and cigars. At the end he made his apologies. 'I must catch the morning aeroplane for London,' he said, 'and I must get some sleep. We shall meet again in London, on the 20th. I shall look forward to that with great pleasure.'

He bade them good-bye, and went out to the lounge. 'Prince Ali Said,' he said. 'He is in his suite?'

The man lifted a telephone; Warren waited, idly studying airline and steamship posters. This was the end, he thought.

'The name, monsieur?'

'Ask if he will receive Mr. Henry Warren.'

The man spoke.

'He says, if you will go up, monsieur.'

He mounted swiftly in the lift; in the sitting-room of the suite the Prince received him, swarthy and immaculate in black and white. 'This is indeed a pleasure, my dear Warren,' he said courteously. 'You are staying in this hotel?'

'No longer than I can help,' said Warren. He glanced around the room, the deep carpets and the garish furniture. 'I came to have a few words with my wife.'

The Arab frowned in bewilderment. 'Surely you are making some mistake,' he said. 'You will not find your wife here.'

'That may be,' said Warren evenly. 'Because if I find her here, she will no longer be my wife.'

He stared at the other reflectively. 'I suppose if I were half a man I'd be knocking the stuffing out of you,' he said, 'or trying to. If you had been the first . . . But as it is, I think I'm through. I'm not going to make a lot of trouble over this. I'm going to get out, and leave you to it.'

He smiled. 'Perhaps, if my wife is not here, you would present me to Miss Naughton,' he said.

'I am afraid you are completely misinformed, Mr. Warren,' said the Arab. 'As you can see for yourself, I am staying here alone. It is true that Miss Naughton dined with me this evening, but she has now returned to her hotel.'

'In that case,' said Warren, 'we can take a look at the next room without disturbing her.' He moved methodically from room to room, opening cupboards and examining curtains.

The Arab watched him with a grave smile. 'A pleasant suite, is it not?' he said. 'I find this a very good hotel.'

'And a complaisant one,' said Warren.

He moved towards the door. 'I see that my wife is not here now,' he said, a little wearily. 'I suppose I ought to offer you my apologies. But I'm not going to.'

He left the Arab standing in the middle of his suite,

and went down to the writing-room upon the mezzanine. He wrote a note, and took it to the porter's desk.

'For Miss Naughton,' he said, and gave it to the man, with twenty francs. 'See that she gets it to-night.'

He went up slowly to his room, threw open the window of his balcony, and stood for a time in the cold air looking out over the roofs of Paris. Beneath him in the street the traffic ran, shadowy and remote; a flake or two of snow slipped past him in the night. His marriage had not been real to him for many years, but now that it was drawing to a close he knew that a great gap was opening in his life, how great he could not say. He only knew that he was coming to great changes, and that itself was difficult for him.

He grew cold at last, and turned back into the room. He unpacked his bag, slowly undressed, and went to bed. He took three tablets of his allonal to make him sleep.

He rose at eight next morning, had a bath and dressed, and ordered coffee in his room. He was seated at his breakfast when he heard a light knock on the outer door. He went to open it; his wife was there.

'Come in,' he said. 'Have some coffee?'

She shook her head, and fumbled with a cigarette. He lit it for her.

'You don't mind if I finish mine?'

She sat down in a chair, and watched him while he ate.

'Well, Henry,' she said at last. 'Where do we go from here?'

He set down his cup and turned to her. 'That's up to you, my dear.'

He considered for a moment. 'I don't know what you're doing here at all, and I'm not sure that I want to know. I didn't come here trailing you, or anything like that. I came on business yesterday, and saw you in the dining-room with Ali Said.'

She said, 'I might have known you came on business. You wouldn't take a day from that for me, would you?'

He said, 'You're probably right. In all these sort of things, there are faults on both sides. I know I've worked long hours for the last two years. But things aren't easy with this slump . . .' He always felt helpless in his dealings with Elise. In most marriages, he thought, the economic tie must make things easier; the wife had her job for which she drew her pay; she could not lightly give it up. Both husband and wife then had to work, he in the office and she in the home. With Elise it was different. She had her own money—plenty of it; a dissolution of their marriage would mean no material loss to her, no unavoidable discomfort. She was not dependent on her job for her security; therefore she took it lightly. To hold her he would have to live a great deal of her life, an idle life to be spent with idle people, following the fashion. It would be possible for him to do so; he had money in plenty to give up his work and retire. But he was only forty-three years old; his work was dear to him. Surely there was some compromise for them?

He said, 'I want you to pack your things and come back home with me to-day. When we get home, I'm going to make some changes.'

She blew a long cloud of cigarette smoke. 'What are they?'

'I'm going to sell the house. We're going to live in the country.'

'Are we, indeed? What part of the country?'

'Somewhere not far from London—Beaconsfield—Dorking—that sort of distance. On my part, I shall spend less time in London, and more at home. We might get some hunting in the winter.'

'Anything else?'

He met her eyes, mocking him. 'Yes,' he said savagely. 'A total exclusion of Prince Ali from your list of friends, and Cathcart, and the Cohens. I'll have no more of them.'

She laughed a little. 'I suppose I've brought that on myself.'

'I suppose you have,' he said.

'It's a pretty joyous sort of life that you've sketched out for me,' she observed. 'You evidently don't trust me in London, so I'm to live in the suburbs. If I'm good you'll take me out with the suburban drag on Saturday mornings. I'm to give up all my friends, and sit in the country alone and grow pansies.'

'That's it exactly,' said Warren. 'Those are my terms if we're going on together. I won't go on as we are. And on my part, I'll do everything I can to make you happy—on those lines.'

'And if I don't accept your terms?'

'I hope you will. If you don't, I shall divorce you.'

There was a little silence.

'Well,' she said, 'you'd better go ahead and do it.'

'You wouldn't like to have another try at carrying on together?'

She shook her head. 'You don't want me, and you know it. All you want is your work. That's all you ever think about, your work and your business friends. It's not as if you had to work as you do in order to live. You do it because that's what you like. You're never at home because you're away on business; you never take a holiday. What sort of a life do you think I lead, married to you? And now you want to shove me away

22

down in the suburbs, away from all my friends and everyone I know. I'm certainly not going to agree to that. If that's the way you feel, the sooner we bring it to an end the better.'

'You mean that?'

'I most certainly do.' She paused. 'I shall be staying here till Monday; then I shall be going down to Cannes, to Nita Menzies. You can send the papers there.'

He stood and stared out of the window at the leaden roofs beneath a leaden sky, the running traffic in the street below.

'As you like,' he said at last. 'I'm sorry that we had to come to this.'

He crossed to London by the midday air service, and went straight to his office. He got there about four o'clock in the afternoon and plunged into his work. He had a long conversation on the telephone with Heinroth, and another with his banking associates in Stockholm. He cleared two days of correspondence in half an hour's dictation; his typist left him with a sense of grievance and a batch of work that would keep her back an hour and spoil her evening.

'Half-past five!' she said to her companion in their room, 'and all these letters to be done! It's too bad! But my dear, have you seen him? He's looking simply awful! Wonder what's been happening?'

In his own room Warren sat with Morgan, his confidential secretary. 'That's the Finnish business, then,' he said. 'We're practically home on that. Get the agreements drawn in draft, and we'll get Heinroth to look over them. Then you can circulate them to the Board. You've got it on the agenda?'

'I have arranged that, sir.'

He passed a hand wearily across his eyes. 'We shan't hear much of Plumberg for a time. The Moresley Corporation thing is dead, I think. I'm not going to do anything with that chap Cantello.'

'There's the Laevatian Oil Development.'

'Let it sweat. I may be irregular at the office for the next week or so. I've got some personal matters to clear up.'

The secretary hesitated. 'If I may say so, why don't you take a holiday? You're looking very tired. I'm sure the Board would wish you not to overdo things, sir.'

'That's all right,' said Warren irritably. 'I may be away for a day or two. Tell Miss Sale to let me have those letters as soon as they're ready. I'm going home then.'

Morgan left him, and he sat alone in his empty office, his fingers drumming nervously upon the leather of the empty desk in front of him. He had said that he was going home; to what sort of home was he going? He pressed a key and spoke into the desk telephone; they were to ring his house and say that he would be in to dinner. He must sell that house, he thought. He must discharge the servants. He would live in a flat, perhaps in Pall Mall or the Albany. He must write to Elise to remove her things. He must see his lawyer. He must go through the tedious, intolerable formalities of a divorce to win a freedom that he did not want. He must start in middle age to build up another life, new interests.

'It's going to be lots of fun,' he said bitterly.

He got up from his desk, and paced up and down the office. In a minute or two he rang irritably for his letters; one or two appeared, which he signed; the remainder were unfinished. He spoke to Morgan on the internal telephone.

'I'm going now. You'd better sign those letters for me.' He put on his hat and coat and left the office.

He dined alone that night in his deserted house, sombre in dinner jacket in the empty dining-room, with shadows flickering in the corners from the candles on the table. His butler served him silently, efficiently; Warren ate very little. He took his coffee in the library before the fire; when he had served it Evans waited for a moment by his side.

Warren looked up. 'What is it, Evans?'

'Could I have a word with you, sir?'

'Certainly. Go ahead.'

The man coughed. 'I am afraid I must give you my notice, sir. I am sorry to inconvenience you, but I would like to leave in a month's time.'

Warren was silent for a minute, sipping his coffee. Then he said, 'I'm sorry to hear that, Evans. Why do you want to go?'

The man hesitated, and then said awkwardly, 'No particular reason, sir. Just that I can't feel settled here.'

'Is the money all right?'

'Oh, quite all right, sir. But I feel that I should be better for a change.'

Warren glanced up at the man, standing deferentially before him. 'I see. As a matter of fact, Evans, I was going to speak to all of you to-morrow. Mrs. Warren will not be coming back to live here. I'm closing down this house, and going to live in chambers.'

'I am very sorry to hear that, sir.'

Warren nodded. 'I was going to give you all a month's notice, with three months' wages. So you needn't feel you're inconveniencing me.'

'That is very generous treatment, sir. I am sure the staff will appreciate your kindness, in the circumstances.' He hesitated. 'With things the way they are, sir, I am sorry that I gave you notice. But I wasn't to know.'

'That's all right. As a matter of interest, why did you want to leave?'

The butler hesitated again. 'I don't know that I can quite answer that, sir. But it hasn't been the sort of house that one would care to spend one's life in, if you understand what I mean.'

Warren said, 'I understand.' He nodded to the man.

'All right Evans—that'll do. I'll see you all in the morning.'

The man left him, and he sat for a long time before the fire, quiet and motionless, full of reflection. So that was it. His house, his mode of life, had become so notorious that decent servants wouldn't stay with him; they had their own lives to consider. He did not blame them. But if that was what his servants thought about it all, what would London and the City think?

Prince Ali Said . . . Already he could frame the limericks and the conundrums in his mind. He knew the Stock Exchange.

He sat on in the library, quiet, without reading; as the fire died the shadows closed in upon him. He had worked hard all his life. He had been in the Gunners in the War and had risen to command a battery; he could still remember the sequence of his firing orders, the colours of the different grades of shell, and that you concentrated when the aiming point was in the rear. He had gone into his father's bank at the Armistice and had worked hard in the City for the last fifteen years.

His life, he thought, was more than half over. He had worked hard since he was a boy; what had he got to show for it?

His wife had left him, had preferred a coloured man. His house was one that decent people would not stay in, even if they were servants. He had few friends; he worked too hard for that. His health was still good, but he had grown nervous and irritable; that was the work again, the difficulty that he had in sleeping due to lack of exercise, perhaps, due also to the drugs he took to make him sleep. In the morning he would take the necessary steps to close the house and put it up for sale. Then, he supposed, he would go and live in a service flat, and try to

27

build up a new life—for what? For more work? He had worked hard for fifteen years and had got nothing, it seemed to him, that was worth having.

Presently he left the library and went up to his room. He stood for a time looking at his face in the mirror; he saw it to be lined and haggard, the face of a man older than his years. He turned away, and went mechanically to the drawer of his dressing-table; he would not sleep that night without the assistance of his allonal.

He took the little vial in his hand. He saw an old face twitching at him from the mirror; the battery major straightened up, a gust of passion swept over him. 'My God,' he said aloud. 'I'm looking like a corpse.' Impulsively he threw the vial in the fire and turned towards his bed.

He hardly slept at all that night.

He set about his business early next morning, the keen mind dulled and impeded with fatigue. He saw the servants after breakfast and gave them, in hard, business-like fashion, the gist of what he had already told the butler; a month's notice with three months' pay. Then he sat down and wrote a letter to Elise, hard and efficient, to ask her to remove her things from the house within the month, before he put the furniture in store. He paid a visit to a house agent. And then he went to his solicitor, and sat in conference with him for an hour.

He lunched at a solitary table in his club, reserved and aloof. In the smoking-room, over his coffee, he fell into an uneasy sleep and woke after twenty minutes of twitching insensibility, dazed and unwell.

He went down to his office.

In the house that he had left the servants gathered round to talk about their notice, dispersed to make pretence of work, and gathered round again. 'I won't say but what three months' pay will be a comfort and a nest egg to put by,' said the cook. 'But what a thing to happen in the house!'

'I never did like black gentlemen,' said Elsie. 'That Prince Ali, he gave me the shudders the first time I saw him. What she could see in him . . .'

Donaghue, the chauffeur, winked at Evans. 'The blacker the berry, the sweeter the juice, as you might say.'

'Not in my kitchen, *if* you please, Mr. Donaghue,' said the cook with dignity.

'Sorry,' said the chauffeur.

'It's a pity that it had to happen now,' said Evans. 'I'd hoped to get away before the bubble bust. It doesn't do one any good in getting a new place, this sort of thing.'

'That's what I say, Mr. Evans,' said the cook. 'It makes things very difficult, I'm sure. Mistresses don't like it, say what you will.'

'Well,' said the chauffeur. 'She's got a nice new place, and no mistake.'

'I wouldn't be too sure she'll keep it,' said Evans.

'Ah,' said the cook darkly. 'The evil stoop and pick up luck.'

They moved away about their work again. Donaghue followed Elsie out into the hall. 'It's a rotten break-up, this,' he said. 'Just as we were beginning to get to know each other, too.' He had only been there for about two months. He was cursing himself, boyishly and miserably, that he had not made more headway with the girl in that two months. He hadn't wanted to rush things. And now this bust-up had come.

'I'm sorry, too,' she said. 'But that's life all over, that is. Just as you think you've got nicely settled down, something happens.'

'That's right,' he said enthusiastically. 'I've often thought it was like that.'

They stood in silent, intimate communion for a moment.

He mustered his courage. 'Were you doing anything to-morrow afternoon? Your half day, isn't it?'

She said, 'I always go and see my Aunt Millie, at Streatham. She's been ever so good to me since I came to London.'

'I was wondering if you'd like to see a picture,' he said awkwardly. 'There's some good ones on . . .'

She smiled radiantly on him. 'That's ever so nice of you, Mr. Donaghue,' she said. 'I could see Aunt Millie on Sunday. I could get ready by half-past two.'

'That's a date,' he said, and went to polish a clean car in an exultant dream.

Warren worked steadily for some hours in his office. He cleared up the arrears of his work with some half-formed idea that he might go away. He was tired and stale. He had no particular desire to take a holiday, but he could not go on in Grosvenor Square alone. He felt that he must have a break in his routine.

'Looking like death again this afternoon,' remarked his typist to her friend. 'I bet there's something wrong.'

He knocked a pencil from his desk in the late afternoon, and stooped to pick it up. A sudden cramp shot through his abdomen and for a minute he was wrung with pain; then it relaxed, and he was sitting motionless in his chair, a little white and breathing very carefully for fear it would come on again. Presently he began to move, cautiously at first, then with increasing confidence. 'Exercise,' he thought. 'I ought to get more exercise. I'll die at fifty if I don't look out.'

He left the office at about seven o'clock and walked part of the way home through the wet, lamp-lit streets in pursuit of his new resolution. He went down Cheapside, over Holborn Viaduct, past Gamage's and Kingsway nearly to Tottenham Court Road. There he was tired and a little faint, and took a taxi to his house in Grosvenor Square. 'I can't go letting myself get run down like this,' he thought. 'I'd better get away and get some exercise.'

He had a whisky and a bath when he got home, and felt refreshed; he put on a dinner jacket and went down to dine alone. With the first mouthful his appetite left him; he ate very little, and went through into the library for coffee. He drank two cups of coffee and a little brandy, and felt better. He sat in his deep chair before the fire, and faced the problem of his sleep.

He knew he would not sleep. He had hardly slept at all the previous night; he knew that it would be the same again. He would not sleep without his allonal, and he had done with that. You need to be physically tired to sleep; it was imperative to him that he should get more exercise, at once, and quickly. He must get away somewhere, and walk. If he walked twenty miles a day for the next week sleep would return to him, he knew; walking was what his body clamoured for. It would rid him of this sick feeling, would clean his mind and body as they needed to be cleaned. Twenty miles a day, and for a week on end.

That was what he would do, to-morrow. But for this night ahead of him, in some way he must get through that. Queer, this matter of his sleep. If he were travelling, in car or train or aeroplane, he would be able to compose his mind, to rest and doze, and fall into a sleep of sorts; in bed he could not sleep without his allonal. But he could sleep in a motor-car.

And that would get him right away, and he could walk. Twenty miles a day; till he was well.

He rose and pressed the bell. He glanced at his watch; it was ten o'clock. When Evans came, he said:

'Is Donaghue about?'

'In the housekeeper's room, sir.'

'Tell him I want the car. In half an hour.'

'Very good, sir.'

'Tell him to get the tank filled up, and put some warm clothes on. I may be going a long way.'

He went up to his room and changed into an old business suit that he had bought in the United States. He put on a heavy ulster and a scarf, and gave Evans a flask to fill with brandy. These completed his preparations for the road; he looked at the contents of his note-case. He had about eighteen pounds. That, he thought, would see him through.

In the housekeeper's room Donaghue was making similar preparations, swearing a little to himself. He had no fancy for a drive of unknown length on a cold night in February.

Elsie came to him with a little packet in her hands.

'I cut you some sandwiches, Mr. Donaghue,' she said, a little shyly, 'and there's a bit of seed cake. I do hope he won't keep you out too late.'

He took them gratefully, and mumbled his thanks. 'See you half-past two to-morrow, anyway,' he said. 'Even if it makes me miss my breakfast.'

She smiled at him. 'You wouldn't rather we put it off?'

'Not much. I'll be back.'

He had already brought the car to the door; he went out to it now, and Evans went into the library.

'The car is quite ready, sir.'

32

Warren rose slowly from his chair, in ulster and scarf. He was feeling unwell, and the prospect of a long night drive seemed less attractive to him now, but he might as well go. He would probably sleep a little, anyway.

'All right, Evans,' he said. 'I may be away for a few days.'

The butler hesitated in surprise. 'Shall I pack a bag, sir?'

'No, thanks. I shan't want that.'

He went out to the car; although the night outside was cold he was glad to be leaving that house. Donaghue, smart in chauffeur's cap and long blue coat with silver buttons, held the door open for him; Warren got in and Evans handed in a couple of rugs. They stood for a moment then, holding open the door of the limousine.

'Where to, sir?' asked Donaghue.

'Get on the Great North Road,' said Warren absently. 'Go on till I tell you to stop.'

Evans and Donaghue exchanged glances of incomprehension. Then the chauffeur said, 'Very good, sir,' and got in to his seat; in turn he wrapped a rug around him and the car moved off. Warren leaned forward and switched off the interior light, and settled down in the back seat.

The car moved forward through Mayfair, up Orchard Street and Baker Street, past Lord's and the Swiss Cottage on to Finchley. A light rain was falling and the streets were wet and empty; Donaghue settled to his wheel and wondered what the night would bring for him. He liked Warren, and was sorry for him; he thought that he had suffered a raw deal. Apart from that, he trusted him implicitly. At the same time, there was no denying that his master was looking mighty queer; Cook had been worried that he ate so little dinner. Maybe he would like a cup of coffee later on.

He drove out on the by-pass, shifted and relaxed into the driving seat, and set himself to the night's work.

In the rear seat of the limousine Warren lay crossways in one corner, quiet and at rest. He was in darkness; for a time he watched the lights and street signs as they passed the windows opposite him. Presently rain blurred the windows and the lights grew more infrequent; soon they were driving through the darkness on a broad, wet ribbon of road lit by the headlights for five hundred yards. The purring of the engine, the wet swish of the tyres, the gentle, easy motion lulled him to a doze, the doze merged into something deeper, and he slept.

Through the wet night the limousine swept on, running at quarter-power at a steady forty-five, untired and effortless. Donaghue had produced a bottle of boiled sweets and sucked them as he drove; occasionally he smoked a cigarette. The rain stopped and began again; it went on intermittently all through the night.

At Welwyn they came out on the old road and drove on north, through Baldock and Biggleswade, past St. Neots and Huntingdon, by Norman Cross, over the bridge at Wansford and to Stamford. There Donaghue slowed down and peered into the rear seat. Warren appeared to be asleep. He shrugged his shoulders, and drove on.

Forty minutes later he ran down the hill into Grantham, slowed down, and finally stopped at a garage to fill up. The all-night hand came sleepily to the pump; Donaghue got down from his seat and busied himself about the car.

Through the rain-spotted window-glass he looked at Warren, saw he was awake. He opened the door.

34

'Stopped here for some petrol, sir,' he said. 'Just about ready to go on.'

'Got enough money?' asked Warren without moving.

'Quite all right, sir.'

Warren turned his head. 'What place is this?'

'Grantham.' The chauffeur hesitated. 'Would you like a cup of coffee, or tea, sir? There's a place open up the road.'

'No thanks. Get one yourself, if you like.'

'I'm all right for the present, thank you, sir. Still straight on north?'

'Straight on,' said Warren. 'Get up into the hills north-west of Newcastle. Between Newcastle and Carlisle.'

'Very good sir,' said the chauffeur. He closed the door, and turned to pay for petrol.

'Going far?' enquired the garage hand.

'Two hundred bloody miles, or so,' said Donaghue. 'I wish I was a dog with a good home.'

He drove out on to the deserted roads in the dark night. From time to time he passed a lorry or an all-night coach roaring along at sixty in a blaze of head-lights; there was nothing else on the road. At Newark he screwed round and peered through the screen behind his back; Warren appeared to be asleep again. He glanced at his watch; it was a quarter to two. Donaghue drove on.

He passed through Tuxford and Retford. Near Bawtry he got out the sandwiches that Elsie had put up for him, and ate them as he drove. It was rotten about the picture he was taking her to; looked as though he'd have to send a telegram. He thought she'd under-stand. He ate her seed cake. He passed through Doncaster.

35

'Another of these bloody towns,' he said. 'Wonder how many more there are?'

He was a young man of a good physique; he was growing tired, but he was not sleepy. He left Ferrybridge behind him, and Wetherby; in Boroughbridge it was pitch dark but there were one or two people in the streets, to his surprise. 'They get up early in these parts,' he thought. It was about half-past four, and still raining a little.

The limousine went flying up the long stretch of Roman road to Catterick, twenty miles away, past Middleton and Leeming Bar. At Scotch Corner he kept north and did not bear away, through Piercebridge and skirting Darlington. He was driving slower now, by map, through Witton-le-Wear and Dan's Castle, where he began to see the shadow of the hedges in the dawn. It had stopped raining. He bore away towards the northwest, leaving Newcastle on the right by ten or fifteen miles; at Rowley it was light enough for him to drive without his lights. Presently he dropped down into Broomhaugh, and drove on a little up the valley of the Tyne.

He screwed round stiffly and looked over his shoulder; Warren was awake. 'This is the Newcastle to Carlisle road, sir,' he said.

'Stop here,' said Warren. 'Let me see your map.'

The chauffeur drew up by the roadside and handed his map through the glass partition. It was about seven o'clock, quite light enough to see the countryside; a raw, windy morning with a wrack of low, scudding cloud down on the hills.

Warren asked, 'Where are we now?'

'That's Corbridge, sir, just over there. The river is the Tyne.'

'I've got it,' said Warren. He studied the map for some minutes, then gave it back to Donaghue. 'Go on towards Carlisle,' he said. 'Stop when you get to that place Greenhead at the top of the pass.'

Donaghue studied the map for a minute, and said, 'Very good, sir.' He slipped round to his wheel again, and drove on.

In half an hour he drew up by the side of the road. 'This is the place you said, sir.'

Warren laid aside his rugs, stretched a little, and got out of the car. The morning air was crisp and bracing to him; he had slept most of the night through, and he was feeling well. He looked around to see what sort of place this was. He saw black, heather-covered hills, a junction of two roads, a railway and a wayside station, one or two houses. The grey clouds went racing past only a few hundred feet above his head to wreathe about the hills; it was infinitely desolate.

'This will do,' he said aloud. He turned back to the car.

'You can leave me here,' he said to Donaghue. 'I'm going to walk a bit. Go down into Carlisle and put up there. I shan't want you any longer. Get some sleep, and then get along back to London.'

'Very good, sir.' The chauffeur hesitated. 'Can I get you anything before I go? Some breakfast, sir?'

'That's all right, thanks. Wait—leave me your map.'

Donaghue offered a selection; Warren picked out a couple of the Ordnance Survey and stuffed them in the pocket of his ulster.

'That will do,' he said. 'Now, off you go. Tell Evans I'll be back in London in about a week.'

The chauffeur was uneasy. He would have liked to have stayed, to have seen his master left in better circumstances, but he had little option in the matter. He said

'Good-bye, sir,' and let in his clutch, and went running down the hill towards Carlisle.

He was a young and vigorous man, not unduly tired by having driven a good car all night. He was three hundred miles from London, where a girl was waiting for him; as he ate his breakfast an idea was forming in his mind. He could make a quick run down the North road in the limousine, average forty-five, easy. Forty-five into three hundred miles, that made six and two-third hours. Allow a bit for going into London—call it seven hours. He looked at his watch; be on the road again by half-past eight. That meant home by half-past three, an hour late, but still with most of her half-day to go. And it wasn't as if he was really tired.

A girl would like a chap to put himself about like that for her.

He paid his bill, and started on the London road.

In the middle of the morning, running at a high speed three miles short of Retford, a small car turned out suddenly across his path. At eighty miles an hour you cannot swerve and dodge; the limousine hit the near-front wheel to off-front wheel and threw the small car to the hedge. Itself it was deflected to the right side of the road to hit a five-ton lorry coming from the town. When finally they got the wreckage off him, Donaghue was dead.

Elsie sat waiting for him all that afternoon. I believe she is waiting for him still.

CHAPTER III

WARREN was hungry. He watched the car depart, then walked down to the station to enquire where he could get some food. A solitary porter cleaning lamps directed him to a cottage half a mile away that in the season sold meals to summer visitors. Warren set out up the road.

As he went, his hand strayed to his unshaven chin. He had no razor, and to get one in this district would be practically impossible; he must give up that. He would have to do something about his teeth, though; washing could wait an opportunity. Savages cleaned their teeth on bits of stick; he could not see himself performing with a bit of heather. It was altogether in a lighter mood that he arrived at the cottage.

A woman, not very old but bent with rheumatism, opened the door to him. Warren asked for breakfast. 'I could do a pair of eggs an' a cup o' tea,' she said doubtfully. 'I haven't any baker's bread this time o' year. Ye'll have to have just what we have ourselves.'

He sat at her kitchen table while she busied herself to get him breakfast. As he waited, he studied the map; he found that he was very near the Wall. North-east seemed to be the best direction if he wanted exercise; a track led up across the moor in the direction of Bellingham and the Cheviots. From the contours it appeared that that would give him all the exercise he wanted for a week or two.

She brought him two fried eggs, a flat home-made loaf

of brownish bread, butter and jam and a pot of strong tea. He ate ravenously at first but with a quickly fading appetite; it was all that he could do to get through the second egg. He had several cups of tea, however, and felt satisfied and well, although he had not eaten very much.

He lit a pipe, paid her the shilling that she asked him for the meal, and, as an afterthought, bought one of her flat and dirty-looking loaves for twopence. From the look of the map it seemed unlikely that he would find a restaurant for lunch; it would be better to take what food he could with him. He broke the loaf into two halves and put one in each pocket of his ulster. Then he set out along the track up on to the moor.

He walked all day, striding along over the black sodden moors, his ulster pulled about his ears. It rained most of the day; a thin, persistent misty drizzle that cleared in the evening as he dropped down into Bellingham. All day he kept to a rough track that wound among the heather-covered hills, always in seeming danger of obliteration, never entirely disappearing. He was not hungry, rather curiously. He ate a few mouthfuls of his bread in the middle of the day; the remainder crumbled in the pockets of his ulster.

He got to Bellingham at about five o'clock after walking for eight hours or so; he covered the last mile in semi-darkness. He was very weary physically, and that same weariness gave him an easy mind; he knew that if he got a decent bed he would sleep naturally that night. Moreover, he was far too tired to think, and that to him was relaxation and relief. He found an inn in the village, where they looked at him askance, wet and unshaven, dirty and with no luggage.

'Aye,' said the landlord, 'we've got beds. Maybe you'll find the house a bit expensive. We charge ten shillings deposit for them as comes without bag or baggage.'

'Seems reasonable enough,' said Warren. He produced his note-case and put down the money; the man's manner altered for the better.

'We has to be careful,' he explained apologetically, 'or you'd be getting queer company. I never see so many on the roads as there are this year.'

'Out of a job?' asked Warren.

'Aye, walking the roads. They say there's more work in the south these days, but I dunno. This is your room. I'll bring up some hot water in a minute.'

He washed and went downstairs to a high tea of ham and eggs, and marmalade, and cherry cake. In the coffee room there was nothing to read but a few copies of the motoring journals of the previous summer, and a queer paper about cattle-breeding that he could not understand. He was tired and disinclined to sit and gossip in the bar with the landlord and his cronies. He went to bed at about half-past seven, leaving his ulster and suit to be dried before the kitchen fire.

He slept in his underclothes, a thing he had not done since the War. It had the pleasure of novelty for him, brought back old times and made him feel a subaltern again. He slept soundly for about five hours, got up and had a drink of water, and then slept again till dawn.

His clothes were stacked outside his door when he got up. The suit had shrunk a little and the ulster was no longer the fine fleecy garment it had been; Warren smiled quietly at his reflection in the glass. He did not mind, in fact he rather welcomed, the change; it made him look a little less conspicuous. He went down to his breakfast with a lighter heart than he had had for some months.

Again he was not hungry, and ate very little.

It was a better morning, cold and raw, but fine. He paid his bill and set out on the road again. Again he kept to moorland tracks all day, trending north-east; now and again he passed through tiny hamlets in the folds of the black hills, or crossed a road. It was better going; from time to time a watery sun lit up the barren country, and was lost again in racing cloud.

Warren walked steadily all through the day. He was not feeling fit; a stale, tired feeling dulled his pleasure in the exercise. Again he had no lunch except a mouthful of bread from his pocket, and did not feel the need of any. Towards sunset he came out on a hill-top; the sky had cleared and over to the east, some ten or fifteen miles away, he saw a grey line of the sea.

He left the hill and dropped down to the valley, where the smoke of houses rose among the trees. Getting over a gate into the main road he dropped down heavily, and in an instant he was wrung with the same stabbing, muscular pain that he had two days before in the office. He sank down on the grass verge of the road and lay there gasping for a moment, white and shaken; slowly the sharpness of the pain eased, and left only a dull ache behind.

'God, but I'm soft,' he muttered to himself. 'I'll never let myself get down like this again.'

After a time he got up from the grass and walked slowly for the half mile to the village. Again he put up at the inn; he felt rested and refreshed after his tea, and went out to the village cinema.

That night he stripped and examined his abdomen with care, thinking of rupture. He found nothing wrong and came to the conclusion that his pain was muscular alone. He sat for a time in bed studying his maps by the light of a flickering candle. It might well be that he was taking things too hard, bearing in mind that he had taken little exercise for years. To-morrow he would not go on the hills. The coast was not so far; he would go gently down to the sea and strike northwards up the coast; then on the following day he could turn north-westwards to the hills again.

Moreover, there were towns down there. He could buy a razor, or perhaps get shaved.

He turned to sleep. Already London and his house seemed infinitely distant to him; his troubles had sunk deep into the background of his mind, things that had happened to him very long ago, that could not touch him now. If anything were needed to expunge them from his mind the little pain that he had had had done it; he rested for the first time in some months with an easy mind, only concerned about the physical circumstances of his present life. He slept.

The morning dawned wet and chilly again. He paid his bill and turned towards the east, tramping in a windy, drizzling rain. The road ran downhill into farming land, a change from the rough moors that he had traversed for the last few days. Although he kept to the road and it was easy walking he was curiously tired; he went slowly with an ache and heaviness where he had had the muscular pain the night before. He began to have his doubts about that muscular pain.

By the middle of the day his doubts were doubts no longer.

He was perhaps five miles from the coast. Tired, he sat down for a few minutes at a cross-roads to smoke a cigarette, when suddenly the pain flared up and pierced him through. He clutched himself and bent up double on the grass; the cigarette fell from his mouth and lay there smouldering beside him.

'God,' he whispered, white to the lips. 'It'll pass off in a minute.'

But it did not pass off. It continued and grew worse, with a throbbing deep down in his abdomen that could not be merely muscular. He lay there for a quarter of an hour in great pain; one or two cars passed by without stopping.

'Better get going somewhere,' he muttered to himself at last. 'It's no good stopping here.'

He struggled to his feet and set himself to walk a quarter of a mile back to a house that he had passed. He covered about a hundred yards, and then he fell by the edge of the road. He heard a rumbling behind him and struggled to a sitting posture, raising one hand.

The lorry drew up to a standstill. The driver remained sitting at his wheel, looking down upon him curiously.

'What's up with you, chum?' he enquired.

Warren said something unintelligible. The driver climbed down and took him by the shoulder, turning him to look into his face. 'Hey, what's the matter, chum?' he said. 'You got it bad?'

'Hell of a pain,' gasped Warren. 'In my guts. Be a good sort. Get me to a doctor.'

The driver paused, irresolute. 'Don't know about a doctor—I'm a stranger in these parts.' And then he said, 'Buck up, chum. I'll see you right.'

Two cars, following each other close, had drawn up at the lorry blocking the road; one of them was full of men. In a minute there was a little crowd around. 'Bloke taken sick,' said the lorry driver. 'Give us a hand with him, an' put him up in the back. I'll take him somewhere.'

The lorry was half full of sacks of cattle food, with a

strange, sweet smell. There was a bustling about, letting down the tail-board, and adjusting sacks; somebody bent over Warren and removed his collar, which was cutting deep into his neck. Then there were many hands about him and he was lifted shoulder-high in a wild blur of pain, passed into the hands of other men standing in the lorry, and deposited on the sacks. The lorry driver made him as comfortable as possible.

'Won't be long now,' he said. 'I'll see you right. That all comfy now?'

'That's all right,' said Warren feebly. 'I'll be all right here. Get me to a doctor.'

'Won't be two jiffys now, chum,' said the driver. He got down from the lorry and put up the tail-board; then with a jerk the vehicle moved on.

Warren lay wedged between the sacks, dazed and in great pain. He had lost his collar and his shirt was open at the neck, for which he felt relief; presently an emptiness about his clothes made him feel his breast pocket, to discover that his wallet was gone. The fact impressed itself upon his consciousness but did not worry him; he was in too much pain for that.

Presently the lorry came to a standstill and he heard the driver speaking from the cab. 'Got a bloke in the back what's taken bad. Picked him up on the road, three, four miles back. Sick in the stomach, I reckon. Says he wants to be taken to a doctor. What'll I do?'

'Sick in the stomach? Let's 'ave a look at him.'

The tail-board was let down, and a constable climbed in on to the sacks. He knelt beside Warren. 'What's all this?' he asked. 'Where's the pain?'

'In my guts,' said Warren. 'It's serious. Is there a doctor here?'

'No doctor here,' said the constable. 'Did it come on sudden-like?' 'Ave you ever had it before?'

'I had spasm of it about three days ago,' said Warren. 'And then I had another yesterday. Just short ones, they were. Nothing like this.' And then he said suddenly, 'I'm going to be sick.' Which he was.

They watched with interest. 'Well,' said the constable at last, 'we can't do nothing for him here. Where you heading for?'

'Burnton,' said the driver. 'I got to dump this load an' get back to Newcastle to-night.'

'Going by Sharples?'

'That's right.'

'Better drop him off at the hospital. You know where that is?'

'Round the back of Palmer Street, ain't it?'

'Aye,' said the constable, 'that's right. You drop him off there, and I'll telephone to say he's coming.' He produced his notebook, and walked round to the back of the lorry. He took the number carefully, took a few particulars, and the lorry drove on.

Warren lay jolting on the sacks in a stupor of pain for many miles. Presently he knew that they were entering a town. They drove on for a time, seemingly on cobbled streets. Then the lorry drew up to a stand-still, and he heard the driver get down.

And presently he heard the driver's voice again. 'You'll want to get a stretcher to him, mate. Sick in the stomach, he is.'

A porter got into the lorry. 'Come, lad,' he said. 'Let's get ye oot o' this.' Warren found himself assisted from the lorry and handled competently in the hospital. They took him down an echoing corridor and put him in the casualty room, and laid him on an examination couch.

46

He wanted to see the lorry driver to thank him, but the man had disappeared. He had no time to lose.

A very young house surgeon came with a sister; together they examined him, and asked a few questions. His abdomen was rigid as a board. 'Peritonitis,' said the young man to the sister. 'And yet—I don't know. Not quite like that, to me.'

He straightened up. 'All right, get him along to the ward and get him ready. 'I'll ring up Dr. Miller.'

The sister said, 'I'd better get the theatre ready. I suppose he'll want to do it at once.'

'I should think so. You'd better give him a shot— quarter grain of the hydrochloride.'

He turned to Warren. 'You've got to have an operation,' he said. 'You've never had one before, have you? Well, it's nothing to worry about. But we'll have to do it at once.'

'All right,' said Warren. He had known for the last hour that this was coming.

The sister came with a hypodermic, wiped his arm deftly, and gave him the injection. Then he was wheeled in a chair down a long corridor and into a ward, and to a bed surrounded by a screen. There he was undressed and washed, and put to bed in a clean shirt.

The morphia began to take firm hold of him; the pain was eased, and he became at rest. A nurse came with a notebook.

'Name?' she asked.

'Henry Warren.'

'Married?'

'Yes. I don't know. She left me—went off with another chap. A black man.'

'Do ye know her address?'

Warren shook his head. 'I don't think she's in England. She wouldn't care, anyway.'

'Next of kin? Have ye got a father, or a mother, any brothers or sisters?'

Warren smiled. 'There's nobody like that. If I peg out, let Mr. Morgan know. Hundred and forty-three, Lisle Court, London, E.C.3.'

'Is he a relation?'

'No. Chap I know in an office.'

'Nobody else?'

'No,' said Warren wearily.

The nurse went away, and he lay quietly for some minutes, in a doze. At the foot of the bed the sister and a maid were sorting out his discarded clothes, and turning out his pockets. He listened quietly to their low commentary.

'That's funny—where's his cards? There ought to be some cards. Funny. What's in the coat pockets? Oh, that's bread—throw it away. He won't want that. Here's his money in the trousers. Eleven and fourpence—no more, is there? All right, write it down, and I'll sign for it. There's his cigarettes and his matches—he'll want those presently. But I can't make out about his cards.'

'Shall I ask him?'

'No, let him be now.'

'What is he, do you think? A clerk?'

The sister turned over the clothes. 'Aye, that'll be it. A clerk, walking down south. They say there's work in the south, but I don't know, I'm sure. Many that's on the road will be glad to be home again, if you ask me.' She was examining the coat. 'They've been good clothes—he's come down from a good position in his time.' She examined the tailor's tab. 'New York! He

48

didn't speak like he was American. I know what he is. He'll have been over in America and been shipped over here when he fell out of work. To Glasgow, like as not, and then be walking south. They do that, I was reading.'

'That's why there wouldn't be any cards,' said the maid.

'Aye, that's it.'

They folded the clothes together and put them in a locker by his bed. Warren lay listening to them in drugged indifference. Their ready acceptance of him as an out-of-work clerk amused him faintly, but he had no intention of refuting their idea at the moment. That would need too much energy; for the next few days his best course was to take the line of least resistance. He did not wonder at the mistake. With three days of stubble on his chin, his soiled and dirty clothes, pockets full of bread, and no wallet he was a very different man from the Henry Warren of Lisle Court off Cornhill. It did not matter. In a few hours he might be dead, for all he knew.

The doctor came back with the sister, bringing with him an older man, grey-haired and thin, and competent. Warren gathered that this was Dr. Miller, the surgeon. He made a careful examination, asked a few questions, prodded the rigid abdomen with searching fingers.

'Acute obstruction,' he said to the younger man. 'Look at it for yourself. I don't think there's any doubt about it.'

'What's that?' asked Warren, interested. They disregarded his question altogether, and he subsided again into his role of patient.

The older man got up. 'I'll do it right away,' he said to the sister. 'You can get him in there soon as you like.' He turned to Warren. 'Soon have you right,' he said

49

confidently. 'I don't suppose you'll be sorry to get rid of the pain, either.'

'I could do without it,' said Warren.

The surgeon and the doctor went away, and shortly after that two porters came with a stretcher, and took Warren to the theatre.

In Godalming, at the same time, Morgan, the confidential secretary, was sitting with old Mortimer, seventy-eight years old and growing feeble in his pleasant house.

'So that's all I know, sir,' he was saying. 'He's been away for three days now. I thought you ought to know.'

The old man considered for a moment. 'You say he told you he might be away for a few days?'

'Yes, sir. But it's quite unlike him not to have let me know when he would be going, or where I could get hold of him.'

'None of the servants knew where he was going to—except the chauffeur?'

'No, sir. And he died.'

'H'm.'

There was a silence for a time. Then Morgan said:

'He's almost certainly somewhere in this country, probably in the north of England or Scotland. If you thought it wise, sir, I could broadcast for him on the B.B.C.'

'Certainly not,' said the old man sharply. There was another pause, and then he said:

'Never do anything to destroy confidence. Always remember, confidence is your chief trading asset. Don't squander it.' He paused again.

'I don't see any reason for extreme measures,' he said. 'Leave him alone, and he'll come home, like the

sheep. And bring his tail behind him—you know.'
Morgan smiled politely. 'You say there's nothing very
urgent. If there is, bring the papers down to me. Tell
everyone he's gone off on a holiday. Tell them the truth
—that that damned woman of his has run off with a
black man, and he's too busy sorting out the mess to
attend to business for a week or two. And keep in touch
with me upon the telephone.'

'Yes, sir.'

The old man stared into the distance. 'He'll come
back all right,' he said. 'But I am afraid he may be very
different. It makes a great change in a man's life, a thing
like this.'

CHAPTER IV

For three days after his operation Warren took little notice of his surroundings. In those three days, without conscious process of thought, he decided upon a policy in regard to his identity. He was in a ward of working-class people, labourers and artisans, in some northern town, he was not quite sure which. He would have to stay there for some weeks, perhaps; he had no desire to be different from the rest, and an object of curiosity. They had assumed, a little curiously, he thought, that he was an out-of-work clerk, and the sister had provided of her own accord a credible story. He was content to accept that story and to maintain it; it was good enough for him. He had no desire to be a merchant banker in a ward of labourers.

On the morning of the third day he asked the sister, as she washed him, 'What place is this?' She looked at him blankly. 'I mean, what's the name of this town?'

'Sharples,' she said. 'Didn't you know?'

'No. I was taken ill on the road a good way from here, I think.'

'Aye, a lorry brought you in. Where did you come from?'

'Glasgow,' he said readily. 'I wanted to get to Hull. I used to work in Hull. I thought maybe they could fix me up with a job.'

She made no comment upon that, and Warren lay digesting what he had heard. Presently he said:

'They build ships here, don't they?'

'Used to, you mean. Barlows shut down five years ago, and the plate mills, and the joineries. There's been no ship built here since then.'

Warren nodded slowly. He knew now where he was. The Barlow proposition had been before him a few years before, not once, but many times. It had been hawked round the City in its later stages like a vacuum cleaner.

He said, 'Used to build a lot of ships here, didn't they?'

'Oh aye—one time. The Heather Line Boats, and the Myers' boats—they all came from Barlows. And then there was a great many for foreigners, and floating docks, and that. There was the Admiralty work, too. There were seven Barlow destroyers at the battle of Jutland—did you know that?' She paused, and then she said, 'It's different here now to what it was in them days.'

She left him, and Warren lay considering what he had learned.

The ward he lay in was a light and airy room, lit with windows down each side. Each bed was neat and tidy, with a red blanket folded methodically at the foot, and a standard locker by the side. Two of the beds had screens around them. For a time Warren lay and studied his surroundings. The ward was neat and clean, and yet there was something wrong about it that he could not place.

It was half an hour before it struck him what was wrong. The ward was overcrowded. There were six windows down each side and one at the end; it was clear that the architect had designed for six beds to a side, one between each window. But now the ward held nineteen beds, nine down each side and one across the bottom of the ward where no bed should have been. And all the beds were full.

He studied the occupants of the beds for a time. They lay inert, a gaunt and listless crew. One or two were reading newspapers and tattered books; most of them were lying still, staring at the ceiling, as though they were already dead. For all his weakness and his discomfort, Warren felt himself to be the only virile man in the whole ward.

He turned his head, and met the eyes of the man in the next bed. A tall, gaunt man of fifty years or so with a grey face; he lay quite motionless.

Warren saw that he was watched. 'Morning,' he said.

There was silence for a moment, and then the man said:

'What's your name?'

'Warren. What's yours?'

'Petersen. Jock Petersen, they call me. Ye're no from these parts?'

'I'm from America,' said Warren. 'I had a job in Philadelphia.'

The grey face showed a flicker of animation. 'Is things good in America? Would a man as was a charge-hand riveter get work oot there?'

'I don't think so. It's pretty bad.'

'Not even holding up?'

'I shouldn't say so. There's over ten million out of a job already over there.'

The animation died from the thin face. Listlessly the next question came.

'What brought ye back to England?'

'I was in a bank,' said Warren. 'I got laid off with fifteen others, last September. Then I bummed around and spent my money, looking for a job. And then they

54

picked me up, and put me on a boat for Glasgow. That's what they do, unless you've taken out your papers.'

'Ye came by Glasgie?' said Petersen. 'Eh, I'd like fine to be in Glasgie again.'

There was a pause, and presently the riveter said: 'What ails ye?'

'A twisted gut,' said Warren. 'They cut out a bit and joined it up again. They say I'll be as good as ever when it's healed, but I wouldn't trust to that.'

'Aye, I wouldna say that's no a fact. Ye've made a fine recovery.'

'What's the matter with you?'

'I had the colic awfu' bad. They took me in for obsairvation, as they say.'

'Have you had it long?'

'Twa three months. It took me sair after eating or drinking. I couldna sleep nights for the colicky pain of it. I come to out-patients, and the wee doctor laddie he said to me to drink three pints o' milk each day—the domned fool. Did ye ever hear o' sich daft talk, with milk three-pence a pint! And that wasn't the end to it. There was baby's food and all sorts I was to take—oot o' thirty-one an' six a week for the four of us, an' nine an' three gaeing for rent. I got nae better, so they took me in for obsairvation.'

'You'll be getting the milk now?' said Warren.

'Aye. An' weary stuff it is.'

On the other side of Warren was a younger man, a dock labourer by the name of Thompson, making a slow recovery from appendicitis. He was largely inarticulate, and apparently had little interest beyond the football pools. He did, however, give one sound piece of advice.

'See here, chum,' he said hoarsely, 'you want to watch that Miss MacMahon. She'll try an' make you pay

55

for what they done to you, but don't you do it. If you got any o' the dibs, don't let on, see? You got a right to be here, same as anyone.'

Warren gathered that Miss MacMahon must be the Almoner.

The bed beyond Thompson was the corner bed; there was a screen around it and an intermittent babble of incoherent talk. From the screen, the delirium, and the movements of the nurses Warren gathered that the case was serious; he asked the ward nurse when she came to him with a drink.

'He's a young man called Tinsley,' she said. 'I think he's a carpenter when he's in work. He ruptured himself lifting some weight or other, and came in for the operation. The wound healed nicely and we thought he was all right, but then it broke out septic. He's very ill.'

Warren wrinkled his brows in perplexity. 'What made it go like that?'

'I don't know, I'm sure. He had terribly neglected teeth. Doctor Miller thinks it might have been from that.'

She went away, and Warren lay puzzling what she had said until he fell asleep. It didn't make sense to him. Bad teeth could not infect a healed wound, unless you turned and bit it. There must be something else wrong with the man; he could not have had an ordinary constitution. But then, were any of these listless people ordinary?

He did not think they were.

That night the young man died. The screen was taken from around the bed, the bed made up, and by lunch time the next day it was occupied again by a man with a crushed foot.

That afternoon the Almoner came to him. He had

56

seen her once or twice before, a slim, dark woman about thirty years of age distributing books and papers in the ward. She came and drew a chair up to his bed; she had a notebook and a pencil in her hand.

'How are you feeling now, Mr. Warren?' she enquired.

'Better, thanks. I'd feel better still if I could get some real food.'

'I don't suppose you'll get that for some time. Now, Mr. Warren, I've come to talk to you about paying for the treatment that you've had. You've had a very big operation that would have cost a great deal of money if a surgeon had done it for you privately, and on top of that there's your expense of living here for at least three weeks.'

'Boiled water,' said Warren.

'Yes,' said Miss MacMahon firmly. 'Later on you'll get expensive foods when you are able to take something—patent milk foods out of tins, white fish, chicken, all that sort of thing, until you are able to get on to a normal diet. It all costs a great deal of money, at least thirty-five shillings a week.'

'I'm afraid I haven't got that much,' said Warren. 'You see, I'm out of a job at the moment.'

She looked at him critically. 'What is your job?'

'I'm a bank clerk,' he said. 'I was over in America, in Philadelphia. Then I fell out of work and the Federal authorities shipped me back here, because I was an Englishman. I was walking down to Hull. I might be able to pick up something there. Otherwise I was going on down to London.'

'Have you got any relations who could help you with this expense?'

He shook his head. 'I don't think so.'

57

'You must make good money when you're in a job.'

He said, 'I was making five pounds ten in England seven years ago, and over in America I was drawing two hundred a month. I don't want you to think I'm trying to dodge this expense. I'll be able to pay it off when I get work again. But I haven't got it now, I'm afraid.'

She looked at him searchingly. 'How much money have you got?'

'Less than a pound,' he said.

She smiled. 'We won't take any of that if you've got to walk to Hull and London. But you must give me an address before you go, and I shall tell you what the treatment has cost the hospital. We shall want you to sign a note acknowledging that you owe the hospital that money. And then you must pay it off in instalments when you get a job.'

'That's right,' said Warren. 'I'll do that.'

Her pencil poised above the pad. 'How much a week will you be able to pay?'

'If I get a job at five pounds a week or more, I could manage ten bob.'

She calculated for a moment. 'That would do.' She smiled at him. 'All right, Mr. Warren—we'll leave it at that for the time being. I shall want you to sign that note before you go, and of course I'll tell you how much we have to charge you. And then you'll pay it off at the rate of ten shillings a week when you get in work again.'

Warren nodded, his conscience more painful than his abdomen. 'I might be able to pay it off quicker than that,' he said. 'If I can, I will.'

She smiled again. 'That's very nice of you. It's not that we want to press you when you're out of a job, but the hospital does need every penny it can get. The poorer a town gets the more it needs its hospital, and of

58

course, the harder it is to make ends meet.'

He was interested, having had to do with hospitals from time to time—generally when they were *in extremis*. 'What's the subscription list like?'

'Terrible. When I came here first Barlows were going. Twopence a week per man and three thousand men —that made twelve hundred pounds a year from Barlows alone. And then there were the rolling-mills, and the little firms—they all had weekly contributions to the hospital. But all that's gone now. And of course the patients can't pay much, either.' She smiled. 'That's why we have to get it back out of them when they get into work again. But in the meantime, you see, the hospital has to do without the money.'

'I see that,' said Warren. 'Are there endowments?'

'Very few.'

He wrinkled his brows. 'What are you using for money then?'

'We get along. Lady Swarland is our sheet anchor; she helps us out each year with a subscription to put us on our feet again. I'm afraid it's a great drain on her, but she keeps on. Year after year.'

'Lady Swarland,' said Warren. 'Isn't her son Lord Cheriton?'

'Yes—he's in the Army, I think. But he lives down in London—we never see him up here.'

She left him, and went down to the little office that she occupied beside the Secretary. She went into the Secretary's office; Mr. Williams was checking invoices at his desk.

'I've seen that man Warren, in the surgical,' she said.

'Can he pay?'

'Not a halfpenny. He's a clerk, out of a job and walking south.'

59

The little man clicked his tongue in consternation.

'Hasn't he got any money?'

'If he had, I'd have got it. I asked the sister what he had when he came in. He's only got a little silver.'

'What sort of man is he?'

'A very good type. He's a payer all right—when he gets in work. But there's no saying when that will be.'

'Aye,' said the Secretary. He stood staring out of the window into the yard, short and rubicund. 'I suppose the men will get in work again—some day.'

'I wouldn't bank on that,' said Miss MacMahon.

Next day a consultation was held upon the riveter in the next bed to Warren. A screen was put around the bed while it was in progress; presently the screen was removed and the doctors and the nurses went away. The riveter leaned over towards Warren.

'Eh, mon,' he said. 'They say I'm to have an operation the morn.'

'I'm sorry to hear that,' said Warren.

' 'Tis the Lord's will, and we must say naething against it.'

'What's the operation for?'

'For the colic I was telling you about. A something ulcer, they was calling it just now. But I don't know.'

He lay back upon his pillows, inert and listless.

'Duodenal ulcer,' said the nurse in response to Warren's enquiry, when she brought him his milk food for lunch. 'Doctor Miller's doing it tomorrow.'

That afternoon the riveter's wife came to sit with him, a woman as tall and gaunt as Petersen himself, dressed in a faded black costume, with straggling grey hair and with appalling shoes. She brought with her a present of a sixpenny packet of cigarettes; the man in the bed smoked one gravely and in perfect silence. The woman stayed with him for about an hour until they told her it was time to go; so far as Warren could detect they exchanged no words at all after the preliminary brief greetings. She came, and sat with him, and went away.

Perhaps, thought Warren, there was nothing to be said.

Next morning there was the bustle of preparation about the riveter in the next bed. They took him to the theatre about half-past ten; an hour later he was back again with the screen drawn close around the bed.

Warren did not see him again. That the case was critical was evident from the attention of the doctors and the nurses. In the middle of the night Warren was roused by what was evidently a consultation of some sort; from behind the screen he heard a laboured breathing that was new to him. All the next day the sound of breathing grew in loudness with a rasping quality, as if the man were gasping for his breath.

'Pneumonia,' said the nurse. 'He's very ill.'

That night the riveter died.

'What did he die of?' Warren asked his nurse. 'How did he come to get pneumonia from an ulcerated stomach?'

She shook her head. 'It just happens. When you're weak enough you can get anything, you know.'

She brought around the packet of cigarettes, from which only one was taken. 'His wife said I was to give these away. Would you like one?'

Warren lay and smoked in meditative silence. He found that he had a great deal to think about.

Three days later, two more patients died on the same day. One was a man of forty-five or so with peritonitis, the other a boy of seventeen who had had an operation

61

on his neck and jaw for some strange bone disease. To Warren, totally unused to hospital routine, there was no apparent reason for the deaths—the men went for operation, and then just died.

The Almoner came down the ward next day distributing her papers and books. He stopped her by his bed. 'Have you got time to stop a minute? I want to know a bit more about this hospital.'

'Why—yes. For a few minutes.'

She sat down by his bed.

He fixed her with his eyes, cold and purposeful; he was becoming very much himself again. 'I don't want to ask anything that you can't answer, or that you ought not to tell me. But there's something wrong here, and I'd like to know what it is.'

'Something wrong?'

'All these deaths.'

She was silent. He went on, 'I've been here ten days now. In that time four people have died in this ward, out of the nineteen beds—all after operations. I suppose there may have been eight or nine operations in that time, counting my own. The way I see it, that's about fifty per cent of deaths. Surely that's not right?'

'I think your figures are a little high. I should have said forty per cent, myself.'

'You mean, that when one has an operation here it's little better than an even chance if one gets through?'

She hesitated. 'I suppose that's what it comes to.'

He was silent for a minute. Then he smiled at her. 'I don't want you to think I'm prying into what isn't my business. After all, I seem to be getting over mine all right, and I suppose that's all that matters to me. But I'd like to understand the reason for these casualties.'

He paused. 'So far as I can see, the nursing here is good —very good indeed. I've nothing to complain about. I can't judge of the surgery, of course. But he seems to have done a good job on me, and I've seen no bloomers on that side. And yet there's this high percentage of deaths. It's unusual, isn't it?'

'Yes. But you know why it happens as well as I do.'

'I promise you I don't.'

In turn, she gave him a coldly, appraising look. 'How long have you been out of work, Mr. Warren?'

He met her eyes. 'About six months,' he said steadily. 'You must remember that I only know conditions in America, and American hospitals. I've only been in this country for a fortnight.'

She softened. 'I forgot.' She glanced at him queerly. 'You've come from the New World, and you don't know anything about your own country. Funny.'

'What do you mean?'

She answered his question with another. 'What did you think of your country when you came back to it again? What did you think of Sharples?'

'I've never seen Sharples.'

'But how did you get here?'

'I got picked up on the road when I was ill, and brought along here on a motor lorry.'

She got up from the bed. 'You've got a lot to learn about this country, Mr. Warren,' she said coldly. 'You'd have done better to have stayed in America. In this country a man on public assistance gets about five shillings a week for his food—not that, unless he's economical. After five years of that you can't expect him to stand operations very well. I should have thought that was obvious, even in America.'

She swept away, and left Warren to his own reflections.

Five shillings a week for food—it didn't seem very much. The riveter had told him that his weekly income from the public assistance committee was thirty-one and six, out of which nine and threepence went for rent. That left twenty-two and threepence for everything else, for four people. If you deducted something for fuel—he did not know how much—and for clothing, it looked as if five shillings was an overstatement.

How much food could you get for five shillings? Like most men, Warren was lamentably ignorant of the price of food. Eggs, he thought, were twopence each; if you lived exclusively on eggs that would be four and a half eggs a day for five shillings a week. You wouldn't get fat on that. There were probably cheaper foods than eggs— bread and stuff. However, there was not much nourishment in those.

And there was no contingency at all to cater for bad management, or ignorance.

The reason for the listlessness of the patients became clear to him. This was the result of unemployment for five years, of living at a gradually decreasing standard of nourishment. Gradually decreasing, because all families would have some capital, something that could be sold from time to time throughout the early period, to add to the family income. There would be things to be picked up, too, at first, firewood from the deserted shipyard, loose coal from the idle slag heaps—trifles unconsidered in the time of general prosperity. Gradually, as time went on, the town would become swept bare, till at last there would be nothing to supplement the weekly dole.

And that, it seemed, meant undernourishment. You did not die when you were drawing public assistance money, but you certainly did not remain alive.

Unlike most hospitals, Warren thought, there was no

wireless laid on to the beds. That evening after tea, however, Miss MacMahon appeared with an electric portable, set it on a table at the end of the ward, and plugged it to a concert of 'old favourites'. The effect upon the ward was magical. Men who had lain inert all day turned their heads and raised themselves on one elbow; the ward woke up. The Almoner strolled over to Warren's bed.

'Good thing, that,' he said. 'Gives them an interest.'

She nodded, 'I wish we could have it laid on properly, with headphones at the beds. Having it like this means you can only have it when there's nobody very ill in the ward.' She smiled at him wryly. 'And as you've pointed out, that isn't very often.'

He said, 'I'm sorry if I spoke out of turn this morning.'

'I was unnecessarily rude,' she said. 'Forget it.'

The ward was thoroughly awake. The men were humming the familiar tunes, singing in low, discordant tones, beating rhythmically with one hand on the counterpane. Warren lay and watched them for a time.

'How much does it cost to put in wireless to the beds?' he asked. 'I should have thought it would have paid.'

'It would pay in results,' she said. 'But there just isn't the money in this town for things like that. We ought to have done it five years ago, when things were good. It costs about five hundred pounds, or a bit more. We got a quotation once.'

The concert was drawing to a close before the News. 'And now,' said the announcer, 'before we finish up we've just got time for one old favourite that we all know.' And the orchestra struck up the opening bars of 'Land of Hope and Glory'.

Warren smiled, a little cynically. The girl saw it, and was angry with him.

65

The music rose and swelled through the ward, lifting the spirits of the men with its derided appeal. Warren, watching, smiling, had the smile wiped off his face, there was nothing here to laugh about. The music rose and swelled through the ward, and now the men were singing from their beds, singing and meaning every word of it.

'Land of Hope and Glory
Mother of the Free——
How shall we extol thee
Who were born of thee? . . .'

'Five shillings a week,' thought Warren. 'My God!'

The music rose, lifted the spirits of the men, held them for a time, and died into silence before the first News. For a moment there was stillness in the ward, then someone moved, and the spell was broken.

Warren turned to the girl. 'Land of Hope and Glory,' he said bitterly. 'I suppose that's Sharples on the dole.'

She eyed him for a moment. 'You're poking fun at us, Mr. Warren,' she said coldly. 'That isn't very nice. We've done our best for you.'

He shook his head. 'I wasn't poking any fun.'

'What did you mean, then?'

'I was wondering what made them sing that thing like that,' he said. 'I suppose they understand the words.' She flushed angrily and was about to speak, but he stopped her. ' "Land of Hope and Glory",' he said quietly. 'The land that gives them five bob a week to live on—and forgets. There's no Glory for them in this land, and very little Hope. And yet they sing that thing like that.

She stood there looking down at him. 'Curious, isn't it?' she said. 'I suppose you'd call it mass hysteria.'

'I might.'

'I might say that it's because they've been born and bred in this country, and they still like it a bit.'

He smiled. 'And you might just as well be right as me.'

Behind her back a steady stream of news, in dulcet tones, flowed from the wireless. 'You mustn't take the unemployment too much to heart, Mr. Warren,' she said seriously. 'Things will come right. You're out of a job, and going through a bad patch. Things are bad all over the country, and here in Sharples they're just terrible. But it *is* only a bad patch. The ships in service are all getting worn out, they say. A lot more ships will be needed before long. It can't be more than a year or two before we're all busy again.'

He was silent.

'Things are terribly bad here now, and they're getting worse each year. But there's a limit to it. We haven't got to stick it out much longer. Then we'll all have jobs again.'

He raised his head and met her eyes, and his heart sank. 'You believe that—really?' he said.

'Absolutely.'

From his own knowledge, deep within himself, he said, 'I'm terribly sorry.' But he said no word aloud, and presently the Fat Stock Prices came upon the air; she went to the wireless, turned it off and took it to another ward, thinking she had reassured him for the future.

Warren lay awake for half the night with mingled feelings. Predominating, curiously, he was deeply ashamed, he did not know of what.

Next day the surgeon on his morning round stopped at his bed, asked a few questions of the house physician, and examined the wound.

'Better start getting him up a bit,' he said to the physician. 'An hour or two each day.'

He turned to Warren. 'Not a Sharples man, are you?'

'No,' said Warren. 'I was on the road.'

'Out of a job?'

'Yes.'

'Where are you going to?'

'I was walking down to Hull. Then if I couldn't get anything there, I was going on to London.'

The surgeon eyed him keenly. 'You're an educated man. What's your job?'

'I'm a bank clerk.'

The surgeon got up from the bed. 'Well,' he said, 'you won't be fit to walk to Hull for a couple of weeks yet.'

He moved on to the next bed. At the end of his round he walked down to the Secretary's office, and through it to the Almoner's little room. He found Miss MacMahon at her desk.

'That bank clerk in the surgical,' he said. 'He'll be ready for discharge in three or four days—say at the end of the week. But I understand he's walking the roads.'

'That's right, sir. He told me he was walking to Hull.'

The surgeon considered for a minute. 'He won't be fit to walk to Hull for a fortnight. You'd better go down to the Labour Exchange and see if he can draw a fortnight's benefit here before he leaves the town. Tell them he's convalescing.'

The Almoner made a little grimace. 'I'll try it on, Doctor, but I don't know that we'll get away with it. You remember that man Halliday?'

The surgeon did; he hesitated. 'Well, try it on. They can't expect us to support a man when he's fit for dis-- charge. Besides, I want the bed.'

68

The Almoner nodded. 'I'll go down right away.'

Behind their backs the Secretary spoke. 'If he's a bank clerk, I could use him for a fortnight here.' They turned to him. 'With Vernon off sick I'm that behind with my books I just don't know how we'll get through. There's the auditors coming in the middle of next month. Could he check the ledgers, do you think?'

'I don't know,' said the Almoner. 'I suppose he could.'

'Let him come down, and let me have a word with him,' said the Secretary. 'I'll know if he can help us, then. It might suit both.'

'We'd have to fit him in somewhere else to sleep for that fortnight,' said the Almoner. 'I could see the Matron about that.'

The surgeon turned away. 'Fix it up that way if you like,' he said. 'We can't afford to keep him after he's fit to walk, though. And get him out of the ward by the end of the week.'

By the end of the week Warren was sitting in the Secretary's office totting up ledgers. It was a great many years since he had served his apprenticeship in his father's bank and he had some difficulty with the work; there are few things so difficult to the amateur as simple addition on the scale required for an audit. Miss Mac-Mahon asked the Secretary after the first day:

'How's your new clerk doing?'

He smiled dourly. 'I'm not surprised he's out of a job.'

She was interested. 'Isn't he any good?'

'He's slow—very slow. A good lad of sixteen would do it quicker.'

'I suppose it's not the sort of work he's used to. If he's no good to you we'll have to think of something else.'

69

The Secretary rubbed his chin. 'Leave him a while. I'd no say that he's no use, only he isn't handy with the books. He was telling me the way they make up the charges in the bank, which is a thing I never rightly understood—no more than anyone else. He was showing me the way we could save half of one per cent on the overdraft. That's over a hundred a year saved—if he's right.'

The girl smiled. 'If he's saved us a hundred a year already we can afford to keep him for the next fortnight,' she said. 'Whether he can tot up books or not.'

'It's no saved yet,' said the Secretary cautiously. 'I must think on it.'

The next afternoon Warren had his first walk in Sharples.

He went first to the Post Office nearby, and sent a post-card to Morgan, giving his address and strict instructions that he was not to be written to except on the most urgent necessity. Having thus satisfied his business conscience, he set off to inspect Sharples, walking slowly with a stick.

The town was dreary with the sad Northern uniformity of long rows of grey houses on a minor scale. Dreary, he thought, but not so bad as some. The houses were better and larger than those which he remembered on his visits to other similar places on the north-east coast, Gateshead, Jarrow, and Sunderland; he judged the town to have been built more recently than those.

It seemed to be a place of about forty thousand inhabitants; later he found that this guess of his was very nearly right. It stood on the edge of the river Haws a mile or so up from the sea; behind the town the hill rose gently to the north, crowned with sparse fields and the gaunt slag heaps of an idle mine.

He found the one main street, Palmer Street, near the hospital. Like all the streets in the town this one was laid out with granite setts; there were rusted tram tracks down the middle of the street, but no trams ran. The shops were mostly small and unpretentious; a great number of them were unoccupied, with windows boarded up. He passed by two closed banks. On a fine corner site an extensive store was shuttered and deserted. On the façade above the windows he traced the outline letters of the sign that had been taken down, and realised that he was standing in a town that could no longer support Woolworths.

He walked the length of Palmer Street. There were very few people to be seen although the afternoon was warm and sunny; he passed a few knots of men standing idle at the corners, but he saw few women and fewer children. Very few vehicles passed him; for a time he was puzzled to identify an aspect of the town that was familiar and that yet eluded him. At last he realised it was the cleanness of the streets. There was no mud upon the granite setts, no rubbish in the gutters of the road, no smoke in the pale sky. The town was clean as a washed corpse.

'It's like Russia,' he muttered to himself. The empty streets, the shuttered shops, the lean, despondent people put him irresistibly in the mind of Leningrad, where he had been some years before.

He very soon grew tired, and was glad to cut his outing short and get back to the hospital. He went through to the Secretary's room to take up his heavy burden of simple addition; he was ruefully conscious that he was not shining as a ledger clerk. Williams was out, but the Almoner was sitting at her desk.

She glanced round as he came in. 'Been out for your

first walk?'

He sank down in his chair. 'I've been looking at Sharples,' he replied. 'It's the first time I've seen it.'

She made no reply.

He drummed with his fingers on the table for a minute. 'What's the unemployment here?' he said at last.

She raised her head. 'About seven thousand five hundred drawing from the P.A.C.,' she said. 'I suppose it's about nine thousand, more or less.'

'That's most of the wage earners, I suppose?'

She nodded without speaking.

He eyed her for a moment. 'What happened here?' he asked gently.

She turned to him. 'I don't know—none of us really know. This is a shipping town—Barlows, you know. Barlows really were Sharples—everyone seemed to work in Barlows, or in the plate mills, or the mine—and those were all mixed up with Barlows. The Yard employed about three thousand people all the time before the War, and in the War, and after the War, it went up to about four thousand, so they say.'

She paused. 'And then about five—no, six years ago, they started to lay off men. There didn't seem to be any more orders for ships coming in.'

'I know,' he said. 'That happened all over the world.'

'It was awful,' she said soberly. 'I've lived here all my life. My father was solicitor to Barlows. It didn't really matter much to us, because he was thinking of retiring anyway. But first of all they had to lay off the men, and then some of the staff. And then the mine shut down, without any warning at all, and that threw over a thousand out of work at once. And there didn't seem to be any reason for it,' she said. 'It wasn't bad management, or anything like that—so far as we could see. It just

72

happened.'

'That was in 1928?' he asked.

'About that time. And then one day, everybody got their notice. They pasted up a placard on the shipyard gates to say that the yard would be suspending work for a time during reorganisation. Everybody thought it would be quite a short time, and it was only a matter of getting a new company going, or something. But it went on—and of course the plate mills closed at the same time. And then, about six months after that, the men started to run out of benefit, and had to go on to the transitional scheme, and then on outdoor relief. And now we've got the P.A.C. and the Means Test.'

He said, 'Has nothing happened to the shipyard since then?'

She shook her head. 'Nothing. They say now that it may never open again.'

He was silent.

'We can't believe that, here in Sharples,' she said quietly. 'Things always do come right, somehow or other. Don't they?'

He did not try to answer that. 'Has there been any attempt to start up other industries?' he asked.

She smiled a little wryly. 'Basket-making, and fancy leather work,' she said. 'The Council of Social Service are doing their best, and I suppose it's a good thing to try and get the men to do something with their hands. But . . . I don't know. There were seven Barlow destroyers at the Battle of Jutland—did you know that, Mr. Warren? I'd have thought they might have found something better for our men to do than fancy leather work.'

'Nobody's tried to start up a light industry—plywood or wireless sets, or anything like that?'

73

She shook her head. 'I haven't heard of anything like that.'

He nodded thoughtfully. A year before a man had come to him with quite a good proposition to manufacture a German type of carpet sweeper under licence. He had proposed to set up a factory in a depressed area of South Wales. Ruefully Warren remembered his own words. 'You must cut out the philanthropy,' he had said. 'Nobody's going to give you money for that. You'll have your work cut out to get this thing established anyway, without planting it in an atmosphere of failure.' A little factory had been put up at Slough, and it was doing well.

She said, 'It's a wicked thing to spread a rumour like the one that's going round now, that the Yard will never open again. It takes all the heart out of the people. It makes them feel there's nothing to look forward to—ever. And besides, it isn't true.'

'Why not?' he asked.

'Ships always have been built in Sharples. All the ships are getting worn out. As soon as this depression lifts, a lot of new ships will be wanted, and things will come right again.'

'That may be,' he said slowly. 'But you've got to face the facts.'

'What do you mean?'

'It seems to me that Barlows is out of the business. No ships have been built here for a long time. Who's going to place the first order?'

She hesitated. 'I suppose somebody will want a ship some day.'

'I know. But put yourself in his shoes. If you were spending fifty thousand pounds of your money on a ship, where would you go to order it? Most probably it wouldn't be your own money. You'd not have that much loose capital; you'd go and borrow most of it from your bank. Would you order the ship from one of the big firms in Belfast, or in Wallsend, or the Clyde? They'd build you the ship in six months, and guarantee delivery to the day. Or would you come and place your order here?'

She was silent.

'The bank wouldn't let you place your order here,' he said. 'They'd be afraid that something would go wrong, that it would be a bad ship and no security for their loan.'

'I know,' she said quietly. 'I know that is the difficulty. One must be practical.'

'It seems to me that it's the first few orders are the difficulty,' he said. 'The goodwill must be absolutely dead.'

'But that means that the Yard never can get started up again,' she said.

He had nothing to say to that.

She rose and faced him, and he rose in turn. 'I know that what you've said is true,' she said. 'And yet I don't believe it. This is a decent world, and things like that don't happen. Sharples is going through a bad patch now, but somehow we're going to get over it. Something we don't see will turn up, or somebody will come and help us get things like they used to be.'

He faced her, and his eyes were very soft. 'That is what you believe?'

'I believe that some day we shall get things right again,' she said.

He smiled. 'If there are many people like you in Sharples, you probably will.'

He turned to his accounts.

He worked on steadily all evening at his books, making up in length of hours what he was well aware was lacking in dexterity. In the middle of the next morning the

Almoner passed through the office; he stopped her as she went.

'I'm going for a walk this afternoon,' he said. 'Is it possible to get into the shipyard? I'd like to see it.'

'The gates are usually open,' she replied. 'Old Robbins is the watchman—he comes up here to out-patients. If you mention me he'll let you in.'

'Thank you so much.'

She considered for a minute. 'I've got visits in Baker Lane and round that way this afternoon. If you like, I'll meet you at the Yard. Say four o'clock.'

'Don't trouble if it's out of your way.'

She turned aside. 'I wouldn't mind seeing it myself— it's over two years since I went there. I'd like to see how tall the grass has grown.'

The Yard stood at a bend in the river, a mile or so up from the sea. It covered, Warren judged, about fifty acres of land; there were three large berths for building and two smaller ones, with quays, wharves, and a small graving dock. The Yard had been placed cleverly upon the bend of the river so that the three large slipways pointed down the stream, enabling quite large vessels to be launched in a small river. All this and other features of the Yard were pointed out by the old watchman, as he hobbled round with Warren and the Almoner.

'Admiralty vessels we built here, too—oh, a many of them,' he quavered. 'Seven Barlow destroyers there was at the Battle of Jutland.'

Warren walked slowly after him, leaning upon his stick and asking keen, incisive questions. He judged the place to be in pretty good shape. The derricks and gantries exposed to the weather had not suffered greatly from corrosion; so far as possible all gear had been removed and put in store, carefully greased and covered with tarpaulins. The woodworking machinery had all been sold; there had been no market for the heavier presses and the plate-manipulating rolls, and these remained in place. The buildings of the Yard were fair; the offices and stores were still quite good.

He lingered there till dusk. At the Yard gate he turned towards the girl.

'Thirty thousand pounds for capital re-equipment,' he said. 'And then the money to finance the order.'

She stared at him. 'What are you talking about?'

He smiled. 'I'm sorry—I was thinking aloud. But that's what it would cost to get it going again.'

'How on earth do you know that?'

He turned towards the hospital. 'I used to do a good bit of that sort of estimating,' he said. 'Over in America, of course.'

She eyed him doubtfully, but said nothing.

During the next week Warren wandered widely through the town on his afternoon walks. He went twice more to the shipyard and talked for a long time with the ancient at the gate. He paid a visit to the rolling-mills. He went down to the fish quay at the harbour mouth and listened to the gossip of the boats—to find if there was any silting of the river. In one swift hour of concentration in the hospital he learned the mystery of football pools, which led him to an hour's talk with a small newsagent that threw a great light on the failure of the Yard. He carried many parcels of washing to the homes of the patients, and for each parcel he was paid in some stray piece of information of the town.

He gained strength rapidly, unlike the people that he lived among. Before many days had passed he could walk long distances without his stick, and knew by that same token that his time in Sharples was drawing to a close.

There was one place more to visit before he left the town. He said to the Almoner, working at her desk:

'I want to see the mine, Miss MacMahon—before I go. Do you think that could be managed?'

She raised her head. 'You can't go down it.'

'I don't want to do that. I'd like to look around about the pithead—see the stores and offices.'

She glanced at him queerly. 'You've seen everything else in Sharples? And now you want to see the mine.'

He smiled. 'I've seen most things,' he admitted. 'Is it possible to see the mine?'

She stared at him, puzzled. 'I know one of the clerks who used to work there,' she said. 'He could show you all there is to see. But what do you want to see it for?'

He smiled. 'To satisfy my curiosity,' he said blandly. 'It would be so kind of you if you'd give me his name.'

She raised her eyebrows. 'I'll come with you this afternoon.'

The man lived in a little house in a row on the top of the hill some way outside the town, not far from the pit-head. He looked white and ill, and very frail. He made no objection to taking them to the offices, and for an hour Warren pored over dirty, dog-eared plans, and talked production costs. He walked through the stores and engine-shops, asking questions that the little clerk found joy in answering, so long it was since he had talked his business with a stranger.

At last they left the mine, and went back to the house. The Almoner went in with the pale clerk; Warren waited for ten minutes in the road outside. Then she rejoined him, and they strolled towards the town.

'That fellow's looking very ill,' he said. 'Is he a patient?'

'Not yet,' she said briefly. 'His wife has been attending

for a long time.'

'What's the matter with him?'

'He isn't getting enough to eat, by the look of him. I've just spoken to him about it.'

Warren frowned. 'Surely the public assistance rates aren't so bad as that? They're revised from time to time, aren't they? You don't just have to starve?'

She shook her head. 'No, you don't have to starve. The rates are all right—in theory, Mr. Warren. You can keep alive and fit on P.A.C. relief—if you happen to have been born an archangel.'

'What do you mean?'

She stopped and faced him. 'It's like this. There's really nothing wrong with the rates of relief. If you are careful, and wise, and prudent, you can live on that amount of money fairly well. And you've got to be intelligent, and well educated, too, and rather selfish. If you were like that you'd get along all right—but you wouldn't have a penny to spare.'

She paused. 'But if you were human—well, you'd be for it. If you got bored stiff with doing nothing so that you went and blued fourpence on going to the pictures— you just wouldn't have enough to eat that week. Or if you couldn't cook very well, and spoiled the food a bit, you'd go hungry. You'd go hungry if your wife had a birthday and you wanted to give her a little present costing a bob —you'd only get eighty per cent of your food that week. And of course, if your wife gets ill and you want to buy her little fancy bits of things . . .'

She shrugged her shoulders. 'You've seen it up there.'

He was silent for a minute. She stood there looking at him, mute; there was no sound but the sighing of the wind over the hill. At last he said, 'That's terrible. Because it's so difficult to change. You can't expect people in work to pay for people who are idle going to the pictures, or giving presents to their wives. We haven't reached that stage of socialism yet. And that means there must always be starvation, in a small degree. Because people are human, and a little foolish sometimes.'

She faced him bitterly. 'There's only one cure for starvation—work! If only we could get some work back here! That's the only thing that allows you to be human and foolish, as you've got to be. My God, if we could get some work back here again . . .'

He moved over to a gate and stood there leaning his arms upon it, looking out over the town. She came and stood beside him. He saw the river running down from the grey moors, the bend by the shipyard, the distant litter of the slips, the graving dock, the grey untidy huddle of the town. All crystal-clear, unsmirched by any smoke of industry.

At last he straightened up, and laid his hand upon her own. 'What would you say,' he said slowly, 'if I were to tell you that within a year there would be work back here again? That there would be ships building in the Yard, the rolling-mills working, and jobs for everybody in the town?'

She caught her breath. There was nothing real to her then but the pressure of his hand, his clear grey eyes, the firm lines of his chin.

'I don't know what you are, or what you've been,' she said unsteadily. 'But if you told me that, I—I'd believe you.'

In silence they walked down into the town.

CHAPTER V

On the next day Warren left the town.

He visited the ward, and said good-bye to the sister in charge. 'Ye've a long walk ahead of you,' she said, 'but it's a nice day ye've got for it. Take things easy now, and remember that ye're not long out of bed. And don't go on if you feel tired, especially about the wound.' He met the Matron in the corridor and said good-bye to her; she told him to call at the porter's lodge for a packet of bread and cheese. And finally, he went down to the Secretary's office.

Mr. Williams and the Almoner were there. 'I'm going now,' he said. 'I just looked in to say good-bye and to thank you for letting me work on here.'

Williams held out his hand. 'Good-bye,' he said, 'and good weather for your walk. Let us know how you get on.'

Miss MacMahon picked up a pen and her pad. 'We'll want to know how you get on,' she said practically. 'Ten bob a week, as soon as you get into a job, we said, didn't we?'

Warren smiled. 'I'm sure I'll be able to manage that,' he said. 'How much do I owe?'

'Four weeks at thirty-five shillings a week,' she said. 'That's seven pounds. I made a note out for you here, acknowledging the debt. Would you mind signing it?'

He took her pen, and signed it 'Henry Warren.'

'One more thing,' she said. 'You said you'd leave an

81

address, where we could get in touch with you at any time.'

He hesitated for a moment. He would be closing down the house in Grosvenor Square, and he shrank from the explanations that would be involved if he were to give his club address in Pall Mall. 'If you write to me at a hundred-and-forty-three Lisle Court, London, E.C.3, it will get to me,' he said. 'I'm afraid I haven't got a very permanent address just now.'

'What is that—a private house?'

He told the truth, simply and boldly, having found in the course of much business that the truth was sometimes the best lie. 'It's an office where I used to work. They forward letters for me still.'

She wrote it down, and then held out her hand. 'Well, good-bye, and good luck. Don't forget us here in Sharples, when you get to London.'

He shook hands with her, and then stood for a moment. 'Everybody has been very kind to me in Sharples,' he said at last, 'and at a time when I most needed it. I promise you I won't forget.'

He smiled at them, and went out of the door. The Secretary turned to the Almoner. 'Yon's a queer customer,' he said.

The Almoner sighed, and shuffled with some papers on her desk. 'He's probably an impostor,' she said wearily. 'If he isn't, he must be a great man. Anyway, he owes us seven pounds.'

'What was that address he was giving you?' asked the Secretary.'

'A hundred-and-forty-three Lisle Court.'

The Secretary reached under his desk and dragged out an old Post Office Guide. 'Let's see what that is. Lisle Court . . . . A hundred-and-forty-three . . .' He ran his finger along the line. 'Hey, come and look at this.'

His finger showed her Warren Sons and Mortimer, Merchant Bankers.

They stared at it in silence.

'It's probably a coincidence,' said the girl. 'Anyway, he's out of the town by now.'

But Warren was not out of the town. Instead of taking the road south, he went to the Post Office and collected a letter that was waiting for him, on his instructions. He signed for it, slit it open, pocketed the twenty pounds and the cheque forms that it contained, and threw away the envelope. Ten minutes later he was calling at the house of Dr. Miller, the surgeon who had done his operation.

The smart maid looked at him askance. 'The surgery is at six o'clock,' she said. 'I don't know as he'll see you now.'

'Ask him if I can see him on business connected with the hospital,' said Warren.

She withdrew into the house, doubtfully, and left him standing at the door. Presently she returned. 'The doctor will see you, if you'll step inside,' she said.

He was shown into a consulting room. The surgeon was standing by the fire, grey-haired, erect, and very competent.

'Well, Warren,' he said, a little sharply. 'What can I do for you? You've got your discharge from the hospital?'

Warren nodded. 'I'm on my way back to London now. I've had a good long holiday. It's time I got back to my office.'

'You're in employment?'

'Yes. They took me for an out-of-work when I was admitted, and I thought it would be more comfortable if I went on like that.'

'I see. Well, what can I do for you now?'

83

'In the first place I want to thank you for the care and attention that I've had. In the second place, I want to pay for it.'

The surgeon smiled, a little grimly. 'Well,' he said. 'We don't turn away money in Sharples, these days. Have you seen Miss MacMahon?'

'I have. She tells me that I owe them seven pounds.' He hesitated for a moment, staring out of the window. 'They were very kind to me,' he said at last, 'thinking I was out of a job, and short of money. So kind that explanations would have been a little difficult. I understand that you are chairman of the House Committee. Would you mind if I give you a cheque?'

The surgeon looked at him incredulously. 'Why—certainly.'

Warren smiled faintly. 'I see your difficulty,' he said. 'Clothes make the man, I know.' He drew a chair up and sat down, taking the cheque forms from his pocket. 'May I have a pen?'

The surgeon passed a fountain pen to him.

Warren paused, pen in hand. 'I think I ought to pay what this operation would normally have cost me,' he said. 'If I had been taken ill in London, I should hardly have got the operation done at less than a hundred guineas. And then the nursing home for four weeks—about twelve guineas a week. If I make it out for a hundred and fifty guineas, payable to the hospital—would that be satisfactory?'

Dr. Miller moistened his lips. 'Perfectly.' He watched in silence while Warren wrote the cheque and blotted it, and examined it curiously when it was handed to him.

'It's a great many years since fees like this were paid in Sharples,' he remarked, '—if ever. This is your own bank —Warren Sons and Mortimer?'

84

Warren nodded.

'And you are Mr. Henry Warren, of that house?'

'That's right.'

The surgeon laid the cheque upon his desk. 'This is exceptionally generous, Mr. Warren. Thank you.'

The banker shook his head. 'That isn't generosity,' he said. 'It's business—I've only paid you what I should expect to pay for a successful operation.'

He paused. 'I have been very kindly treated here,' he said. 'I should like to do something for the hospital, apart from paying for my operation, if you would allow me.'

'Our hospital is in need of money,' said the surgeon. 'All hospitals are—but this one more than most.'

'I know. Are you in trouble with the current running expenses?'

'Not at the moment. Lady Swarland gives us a cheque each year, even in these difficult times.'

Warren nodded. 'From my own experience,' he said, 'I would have said that the installation of wireless to the beds was one of your great needs—for psychological reasons. But I know nothing of your technical requirements. Is there anything in the way of equipment that you need more than that?'

The surgeon thought for a long time. At last he said, 'I think you're right. Morbidity is our great trouble here —depression. The men get listless, and let go. We need the wireless very badly, certainly. As much as anything.'

'I took the liberty of looking through your files,' said Warren, 'while I was working with the Secretary.' He took the pen, and wrote another cheque. 'You got your last quotation two years ago. I think that ought to cover it.'

He passed the slip of paper to the surgeon. 'I don't want you to make any parade of this,' he said. 'I should prefer this gift to remain anonymous—for a number of reasons. That's why I took the liberty of calling upon you. Do you think that can be arranged?'

The surgeon nodded. 'I can arrange that, if you would prefer it. In that case, I can only thank you myself for your very generous gift. But even if you remain anonymous, I hope you will come down and stay a night with me, to see the installation when it is complete.'

Warren smiled. 'I shall look forward to that.'

They talked about the hospital for a few minutes. Then the surgeon said:

'I understand, Mr. Warren, that you are the head of a banking house. What exactly does that mean? Are you concerned with industry?'

Warren nodded. 'My family started the business in about 1750. We ran as a private bank in Exeter till 1873. Then we moved the headquarters of the business to London, and finally the Exeter business was absorbed by one of the joint stock banks. We do very little business now with private accounts. We mostly handle loans for the various Corporations and the smaller Governments, placing them on the London market. We do a lot of Continental business.'

'Do you touch shipping?'

'Not directly. Are you thinking of shipbuilding, and of your Yard here?'

The surgeon nodded. 'I was wondering if you had seen any sign yet of the revival in shipbuilding industry.'

Warren shook his head. 'I'm not a shipping man,' he said. 'But I know of nothing that would benefit you here.'

There was a pause.

'I was afraid that would be the answer.'

'It's better to be frank about these things,' said

Warren. 'I've been in this town now for a month, and walking about it for ten days. I've seen your shipyard, your plate mills, and your mine. And I've been in most of the smaller workshops, too—or heard about them. I've done my level best to think of work that could be profitably carried on here.

'I can think of nothing,' he said. 'Nothing that would make any difference to the town.'

'You mean we've got to wait for a general revival of prosperity in the country?'

Warren was silent.

The surgeon turned and faced him. 'Or do you mean that we shall never work again?'

Warren met his eyes. 'That's what I mean,' he said gently. 'I think you know it yourself, and anyway, it's better to face up to the facts.' He considered for a minute, and then said, 'If prosperity comes back to the country, as I think it will, I'm afraid Sharples will be left behind. It's five years now since your shipyard closed down, since your mine stopped and the rolling-mills. Your executives have gone to other jobs, and your workmen have grown weak and flabby on out-door relief. If you got a ship to build now, at a bumper price, you couldn't build it profitably, or complete it to time. And it's the same in the plate mills, and the mine.'

'You don't think any work will come back here when shipbuilding revives?'

'It depends on the extent of the revival. Another war might do it. Nothing less.'

'Well,' said the surgeon at last, a little heavily, 'as you say, it's better to have the truth.' He glanced again at Warren. 'I have always understood that you people in the City controlled industry,' he said. 'That you moved companies and businesses about like chessmen. I've

87

seen a great deal in the papers about the banks assisting industry. Don't they assist places like Sharples?

'This place built fine ships once, and not so long ago,' he said. 'There were seven Barlow destroyers at the Battle of Jutland. Seven, no less.'

'I have heard that,' said Warren gravely. 'It's very creditable.

'What you say about the City is only partly true,' he said. 'People deposit money in the banks, or lend it out to companies, and our job is to see that that money is kept reasonably safe. That is what we call legitimate business. In this case, to give ships out to be built in Sharples would entail a risk of non-completion or bad work that nobody would dare to take.'

'I quite understand,' said the surgeon.

Warren rose to take his leave. 'I am afraid that I see nothing whatsoever to be done for Sharples,' he said evenly. 'Legitimately, that is to say . . .'

He turned to the other. 'It has been so kind of you . . .' he said formally. They walked together to the door.

'I'll let you know when our wireless installation is complete,' said Dr. Miller. They said good-bye, and he closed his door again, and turned back to the consulting room. There he stood for a long time fingering two cheques. He wore the expression of a man who at the age of fifty-six no longer believes in fairies, and has received indisputable proof of their existence.

Warren sat in the train till evening, as it roared the length of England down to London. He was alone in his compartment; most of the time he lay in one corner, motionless, staring out of the window. It seemed to him that he had come to one of the turning points in his life, in his career. He knew what he was going back to. He was returning to the work that he had been doing for the last fifteen years, with the distinction that now he would have to live in chambers, quite alone. He was already a wealthy man; he would go on working, making more money, because that was the only interest he knew. He felt that before long that interest would desert him. It would be difficult to keep an interest in the work if he were working only for himself . . .

Of course, he might marry again after his divorce. That might be. But next time, he would marry somebody who knew the discipline of work.

Darlington swept past him, and Northallerton; he passed through York. With every mile that took him south he grew a little more depressed; it seemed to him that he was leaving a place where people had been kind to him, to go back to an empty life of nothing but his work. He felt that the people he had known in Sharples needed him, and that he was running away back to his own life. He had given them several hundred pounds; surely that was enough to quiet the conscience of anyone but a fool. But it wasn't.

He passed through Doncaster. There were fifty acres of the shipyard, more or less—one wouldn't give a bean more than five thousand pounds for the whole thing, lock, stock and barrel. It wasn't worth that—it wasn't worth a halfpenny, because it wasn't earning anything. He could do that himself. But one would have to get the public in on it—to pay the losses. No one man could support the loss that that shipyard would make if it built ships again.

He pulled himself up with a jerk. This was sheer madness. He was thinking Hatry stuff.

He passed through Newark. If that Yard ever was to start again, the difficulty would lie with the first order. The order would be obtained for such a place

89

with difficulty; that probably would mean at a cut price. Therefore, it would probably be done at a colossal loss, and the ship would be late in delivery. You would have to find a pretty complacent shipowner to order from a yard like Barlows. Somebody that you had some sort of hold upon, perhaps . . .

There was always a *quid pro quo*. One of the Latin countries, or perhaps the Balkans, now. One might be able to do something there. They were always pressing him to advance a little further than he cared to go. Perhaps, however, if they placed an order for a ship . . .

He thought of his old father, dead for many years. He closed his eyes, and he could see the old man sitting at his desk. 'That stuff won't do,' he muttered to himself. 'That isn't how our business was built up.'

Grantham swept past him, and away into the dusk behind. The yard employed three thousand men when it was working at full bore—a wage bill of perhaps seven thousand pounds a week. Three hundred and fifty thousand pounds a year. That meant, perhaps, that they would build ships to the value of seven hundred thousand pounds a year, allowing for materials and overheads. That meant at least six ships of ten thousand tons, or smaller vessels in proportion.

It was impossible. Nobody, in this time of depression, could find an order for one single ship of such a size—let along a flock of them.

There was the staff. That might not be so difficult; most of the chief executives of the old team were working in the industry at lower salaries and many of them not so far away—at Wallsend and in Sunderland. He could probably get them together again at a twenty per cent rise in salary—if they were any good. But how was he to judge of that?

The whole thing was impossible, sheer madness to attempt. He must be sensible, and put it from his mind.

He passed through Peterborough.

It would be damn good fun . . .

CHAPTER VI

THREE weeks later Barlows' Yard became the property of Mr. Henry Warren.

He bought it through a solicitor; it was a long time before the news leaked out of the new ownership. He did not use his firm's solicitors, which might have led the rumours straight to him, but used a firm called Matheson and Donkin who had done some work for him before. He summoned Matheson on the morning after he reached London, and gave him his directions.

Two days later Matheson reported back to Warren in his office. 'The shipyard is the property of Mrs. Hector Barlow,' he said. 'She's in Le Touquet at the moment—or else the south of France. Jacobson and Priestly are acting for her. There's a son, too. He's something in the cinema industry, but I don't think he comes into the picture.'

Warren nodded. 'How much did they take out of the business?'

The solicitor glanced at a pencilled note. 'It's a little difficult to say. Between 1914 and 1929—not less than four hundred thousand pounds. Probably rather more.'

'Not very pretty.'

'I beg your pardon, sir?'

'I said,' said Warren grimly, 'that it wasn't very pretty. If I understand you right, they took all the cash out of the business in the good years. When the bad years came they let it bust, and left the town to starve.'

'That's broadly what happened,' said the solicitor.

'They cashed in. Of course, it was their own business. Still, put in that way it's not a very pretty story.'

'What do they want for it now?'

The solicitor picked up another paper. 'I had an hour with Jacobson. He wants fifty thousand for the goodwill, and another twenty thousand for the property as it stands, the freehold site, buildings, plant, machinery, fixtures and fittings—as a going concern.'

'Does he expect to get that?'

'I don't think so. It's an asking price.'

'You'd better tell him to go to Sharples and have a look at it—and then come back and talk sense.'

'You've seen it, have you?'

Warren nodded.

'It's very bad?'

'It's awful—the worst you ever saw. They haven't built a ship there for five years. There's no goodwill. I won't pay a sausage for that. There's fifty acres of land encumbered with useless junk. I'll give him three thousand for that fifty acres, and anything he wants to take away before he sells, he can.'

He got up from his desk. 'Tell him that. Tell him to go and have a look at what he's selling. And tell him to remember that there's somebody fool enough to offer him three thousand pounds for what he's looking at.'

He paid five thousand five hundred in the end.

Matheson bought it for him in his own name, transferring it next day to Lisle Court Securities Ltd., the company which represented Warren's personal fortune. Robbins the watchman continued to receive his weekly wage from Jacobson, as formerly. The deal concluded, Warren placed it in the background of his mind and plunged into the arrears of his work.

He left the house in Grosvenor Square and went to

live in the chambers in Pall Mall, opposite his club. His divorce proceeded on its way; he treated it as a matter of minor business, to the distress of his solicitor. It seemed to Warren that his divorce was an affair of little consequence; he had started it off, and it would happen; let the lawyers get on with it. His entire waking thoughts were centred in his work, but with an added interest. He was looking for ships.

In the next few weeks he learned a good deal about ships. With ships laid up in every creek and every river in the country, orders for new ships were a rarity. He heard of empty shipyards everywhere, of a few scattered orders bitterly competed for, and taken at prices that meant certain loss, but less loss than an empty yard. He heard of Government-assisted German and Italian yards competing in the slender markets that remained, content to make a loss on every ship to take the opportunity of world depression to build up their industry. He heard of queer ships for queer trades, and of rum runners.

In the office one day Morgan said, 'The Laevatian Oil Development, sir. You remember you said it could wait over. Colonel Mavrogadato was on the telephone about a week ago. He wanted to talk it over with you.'

'Elias Mavrogadato? The one who was Minister for Home Affairs?'

'No, sir. This is Demetrios Mavrogadato. I think he's a cousin—a cousin or a nephew. He's over here with the Commission.'

Warren nodded. 'I remember. How long was the pipe line going to be?'

'About forty-eight miles from the wells to the coast, at Pitlonas.'

Warren raised his head. 'What were they going to do with the oil then?'

'Ship it, I suppose. They can place the greater part of the output in Italy.'

'They'd want tankers.'

'I couldn't say, sir.'

Later that day Warren rang up Colonel Demetrios Mavrogadato and invited him to lunch at the Savoy.

Colonel Mavrogadato was pleased to detach himself from the Commission and to accept the invitation. It pleased him to lunch at the Savoy. He prided himself on his capacity as *un homme d'affaires*; he considered the language of his country to be uncouth, and endeavoured to avoid the use of it. He had travelled widely. He had been to Belgrade twice and several times to Sofia; his brother had been to Berlin. With this wealth of experience behind him he knew exactly what was implied by the invitation; he would be expected to eat in one meal the value of his salary for a month, and it would cost him nothing at all. It would cost him less than nothing, in fact, since by common consent the Laevatian Commission had resolved that private hospitality could not affect expense accounts. He was pleased, too, at the prospect of lunching alone with Mr. Henry Warren. It must be that the banker required his help. On his side, Colonel Mavrogadato was willing, nay, even anxious to assist Mr. Warren. In the nature of things, he could hardly expect to serve upon another Commission for some years, and he must make sufficient out of this one to augment his salary till Fortune's wheel came round again.

They met in the entrance hall. 'My dear Colonel,' said Warren in French. 'This is indeed a pleasure.'

The swarthy features broke into a smile. '*Enchanté, cher monsieur,*' said the colonel, and bowed stiffly from the waist. They went down into the dining-room, talking

95

amiable politenesses in bad French, and having some little difficulty in understanding each other.

Warren, who had had some experience of the Balkan peoples, was nevertheless surprised at what the colonel put away. He began, reasonably enough, with a plate of iced melon, followed by hors d'œuvres and caviar. At Warren's suggestion he followed this up with a couple of dozen oysters and half a bottle of Chablis. He then expressed a preference for turtle soup and *sole meunière,* and was so delighted with pheasant that Warren had little difficulty in inducing him to consume a second portion. With the tournedos they broached the second bottle of champagne. The sweet demanded serious concentration; the colonel took the card and studied it.

'*Qu'est celyui-là?*' he enquired. 'Jam Roly Poly?'

'*C'est un plat du pays,*' said Warren, '*avec confiture. C'est bien délicieux—mais solide.*'

'*Bien,*' said the colonel. '*J'ai encore un peu de faim.*'

Coffee and kummel; with the blue smoke wreathing up from their cigars Warren approached the subject of their business. 'It has been a great sorrow to me,' he said in French, 'that I have been unable to see more of your beautiful country. Two visits only I have made there, for the business of the Visgrad waterworks.'

'The Visgrad waterworks,' said the colonel, a little thickly. 'That was a very good business, I think. For everybody, that was very good business.' He leaned a little towards Warren. 'But our oil development—that will be a good business too, I think.'

'I understand,' said Warren, 'that it is the intention of your Government to raise the finance for the oil development from external sources. It is for this reason that I ventured to ask if you could spare the time to talk the matter over with me, as between two friends, or business associates.' The dark eyes watching him narrowed a little. 'As I understand the matter, it is not the intention of your Government to seek a loan?'

They'd never have the nerve to ask for a loan, thought Warren to himself. Not after what happened to the last one.

The Laevatian leaned over a little closer to him. 'Not a loan,' he said. 'There will be a company, an incorporated company of the highest integrity, supported by our Government. There will be two classes of the shares. The first class will be held entirely by the Laevatian Government. The second class will be issued to the public in London, perhaps also in Paris and in New York. But London alone, I think, is better.'

They know it's the only place where they could raise money for a thing like this, thought Warren. I'd like to see them try it on in Paris.

Aloud, he said, 'The Laevatian Government, will they subscribe in cash for any portion of their shares?'

He knew the answer before he asked the question.

'It is not necessary,' declared the colonel. 'The Laevatian Government is the owner of all the oil that is in the land. It is not necessary that they should give money also to the company, besides the oil. That is for the public to subscribe.'

Warren nodded slowly. He sat there smoking meditatively for a few minutes. In the course of his working life he had examined many such proposals for Government-controlled companies, and he thought little of them. His experience warned him at the outset that this was probably a wrong 'un. It might not be consciously fraudulent in its inception, though he would not rule that out, but in the end the investors would probably lose their money.

97

He turned to the colonel. 'It may be that it would be possible to float such a company,' he said. 'But as a first step, I think it would be necessary to offer some collateral security to the investors.'

The other nodded. 'That might be arranged,' he said. 'For example, the profit from the railways.'

Warren nodded. This thing had been carefully prepared; his sense of the unsoundness of it grew stronger. He had successfully avoided the railways as a security when he was dealing with the waterworks; in his view they were no security at all. But they would do to dress up a prospectus with.

God, he couldn't touch this thing. He must be crazy to be thinking of it.

'As I understand it,' he said, 'the proposal is that a pipe line should be laid from the wells to Pitlonas, on the coast, to get the oil to the coast for shipment. I take it that you have had suitable consultants on that portion of the project?'

'Everything,' said the colonel, 'has been examined with a care that is incredible. Everything is in order for the work to begin now. The reports of the engineers are at your disposal.'

Warren nodded. That part of the thing was probably all right; it was not there that the swindle would lie.

He thought for a minute, and then said, 'After the oil reaches the coast, how is it transported? In whose ships?'

The colonel shrugged his shoulders, and spread his hands. 'You understand—that is a concern of detail, for the management of the company.'

Warren considered for a moment. He decided that there was no objection to indicating his line, even at this early stage. This would be a long business, and must be shortened as much as possible. 'My dear Colonel,' he said. 'You must understand the position of our finance in this country. In this time of depression, our business in the financial world is so to direct the facilities that we offer that they produce the greatest assistance to the trade of this country—in which also we have great interests.'

'*Parfaitement*,' said the colonel. He helped himself to a little more of the hotel's excellent brandy.

'The construction of the pipe line,' said Warren. 'It would be necessary, of course, for that contract to be placed in this country.'

'That could perhaps be arranged.'

Warren thought, This is a damn sight too easy. They must have tried Paris. I wonder if they've tried New York? Aloud, he said, 'What would be the cost of that contract?'

'About three hundred thousand of your English pounds, in sterling.'

'And the working capital that would be required?'

'About another three hundred thousand of your sterling.'

There was a long pause. In the end Warren said, 'You understand, I speak only of my own group. But, in my view, that prospect would not be very attractive. The contracts are too small in relation to the risk.' The colonel was about to say something impetuous, but thought better of it. 'On the other hand,' said Warren, 'if it were possible for the company to reconsider its plan of operation so that it would operate its own fleet of oil tankers, and if the order for the tankers were to be placed through my group in this country, then I think the position might be greatly eased.'

The Laevatian was silent for a minute, his swarthy

features a mask. And then, 'I cannot say,' he said. 'It will be difficult. It will be necessary to satisfy the Minister of Marine, M. Theopoulos.'

Satisfy is right, thought Warren grimly. I'll have to satisfy the whole bloody Cabinet before I'm through with this.

'You understand,' said the Laevatian, 'there is the Trade Agreement with Germany that would require to be considered.'

Warren nodded slowly. He had not thought of that. The Laevatians some years before had bartered the whole of their output of pseudo-Turkish tobacco to Germany in exchange for manufactured goods. In normal markets the stuff was practically unsaleable, but in totalitarian countries people smoked what they were told to smoke. The Laevatians had not taken from Germany the value of the stuff they sent; there were large credits tied up in that country. If any ships were to be bought they would be German ships.

He must stand firm on that, however. No ships, no money. One didn't finance a muck-heap of a country like Laevatia for fun.

He smiled at the Laevatian. 'We will turn it over in our minds,' he said. 'On my part, I feel that it would make the scheme complete if the company were to operate its own ships. It would assist a flotation. It would make a flotation very much easier if part of the issue were to be expended in orders for ships in this country.'

He paused. 'On your part, you will consult with your colleagues, and obtain their views. Then, perhaps, we may meet again to take the matter a stage further.'

'With pleasure,' said the colonel, and paused expectantly.

Warren chose his words carefully. 'I am sure that we can bring about this business if we work together, my dear Colonel,' he said smoothly, 'as business associates. We shall do everything within our power to—satisfy— any reasonable request that you may make.'

Their eyes met. 'I will see what I can do,' said the colonel.

Warren turned and motioned to the waiter for his bill; the colonel surreptitiously pocketed a couple of cigars from the box upon the table. They left the dining-room, and parted with mutual expressions of esteem.

Two days later Warren received a letter from Dr. Miller in Sharples. His wireless installation in the hospital was complete; would he care to come down to see it, staying a couple of nights with the doctor? He thought it over for a minute, and decided to go down at the week-end.

He arrived in Sharples late on Friday night, had a whisky and soda with the doctor, and went to bed.

Next morning they drove down to the hospital. 'I feel a bit of an impostor,' said Warren uneasily. 'Does anybody know that I gave the damn thing?'

'Not a soul,' said the surgeon cheerfully. 'I gave out that it was an anonymous donor and that's all they know.' He smiled. 'I don't suppose anyone will recognise you.'

'I hope you're right,' said Warren.

He was not. In the corridor, on their way down to the installation in the basement, they met Miss MacMahon. She nodded to the surgeon, glanced at Warren, stopped, and stared hard at him.

Warren smiled. 'I'm afraid so,' he said.

She said, 'You are Warren, aren't you?'

'Yes, I'm Warren.'

She smiled. 'Have you come back to pay me your seven pounds?'

The surgeon smiled. 'You'll have to strike that off your books, Mr. Warren has already paid that—to me. I dealt with it at the last committee.'

'Oh. Is he the patient who paid a hundred and fifty guineas?'

The surgeon nodded.

She thought for a minute, and then turned to Warren. 'I suppose you put in the wireless, too. Or was that some other tramp?'

'I'm afraid that was me. But it was supposed to be anonymous.'

'That's all very well,' said Miss MacMahon. 'But we've got the books to keep straight, Mr. Williams and I. Somebody's got to know who gives anonymous gifts, or you couldn't cash any cheques. As it is, I don't know what I shall say to Mr. Williams about that seven pounds. You see, it's entered in the ledger. I suppose I shall have to tell him that I can't collect it from you, and he's got to write it off as a bad debt. I'll probably get the sack over it.'

'I'd better pay up.'

'That wouldn't be fair. You'd better let me tell Mr. Williams. You see, it's not so easy to hide your light under a bushel.'

He smiled. 'I ought to have stayed in London.'

'That wouldn't have done you any good. I was going to get after you for it next week—you remember you left an address.' She paused. 'I suppose I should have found that you were head of the firm, or something.'

'I suppose you would.'

'Why did you say you were out of a job?'

'I didn't say it first—somebody told me that was what I was—one of the nurses. I thought it was easier to carry on that way.'

She sighed a little. 'I suppose it was a natural mistake. We don't get many of the other sort here these days.'

He nodded slowly. 'I suppose things are still very bad. There's been no improvement?'

She shook her head.

The surgeon said, 'Things are getting terrible, Mr. Warren. In the last few months—the place seems to have changed. It's as if the disease had become chronic.'

The Almoner broke in, 'I've noticed that, too, Dr. Miller. Last spring, things seemed to pick up a bit. People seemed more cheerful, and the out-patients went down quite a lot. I could show you in the records. But this year it's just flat—the same all the time. The people aren't so . . . so buoyant as they were last year.'

Warren said nothing.

They went down to inspect the apparatus, and then walked through the hospital. In practically every bed the patient was wearing headphones; there was a better atmosphere about the place than Warren had remembered. 'It's made a difference,' said the surgeon. 'There's no doubt about it. And the beauty of it is, it's always new. Hardly any of them have it in their homes. So when they come in here, it gives them something fresh to think about.'

Warren said nothing.

They went back to the entrance hall; Warren turned to the Almoner. 'I'm staying here to-night,' he said, 'with Dr. Miller. There are one or two things I'd like to see this afternoon, before I go back. Would you take me down to the shipyard again?'

'Why—certainly, Mr. Warren. I'm free.'

He smiled. 'That's terribly good of you. I'll call round for you here at about half-past two.'

He met her at the hospital, and they walked down through the town together. It was a bright, sunny afternoon with a fresh wind; the wind blew through the bare grey streets with all the freshness of the moors behind the town, untainted by the smoke of industry. A few men stood about at street corners and eyed them curiously as they passed; one or two women sat on doorsteps in the sun in sheltered corners. It surprised Warren that in spite of the fine day there were so few people to be seen about, and he said so.

'The wind's quite sharp,' said the Almoner, 'and they've got very little resistance to cold. They mostly stay indoors on days like this.'

Warren's heart sank. He might perhaps get orders for a ship or two, but could these people ever build them?

They passed the old watchman with a word, and went into the Yard. To all appearances it was as it had been before, the buildings and the wharves deserted and a little fresh grass growing on the slips. The wind sighed through the derricks and the gantries overhead. Again Warren got the impression that there was not much wrong with the place; so far as he could see, nothing had been removed before the sale.

'Well, here we are,' said the girl. 'What did you want to see?'

Warren laughed. 'Just that it was all still here,' he said. 'I don't see much altered since I was here before.'

She smiled, a little bitterly. 'You needn't be afraid of that. You'll see it just the same if you come here next year, or the year after that. Only some of the derricks may have fallen down by then.'

He eyed her for a moment. 'You've lived in Sharples all your life, have you?'

'Most of it. I went away to school, of course. And then

I went to Durham University. But my home was always here.' She turned to him. 'You see, I knew it all as it used to be, when you couldn't hear yourself speak standing here, because of the riveters. And then, there was a launch every couple of months or so, with the flags and cheering, and champagne, and everything. And we always used to look at the shipping news in *The Times,* to see where our ships had got to. . . . It makes one feel bad to see it all just rotting away like this.'

He asked, 'What did you read at Durham?'

'Law,' she said unexpectedly. 'But I never practised.'

He rested one foot upon a baulk of timber, and leaned forward on the knee. 'You ought to get away from here,' he said. 'It's not good for you, or anyone, to spend their life in a dead place like this.'

She nodded. 'That's one way of looking at it, I know.'

'What is the other?'

She raised her head and looked him in the eyes. 'I had a fine time here when I was young,' she said simply. 'From the earliest I can remember, up to the time when I was twenty-five, when the depression came. All those years—I was terribly happy. I knew everybody here, and they were kind, and decent—and it was all so interesting. It's different now, of course, but you've got to take the rough with the smooth.

'I don't say that I'm going to stay here all my life,' she said. 'But I wouldn't want to go away from here till things get right again.'

They moved slowly through the yard, between the heaps of rusty scrap and stinging-nettles, under the towering gantries. A few white-faced children were playing listlessly upon a heap of rotting plate.

'Not a very good place for them to play,' he said. 'They'd get a nasty cut if they fell down on that stuff.'

'They do from time to time. Then we get them up as out-patients—after it's had time to get nicely septic.'

'Can't the watchman keep them out?'

She shook her head. 'There are holes all along the fence where they get in.' She pointed. 'There.'

He nodded. 'I'll have that seen to.'

She turned and stared at him. 'What do you mean—you'll have it seen to?'

'I own this yard,' he said. 'I bought it three weeks ago.'

There was a long silence. The gantries overhead rattled and groaned a little; somewhere a sheet of corrugated iron was flapping in the wind.

'That's a change, anyway,' she said at last. 'I sometimes thought that nothing would ever happen here again.' She stared at him curiously. 'Who are you, Mr. Warren? What do you do?'

'I'm a banker. If you wanted to be rude, you might say that we're an issuing house.'

She wrinkled her brows. 'Does that mean that you start companies?'

He hesitated. 'Sometimes we do that.'

'Are you going to start one here?'

He eyed her for a minute. 'If you were in my shoes, would you go and tell a lot of shareholders that you could make money by building ships here?'

She hesitated. 'I—I don't know.'

'Nor do I,' he said grimly.

'I see it's difficult,' she said. 'But what are you going to do with it, now that you've bought it?'

He shook his head. 'I don't know that I really know myself. I bought it because I was afraid that the National Shipbuilders Security would get hold of it, and close it down for ever. But . . .'

He stared around. 'I don't know what to do with it. I'm just hoping something may turn up.'

'It would put fresh life into the town if they knew there was some chance of work again,' she said. 'May it be talked about?'

He shook his head. 'I'd rather not, if you don't mind. It may be that I shan't be able to do anything at all. In that case I should sell it again—if I could. And that would be a disappointment to them.'

She nodded. 'All right. I won't say anything.'

They turned and walked towards the gate. 'If there is anything that I can do to help this thing,' she said, 'I hope you'll let me know.' She smiled a little ruefully. 'Not that I'd be much help to you in starting companies.'

He said, 'You might let me know from time to time how things go on down here. Old Robbins, at the gate, he ought to be getting his money regularly every week in the same way that he always has. Let me know if there should be any hitch there.'

She nodded.

'There's another thing. You used to know all the heads of the departments in this Yard?'

She nodded. 'Daddy knew everyone, and they all used to come to our house. And we'd go to theirs.'

'Some day,' he said, 'we may want a General Manager. It ought to be someone who knows the place, and the men. And he must be young—not more than forty. And he must be working in shipbuilding now. He'd have to be cheerful and tactful, because he'd have the hell of a job ahead of him if we got this thing started up again. But we'd pay him well.'

She said, 'I'd like to think that over, Mr. Warren. I know the sort of man you mean. I'll write to you if I can think of anyone.'

They walked up to the hospital. At the gates she turned towards him as they said good-bye.

'Mr. Warren,' she said. 'You're serious about this? You're really trying to start something here again—after all these years?'

He met her eyes. 'I'm serious enough,' he said. 'If I could get this yard cracking again I'd be a very happy man. But whether I can do it—that's another matter.'

'It's good to hear that much,' she said quietly. 'The only thing that I can do is wish you all the luck in the world.'

He changed his plans, and went back to London on a sleeper train. Next day was Sunday; he spent it going through the papers relating to the Laevatian Oil Development that Morgan had prepared for him. At the end of five hours' work he had developed and increased his first suspicion that the thing was basically unsound.

It was, however, the one thing he had in sight that held out any prospect of orders for ships.

CHAPTER VII

A MONTH later Warren arrived in Visgrad from Berlin by air, and went to the Hotel des Nations. The hall porter, with encyclopaedic memory, greeted him as an old friend.

He had met the Laevatian Commission in London in conference, not once, but four times. He had stated his terms courteously, but firmly, from the first. Three oil tankers, of ten thousand tons each, were to be built in England by a concern that he would nominate at a later stage. On that basis he would proceed to use his best endeavours to promote their issue on the London market.

They were grieved, and went away. They came back in a few days, and went away again; Warren sat quiet, and watched them go from house to house with their proposal. In that time of depression he had little fear that anyone would entertain it for a moment, without some powerful outside motive.

After the third meeting he lunched again with Colonel Mavrogadato. 'I think it is very difficult, this business,' said the colonel. 'It is M. Theopoulos. They are all afraid of what M. Theopoulos may say. M. Theopoulos will say that the ships must be built in Germany.'

He paused. 'M. Theopoulos has had great kindness from many German firms, on many occasions,' he said confidentially. 'He was a poor man, as I am myself, when first he came to office. Now he is very wealthy, but—you understand—he does not make a display of his wealth. It is natural that he would not wish to disappoint his friends in Germany.'

Warren nodded slowly. He knew the Balkans. 'M. Theopoulos will not be disappointed with our business,' he said. 'You understand—one would not wish to talk of money with a man so highly placed. Has he no friend on the Commission with whom we could discuss the matter, and who could put it to him in the proper light?'

There was generally an agent in the background somewhere, to negotiate the bribe.

The colonel slammed his hands down on the table. 'It is three times—no, four times—unfortunate,' he exclaimed. 'M. Hassanein, it was arranged, should be of the Commission. He is married to the divorced wife of the brother of the wife to Mr. Theopoulos. But he fell ill, and was unable to accompany the Commission.'

'That is indeed unfortunate,' said Warren gravely.

Three days later he met the Commission again.

'It appears to me,' he said, 'that a matter of such importance to your country can hardly be negotiated except in Visgrad, where it will be possible for you to consult with your Government at every stage. If the proposals of my group are such as to justify your further consideration, I would suggest that you invite me to wait upon you in Visgrad, to take the matter farther.'

They glanced at each other.

Mr. Potiscu, the chairman, said, 'That we had intended to suggest. It will, perhaps, be better that you should meet with M. Theopoulos, and with M. Deleben, the Prime Minister. In that event, the Commission would return to Visgrad, via Paris, on Friday of the week after next.'

'I would not ask the Commission to wait so long on my

account,' said Warren, a little tactlessly. 'I am completely at your disposal.'

Mr. Potiscu looked a little pained. 'There is a race of horses,' he explained. 'Your Grand National . . .'

Warren smiled. 'I should have thought of that,' he said. 'It would give me infinite pleasure if the Commission would regard themselves as my guests for that day.'

He was forced to submit to the delay. He was able, however, to ensure that they did not tarry in Paris on the way home by presenting them with through tickets to Visgrad at fifty per cent discount, sending each member home happy with a few pounds extra gleaned from the expense account.

A few days later he followed them to Visgrad.

He knew the city well. It lay in a bowl of the hills, snow-capped to the south; the river ran beside it. It sprawled in Eastern fashion, indeterminately; a litter of mud-houses set upon bare earth, whitewashed and dazzling in the sun, flat-roofed. Olives clothed the surrounding hills with a grey sheen; in the city itself palm trees and oleanders lined the principal roads.

All this could be seen before you landed at the aerodrome. You stepped from the machine, and the interminable formalities of entrance to Laevatia began. Dirty, unshaven soldiery in buttonless uniforms laid loaded rifles on the table with alarming insouciance, while they pawed your passport in a pretence at reading. Illiterate clerks asked interminable questions about the religion and habits of your grandparents; it was better to provide an answer, right or wrong. Fingerprints were taken, for the greater security of Laevatia against its enemies. And finally, a grudging permit was given to depart on the dusty seven-mile drive into the city.

The road wound from the aerodrome through olive woods, and an occasional village. Ox-carts impeded the way, yoked picturesquely to low, high-wheeled carts. In the villages the veiled women and the mosques added to the Eastern atmosphere; usually a very new church stood unused on the outskirts. In the country districts Laevatia was principally Mohammedan.

On the morning following his arrival, Warren visited the British Embassy. He left cards on the Minister and had a short talk with the Counsellor. Then he found himself in the office of the Commercial Secretary, a high, sunny room, with a window wide open on a garden full of lilac in bloom. Mr. Pennington received him cordially, and gave him a cigarette.

'We've heard a lot about you, Mr. Warren,' he said. 'From the Foreign Office, of course—but also here. Yes. When the Commission came back last week and old Potiscu reported, they had something like a free fight in the Cabinet over your visit. The Prime Minister was non-commital; he really prefers to do business with us. But Theopoulos went straight up in the air, of course. He made a speech in the Assembly about you—I'll let you have a copy, translated, this afternoon. The gist of it was that your proposals were an insult to a friendly nation— meaning Germany, of course.'

He paused. 'Two representatives of the Hamburger Metallgeschellschaft arrived here the day before yesterday—Herren Braum and Linersoppe. They're staying at your hotel.'

Warren asked, 'What sort of following has Theopoulos in the Assembly?'

'Not so strong—perhaps twenty per cent. But if things got too difficult it might create a split: in that case. Theopoulos would leave the present Government—the

People's Party—and go to the Social Reform Party. They'll very likely be the next Government.'

'When will that be?'

Mr. Pennington shrugged his shoulders. 'We haven't had a change of Government for some time. Perhaps next month—perhaps not for three years.' He considered for a moment. 'Of course, your business might cause enough stir to change the Government, in itself.'

'It seems to me,' said Warren, 'that first of all I've got to make a contact with Theopoulos. Unless I can get him sweet, I don't think it looks so good.'

'I should say you're right,' said the Commercial Secretary gravely. 'But I'm afraid you've taken on something. The Germans have got him in their pocket, properly.'

'How would you set about it, if you were me?'

Mr. Pennington considered for a minute. 'I'd get hold of the Prime Minister first,' he said, 'old Deleben, and make him sweet. We might be able to help you there a bit; the Minister's pretty thick with the old boy. If you could get him on your side, at any rate you'd have a good representation in the Cabinet.'

He took Warren across the road, made him a member of the English Club, introduced him to the Military and Air Attachés, and gave him a pink gin.

Warren went back to his hotel, lunched thoughtfully, and spent a quiet hour in meditation afterwards. Then he wrote a short letter to the Prime Minister, asking for an interview.

He spent the remainder of the day in taking stock of his surroundings. Little seemed to have changed about the town since his last visit, three years previously. In the squares people sat in front of cafés with queer drinks of alcoholic aniseed. All serious business negotiation was still done in the long bar of his hotel, between the hours of seven and nine. He met the Military Attaché there and had a drink with him, dined alone, and went early to his bed.

Next morning he waited on the Prime Minister in the House of Assembly. He had not previously met M. Deleben, and found him amiable enough, a rotund, black-visaged little man. When out of office he was a lawyer in a small country town.

They talked in French for some time. Warren was told that the Commission, headed by M. Potiscu, would continue to function and to deal with the Oil Development. They were, of course, primarily answerable to M. Theopoulos, who would bring their decisions to the Cabinet.

'I had the honour of meeting Mr. Potiscu several times in London,' said Warren, who thought nothing of him. 'I feel that a more able man for the position could hardly have been chosen. M. Theopoulos I have not yet met.'

'That we must arrange,' said the Prime Minister.

'It will be indeed a pleasure,' said Warren. He thought for a moment. 'It has occurred to me,' he continued, 'that a matter of such importance to your country will naturally take a little time to negotiate. Such matters can hardly be hurried.'

'That is very true,' said the Prime Minister.

'It may be necessary that I should travel to England, or to Paris, before the matter is finally concluded—possibly more than once, in order to assist the business from our side. Such absences on my part may be very inconvenient to you, and that I wish to avoid. It is in my mind to employ an agent here in Visgrad, a confidential agent— you understand, a man of complete discretion, in whom you would have confidence.'

The little beady eyes were watching him intently. 'Such agents are not very easy to find, Mr. Warren.'

Warren smiled. 'If this were an easy matter,' he said smoothly, 'I should not have troubled the Prime Minister of this country with it. On my side, I should be prepared to pay the highest fee for the services of the right man, on the assumption that the business should develop to our satisfaction. I realise that to employ the wrong man would be a disaster. It is because of this, and because of the importance of this matter to the State of Laevatia, that I have come to you.'

He met the little black eyes fixed on him in all innocence.

'Could you recommend to me the services of a good agent for this very delicate purpose?'

There was silence in the room. At last the Laevatian arose, and Warren got up with him. 'Such a matter would take much consideration, Mr. Warren,' he said. 'Something may perhaps be arranged. I will think about it, and communicate with you at your hotel.'

'I shall be infinitely obliged,' said Warren.

He left the Assembly, and went over to the English Club. The Air Attaché introduced him to the Consul. The Consul stood him a drink. 'I've read about you in the local papers,' he remarked. 'Will you be here for long?'.

'Six months,' said the Air Attaché. 'It'll take him that long to appreciate the—er—atmosphere they do business in out here.'

Warren raised his glass. 'You forget,' he said gravely, 'that I know a little bit about the atmosphere. I've been out here before.'

The Air Attaché grinned. 'I'll come to you for a course of lectures. If you can tell me how to get our aircraft in. . . . Though why we want to get our aircraft into a dud place like this beats me.'

'Member of the League,' said the Consul gravely. 'Horse, foot, guns, *and* aeroplanes all march to our assistance when we get attacked.'

'Like hell they will,' said the Attaché.

Warren returned to his hotel for lunch. In the middle of the afternoon the porter brought a note to him in the lounge.

'For m'sieur,' he said. 'Delivered by a messenger.'

'Thank you,' said Warren, and dismissed the man. He went up to his bedroom, sat down on his bed, and opened it. Inside there was a single sentence written in precise, clerkly characters upon a single sheet of blank paper, unsigned. It read:

I think M. Petre Vislan, Amontadeo 4, will make for you a suitable agent.

He sat for a time waving it to and fro between his fingers, deep in thought. Then he copied the name and address into his diary, put a match to the paper and destroyed it.

He rang up the Commercial Secretary from his bedroom. 'Can I come round and have a cup o' tea?' he inquired.

'Never touch it,' said Mr. Pennington. 'It doesn't taste right out here. But come round, by all means.'

In the lilac-scented office Warren asked:

'Who is Mr. Petre Vislan, who lives at Amontadeo 4?'

'Search me,' said Mr. Pennington. 'But I'll find out for you.'

'How long would that take?'

The Secretary looked at his watch. 'Couple of hours,

perhaps. Let you know all we can find out about him by then.' He hesitated. 'I could ring up the Chief of the Civic Guard, of course, and probably tell you at once. But perhaps you'd rather not do that?'

'It might be better not to worry them,' said Warren considerately.

'All right. Is he an official?'

'I know literally nothing about him.'

Mr. Pennington nodded. 'I'll do what I can. You're in the Hotel des Nations? I'll look in there at cocktail-time—about seven, and tell you what I can.'

At seven-fifteen they were seated in an alcove with cigarettes and glasses of hulse, which is the same as the Greek ouzo. Warren poured the water into the clear liquid and watched the white precipitate.

'Here's luck,' said Pennington. He drank. 'I got a little on your man through the Embassy servants. He's a nephew of Deleben—the son of a brother of Deleben's wife.'

Warren nodded slowly.

'He's quite a young man—twenty-two or twenty-three. He's supposed to be an artist. He spent a year in Paris about three years ago. Does nothing in particular. Rather a pansy, from what I can gather. Keeps a mistress on the other side of the river, but I don't suppose that interests you. Yes, he's unmarried. Lives alone in a flat—unless you count the girl.'

'That's all?'

'That's all I can easily find out. We don't keep any sort of secret service, or anything of that sort, you know. It wouldn't do. At the same time—we aim to please.'

Warren smiled. 'That's given me enough to be going on with.'

Mr. Pennington cocked an experienced eye at him.

117

'I must say, you don't waste a lot of time. This is going to be a pleasure to watch.'

Warren spent the evening in infinite boredom, the first of several. He dined alone, and sat for a little time alone in the lounge. Then, the night being fine, he strolled out into the main streets of the city. At eleven o'clock the city was just beginning to wake up; theatre and cinema crowds were going to their seats; the shops were all open and ablaze with lights. He paused for a moment outside a wide portal, all chromium and glass; from within came a sound of a dance band. It was a night-club of some sort. Over his head a neon sign blazoned the one word, Gonea.

'γυνη,' he said. 'It's half Greek, this language. Woman. Not bad for a title. Says what it means. A trifle crude?'

He went back to his hotel to bed.

Next day he made contact on the telephone with M. Petre Vislan, and went to see him at his flat. M. Vislan came swaying to meet him, a willowy, dark-haired young man, with a pale, fleshy face, heavily scented. He was refreshingly direct.

'My uncle has told me,' he said in French, 'that you must pay twenty thousand dinars, net—you understand? Without deduction for any other parties.'

Warren made a rapid mental calculation. 'If the entire business is completed,' he said, 'that would be possible. But it would be necessary that the order for the ships should be placed with my group. Apart from that—nothing. The business would not then be interesting to me.'

The other waved a languid handkerchief, flooding the air with scent. 'It is a difficulty, so my uncle says. M. Theopoulos is very angry, and he will not wish to disappoint his friends in Germany.'

'It is a difficulty which we must get over,' said Warren.
'I shall expect your uncle to assist in persuading
M. Theopoulos to place the order with my group.'

The other sighed. 'I will tell my uncle. But it is a
great difficulty.'

'Are you able to arrange a meeting for me with
M. Theopoulos?'

'I do not know. I will try if I can arrange a meeting.
I will talk with my uncle. It is a great difficulty.'

'When will you know if you can arrange a meeting?'

'I do not know. Perhaps I can talk with my uncle to-
day. He may telephone to M. Theopoulos—I do not
know. Perhaps, this evening, we meet again—in the bar
of the Hotel des Nations?'

'That will be a great pleasure,' said Warren formally.

He spent the remainder of the day walking round
Visgrad, infinitely bored. In the evening he sat for half
an hour in the bar before M. Vislan put in an appearance.

'M. Theopoulos, he is a very busy man,' he said.
'Two days—three days—perhaps then you will have an
interview with him. My uncle has spoken to him by
telephone. But it is a great difficulty.'

Warren wrinkled his brows. 'I will write formally to
ask him for an interview,' he said. 'Your uncle will then
be able to remind him.'

'That you may do,' said M. Vislan mournfully. 'But
M. Theopoulos is very busy.'

Warren dined alone, wrote his formal letter, and went
for another walk.

Nothing whatever happened on the following day; he
got no answer to his letter. In the afternoon he took a
car to the summit of Monte Turcu, and sat for an hour
over a glass of hulse, looking out over the city. He

returned to the hotel, read a novel in his bedroom for a couple of hours, and dined alone.

All day he had not spoken to a soul except the hotel servants and the driver of his taxicab. He was most paralytically bored.

He went out to the Gonea.

The tables rose in tiers and little boxes, separated by waist-high partitions, above the oval dancing floor. The place was only scantily filled; it was early. Over by the floor the band were twanging at their instruments, moving restlessly about, and shuffling their music. Warren settled into a small box at the back of the hall, ordered a coffee and a cognac, and waited upon events.

He had not long to wait. Within ten minutes a slim, dark girl was leaning over the back of his box. 'You look so sad,' she said in French, with a mocking tone. 'It is a great pity. But no doubt you would prefer to be alone?'

He smiled. 'It would be very kind of you to join me. I have spoken to nobody all day.'

She slipped into a seat beside him. 'It is the business,' she said. 'All of you Americans are the same. The business makes you grow so sad.'

'That may be. But I'm English.'

She rippled into laughter. 'The English, they are the worst of all.'

Spangles covered the black stuff of her corsage and her dress; her lips and finger-nails were very red, her eyebrows pencilled black. 'And you,' he said thoughtfully, 'must be Sicilian.'

She pouted. 'I declare—it is an insult.'

'A thousand pardons, Mademoiselle.' She threw him a swift, brilliant smile. 'I am entirely deceived. From what country do you come?'

'From Corsica. There is my home. In Sulina. You have perhaps travelled in Corsica?'

He shook his head. 'Mademoiselle,' he said. 'It would be a great pleasure to me if you would drink a glass of wine.'

'Of a certainty. What wine would you prefer?' She fingered the list.

He smiled. 'Mademoiselle, I would prefer that wine which carries the most generous commission with the cork, for this first meeting. Later, on future evenings, we drink lemonade.'

She threw her head back and laughed merrily. 'You are droll, Monsieur,' she said. 'The most droll Englishman that I have ever met. It would amuse me to drink lemonade with you. But for this first evening, we will drink French champagne.'

A waiter appeared behind them swiftly with a bottle and the glasses. She stopped him as he was retiring. 'Give me the cork,' she said. He left it on the table with a smile; presently it was joined by another.

She told Warren that her name was Pepita. In a little while they went and danced, talked for a little, and then danced again. Once in the course of the evening she left him for a quarter of an hour to do her turn in cabaret, a Spanish song and dance with castanets; then she came back to him, and they danced again.

At midnight he went back to his hotel. She pouted as he left her. 'It is too early,' she said. 'I declare—the English are so sleepy. This place is not yet alive.'

'What time do you get home?' he asked.

'Five o'clock, usually.'

'And then you get up in the middle of the afternoon?'

'But no. At twelve o'clock. That is sufficient sleep for anybody but an Englishman.'

She smiled at him, and he went back to his hotel to bed.

He saw M. Vislan again next morning. 'I do not think it is possible to do anything,' he said, waving a scented handkerchief in languid manner. 'M. Theopoulos is very busy. I think he will see you before long.'

'I trust so,' said Warren equably. 'But I have other business to attend to; it will not be possible for me to wait in Visgrad unless it is possible for the business to progress. Tell your uncle that.'

The other sighed. 'It is very difficult. I will talk with my uncle, and I will tell you what he has said.'

Warren went and had a cocktail in the English Club. 'Not so good, to-day,' he said in answer to a question from the Consul. 'I'm trying to get in to see Theopoulos —without any very great success.'

The Air Attaché smiled. 'I thought you knew this town,' he said. 'This is Heartbreak House.'

'I guessed as much,' said Warren.

He spent the afternoon asleep upon his bed, in common with the remainder of Visgrad. That night he went again to the Gonea and danced with Pepita.

She told him, as the evening progressed, something about her life. She rarely spent more than six weeks in one cabaret. She had come to Visgrad a fortnight previously from Athens; before that she had been in Belgrade. She knew Istanbul and Cairo, Bucharest and Tripoli. She spent her life, in fact, in journeying from cabaret to cabaret around the Mediterranean.

He asked, 'Do you ever take a holiday?'

She said, 'I go to Sulina once a year, to be with my little one. I stay one week—two weeks. But you understand, it is necessary to work.'

He nodded. 'Is your little one a boy or a girl?'

She smiled. 'A girl, of five years. I go in the spring,

or early in the summer. Then I can take her out on to the hill-side, where the flowers are. We make little crowns of the flowers . . .' She broke off. 'M'sieur no doubt would like to dance again?'

Later in the evening he said, 'You are perhaps engaged to-morrow afternoon, Mademoiselle? I find,' he explained, 'that one does not do business in Visgrad in the afternoon. I have the intention to take an automobile into the mountains for two or three hours—beyond Monte Turcu. It would give me great pleasure if you would accompany me.'

She smiled. 'To the high mountains? M'sieur, I would be enchanted. But it will be necessary that I return to Visgrad by six o'clock precisely, for my meal and for my rest. You understand, one must think of one's profession. . . .'

She came to the hotel next day, dressed a little extravagantly in black and white; he took her in and gave her lunch. He found that she was known to many of the people lunching in the dining-room; from time to time somebody would catch her eye, and she would smile.

'You know more people than I do, Mademoiselle,' he said.

She shrugged her shoulders. 'It is the same everywhere. In Visgrad all the world visits the Gonea—the men, that is to say. It is so in Athens also, in Sofia, in Aleppo—everywhere.' She turned to him. 'M'sieur, I have said that I must return by six o'clock. But now, I have things that I must buy to-day in the shops. Would it be possible that we should return by half-past five?'

'But certainly,' he said.

She threw him one of her swift, brilliant smiles. 'M'sieur, you are too kind.'

They left the hotel after coffee, and went out to the

E

car he had engaged. From Visgrad the road ran for ten kilometres across the plain, then rose swiftly into the mountains, first through the grey olive woods and then through pine forest. Warren sat chatting with the girl in the warm sun, content and at rest; the chauffeur drove them at an easy pace.

In the middle of the afternoon they came to a small lake, bordered by a meadow of white flowers, the pine trees dark behind. The girl caught at his arm.

'M'sieur,' she said, 'the flowers! They are marvellous! M'sieur, stop the car, and let me walk here for a little.'

He stopped the car and they got out; the chauffeur said something rapidly in Laevatian that Warren could not understand.

'He says that one kilometre farther on there is a café by the lake,' she said. 'I will tell him to wait for us there.'

They strolled down to the lake side; the girl picked a handful of the celandines, and put one in his button-hole. 'It is so beautiful,' she said. 'Twice before I have been in Visgrad, but I have never seen this place. Do you know the name?'

He shook his head. 'I will ask the chauffeur when we reach the café.' He smiled. 'Your little one would like to be here, Mademoiselle?'

She nodded quickly. 'M'sieur, it is to places such as this that I take my little one when I am in Sulina, so that when I am away she may remember me with the flowers, and things that are beautiful, and good. I have to be away so much; it is only for one week or for two weeks in each year that I can see her.'

'That is a very little time,' he said.

She nodded again. 'It is true. It is not right that a mother should not see her little one more than two weeks in the year. And it is for that, M'sieur, that I spend no money that I can help, and,' she flashed a smile at him, 'we do not drink lemonade, M'sieur, but champagne. In five years more, perhaps I shall have saved enough to return to live in Sulina.'

'How much is necessary for that?'

She shrugged her shoulders. 'It would not be prudent that I should give up my career as artiste till I had saved a hundred and fifty thousand francs.'

'That is a very large sum, Mademoiselle.'

She nodded. 'Terrifying. Five years ago, when my little one was born and I became responsible—you understand, M'sieur? At that time I determined on that sum—I declare, I was terrified, it seemed so long to make it, and to leave my little one alone for all these years—insupportable. But now it is already five years, and I have saved nearly the half, and now I demand more money. Twenty dinars a night—I will not dance for less. I have told them in the Gonea—I am artiste, and known to the clientèle.'

They walked down the shore of the lake among the flowers; the air was cool and refreshing after the heat of Visgrad. At the café they sat for a while and drank Turkish coffee, served to them by a veiled girl.

'They are not civilised, these people,' said Pepita.

They drove back to Visgrad and entered the city a few minutes before half-past five. Warren turned to the girl. 'Where shall I put you down, Mademoiselle? You wish to do some shopping?'

She thought for a moment. 'There is a large shop in the Litescu.' She spoke rapidly to the driver through the screen; he nodded his head. 'I have asked him if he will stop in the Litescu; it is on the way to your hotel.'

The car ran swiftly through the streets, and slowed down in the shopping quarter. 'M'sieur,' she said. 'I have enjoyed this afternoon; I thank you infinitely. We will dance again this evening?'

'But certainly,' he said. The car drew up to a standstill by the broken pavement; Warren looked at the shop. It was a toy shop.

He smiled. 'You go to buy toys, Mademoiselle?'

'M'sieur,' she said, 'I declare—I am ashamed. All of the afternoon I have talked to you of my little one—it was not *gentil*, that. But in ten days will arrive her day of birth, and it is necessary that I should post her present now, or it will be late.'

'You would prefer to be alone, perhaps?'

'But no, M'sieur. But for you—it is not interesting— to buy a doll?'

'Mademoiselle,' he said, 'I should enjoy it infinitely.'

She threw back her head and laughed. 'Come, M'sieur, and we will choose a doll together.'

In the shop she hesitated for a long time over the choice. There were dolls in Greek peasant costume, in Laevatian peasant costume, in Albanian peasant costume; baby dolls, little girl dolls, soldier dolls, black dolls. After endless discussion in broken Laevatian with the old lady of the shop she chose a large baby doll, with long draperies.

'Mademoiselle,' said Warren, 'I have never been a father. But I understand that a young child like that requires a perambulator. Is it permitted that I should send a perambulator for the doll, that your little one may wheel her about?'

The old lady dragged forward a selection of doll's perambulators.

'M'sieur,' said the girl, a little huskily, 'you are too kind. My little one will be enchanted.'

They chose a perambulator and gave instructions for

126

the packing and the carriage to Sulina, in Corsica. Then he went back to his hotel. In the evening he danced a little with the girl, and was in bed by midnight.

He went down next day to the Embassy and had a talk with Pennington. 'I seem to be at a dead end,' he said. 'Unless I can get on the right side of Theopoulos I may as well go home. I haven't yet been able even to have a word with him.'

The Secretary rubbed his chin. 'That often happens here, you know. I'm glad you got on well with Deleben. But if he can't get you in to see Theopoulos, it certainly is difficult.'

'I think I'll go direct to his office,' said Warren. 'Send in a card, and see what happens.'

'You may get a rebuff,' said Pennington.

'I don't know that I greatly care. If there's nothing to be done here, the sooner I know about it the better.'

He left the Embassy and went down to the Ministry of Marine. The doorway was guarded by a sailor, unshaven and dirty and armed with rifle and bayonet. He barred the entrance.

Warren produced his card. A non-commissioned officer of the army strolled up from behind the sailor, took the card and scrutinised it.

'For M. Theopoulos,' said Warren. 'Take the card to him; he will wish to see me.'

The man looked at him insolently. 'You are the Englishman from London,' he said in broken French. 'M. Theopoulos is too busy to see you.'

'Nevertheless,' said Warren, 'you will take the card to him.'

For answer, the man tore the card in two and threw it on the ground. Then he spat, ostensibly towards the

127

gutter. The saliva hit the leg of Warren's trouser and trickled down.

The man turned back into the hall. 'M. Theopoulos is busy,' he said indifferently. 'You must come another day.'

Warren turned back into the street, black with anger. He stopped a few paces from the door and wiped his trouser with his handkerchief. Behind him a taxi drew up at the door of the Ministry; he turned and saw the two Germans get out, Herr Braum and Herr Linersoppe. They were immediately admitted.

Warren walked back to his hotel and rang up Vislan. 'You must tell M. Deleben,' he said, 'that I can wait no longer. I shall be at the hotel for the remainder of to-day, but to-morrow I return to London. If the business should move at all to-day, I will put off my return, otherwise I leave on the first plane.'

He heard the other sigh. 'It is so difficult,' he complained. 'But I will see my uncle, and I will tell him.'

In the late afternoon he went down to the Embassy again. He told Pennington what had happened. Then he walked over to the window, and stood there for a minute looking out upon the garden, sweetly scented by the lilac trees. 'I think I'm through,' he said. 'I've made a mistake; I was too eager to get the business. I should not have come here till the deal was much farther advanced.'

'We get a lot of this out here, you know,' said Pennington. 'They're not very good people to deal with.'

Warren turned back into the room. 'I know.' He took up his hat and stick. 'I'm leaving for London on the morning plane to-morrow,' he said. 'It's been terribly good of you to give me all the help you have.'

He went back to his hotel and booked a seat upon the Berlin plane; he would have to go by Berlin to get to London. Then he rang up Vislan, and told him again that he was leaving.

'My uncle is very much upset that you are going,' said the Laevatian. 'He says that it is a great pity. He has said to me to tell you that he is sure that M. Theopoulos will be able to see you in a day or two.'

Warren laughed. 'He will have to come to London if he wishes to see me in a day or two,' he said. 'Tell M. Deleben that I am desolated that I have not had the opportunity to do business in your country. It would have been the greatest pleasure to me.'

'I will tell him so.'

Warren dined alone, and went out to the Gonea. Pepita rose and came to meet him; they danced once or twice.

'Mademoiselle,' he said presently, 'this evening is the last that I come here. I leave for London in the morning.'

She stared at him. 'M'sieur . . . you are leaving Visgrad to-morrow?'

He smiled. 'I have to go.'

She pouted. 'I declare, M'sieur—I am not at all content. You have told me that you would be here, perhaps, for several weeks, and I have looked forward to dancing with you. And now, you say that you must go back to London. No, M'sieur—I declare—I have been badly used! This business that takes you back to London—can it not wait for a few days?'

He smiled. 'It is not business that takes me back to London,' he said. 'But I can do no business here, and so I must go back to my own country.'

She leaned her elbows on the table. 'M'sieur, I have read about your business in the journal. I do not understand why you must go away. They say here that you are very close to M. Deleben. No, I do not understand at all.'

'You understand a great deal of Visgrad politics, Mademoiselle. I did not know you understood so much.'

'Bah! Everybody comes here, and in the early morning, late, you understand, one hears much talk of politics.'

He nodded slowly. 'You may know, perhaps, Mademoiselle, that in my business nothing can be done without the goodwill of M. Theopoulos. I have not that goodwill, and I find that I am unable to get it. I cannot even get to see Theopoulos—he finds himself too busy to give me an appointment. My business, which is finance, can only flourish with goodwill on either side. Therefore, I must return to London.'

She stretched her hands out on the table before her. 'M'sieur has been unable to meet M. Theopoulos?'

'That is so.'

A smile wreathed about her lips. 'And for that reason you return to London?'

'Certainly.'

She threw her head back, and burst into a peal of laughter. 'Oh, M'sieur—it is droll, that.' She laughed again, continuously.

Warren smiled. 'Mademoiselle,' he said, 'I am glad that I am able to amuse.'

She turned to him, choking with laughter, wiping the tears from her eyes. 'M'sieur, I ask your pardon. It is not *gentil* that I should laugh. But M'sieur—you must understand—M. Theopoulos comes here every night. All the Ministers of the Cabinet come here, every night. If M'sieur wishes to meet M. Theopoulos, nothing is more easy.'

'You could arrange that?'

She burst again into a peal of helpless laughter. 'M'sieur, it could have been arranged on that first night that you were here. Always M. Theopoulos will arrive at half-past one or two in the morning. But, M'sieur . . . the English . . . they—go—to—bed—too—soon!'

He calmed her with kind words and French champagne. 'M'sieur,' she said, wiping her eyes, 'ten thousand pardons. It is wrong that I should laugh. But as for M. Theopoulos, we will arrange a meeting for to-night. It is of all things the most easy. If M'sieur will arrange a little party with a few of the demoiselles of the house—especially Hélène—and with plenty of champagne, M. Theopoulos will join us of his own accord. It will not be necessary for M'sieur to go to M. Theopoulos. He will come to M'sieur.'

'It would be most kind if you would arrange such a meeting, Mademoiselle.'

She leaned back in her chair and beckoned to a waiter. 'Hélène—and Rita—and Virginio,' she said. 'Ask them to come to meet M'sieur—we make a party for to-night.'

'You may bring, for a commencement,' said Warren, 'another half-dozen bottles.'

His guests arrived in a few minutes, a couple of magnificently-built young women and a saturnine young man, who partnered one of the young women—Rita—in an acrobatic dance. Pepita did the honours.

'Hélène,' she said, 'permit that I present you to M'sieur Ouarren.' He bowed. 'Also, Mademoiselle Rita, and M'sieur Virginio.'

'I am enchanted,' said Warren.

Hélène turned to him. 'M'sieur,' she said, 'I have longed to meet you.' He could hardly follow her Rumanian French. 'The patron who has bought the perambulator for the doll.' There was laughter; she turned upon them. 'No—no—no! It is not to laugh. It was *bien aimable*, that.'

'It is true,' said Pepita. 'M. Potiscu has said the same.'

Warren wrinkled his brows. 'M. Potiscu?' he inquired. 'Does he know about it?'

'But certainly,' said Pepita. 'You understand, M. Potiscu is of the department of the Treasury, which controls the Customs. In the ordinary way, a parcel such as that—there would be much delay. There would be declarations—and forms—and carnets—and attestations—and very, very many dinars to be paid. It would be insupportable, that. But last night I have seen and danced with M. Potiscu and I have told him that the parcel is a gift for my little one. So all is arranged.'

'It is good to give presents to little children,' said the saturnine Virginio. 'I myself very much enjoy doing that.'

Pepita turned to Hélène. 'It is necessary that M'sieur here should become acquainted with M. Theopoulos,' she said. 'Perhaps we can assist M'sieur—yes?'

'Of a certainty,' said Hélène. She added something in a language that Warren could not understand, which left the table convulsed with laughter. Pepita explained in French to Warren. 'She has said, if you would take him away from her and put him in the closet—you understand?' She made a motion as of one who pulls a chain.

Warren laughed. 'Mademoiselle,' he said to Hélène, 'I will do my utmost to engage his entire attention.'

'That,' she said, 'will be a very considerable relief.'

Virginio interposed. 'M. Theopoulos also plays cards,' he said. He bowed slightly to Hélène. 'It is his other amusement. M'sieur is acquainted with the game of Polski Bank, perhaps?'

Warren shook his head.

'It would perhaps assist M'sieur,' said Virginio, 'if he were to play cards with M. Theopoulos. To win a little money—forty, fifty dinars, no more—makes M. Theopoulos very happy. It will be easy for you, then.'

'That is true,' said Hélène. 'I have seen it many times.'

Virginio said, 'If M'sieur wishes, I will show him how the cards should be played.'

Irresolute, Warren glanced at Pepita; she nodded slightly. 'That would be a great pleasure,' he said.

Virginio departed to get cards; Pepita leaned across to Warren. 'He is safe for you to trust,' she said. 'He is very clever with the cards—I knew him before, in Beirut. He has been croupier in a casino. He is also conjuror a little, for the cards to go as he wishes. But he will not cheat you, because you are my friend. You should make an arrangement with him to give him, perhaps, ten per cent of what you wish to win or lose.'

Warren considered for a moment. He had nothing to lose. Before he had come into the place he had thrown up the sponge, booked his ticket for London, acknowledging defeat. If now he could reverse the position by these means, why not? But to play cards with a conjuror . . .

Abruptly there returned to him the memory of his conversation about Sharples. 'Nothing whatever can be done,' he had said, 'legitimately. . . .'

Virginio returned with the cards. Warren retired with him to an adjoining table. 'See, M'sieur,' he said, 'the game of Polski Bank is so. I am the Bank. I deal the three cards—so—face down. . . .'

In five minutes Warren had mastered the intricacies of the game. It seemed to him to be suitable for very young children, or for the feeble-minded, but with an added tang of viciousness about it. He found it not unlike the three-card trick.

At the conclusion of the lesson he eyed Virginio for a moment. 'It would be well that I should lose this evening forty or fifty dinars to M. Theopoulos,' he said. 'But in a game where chance must play so great a part, that may not, perhaps, be very easy.'

'That can be arranged, M'sieur.'

'I should be infinitely obliged. Should we say ten per cent of the winnings of M. Theopoulos, up to fifty dinars?'

Virginio bowed slightly. 'M'sieur is too kind. Now, if M'sieur will note carefully—when I have the Bank, and perhaps also at some other times, if a court card should be the highest, then in the next hand the highest card will find itself on the right. If the highest card should be from ace to seven, then in the next hand the highest card will find itself on the left—so. Eight, nine, or ten, then in the next hand the highest card will find itself in the centre. That will be easy to remember, is that not so?'

'But certainly. That will be of a great assistance.'

They rejoined the ladies.

It was at a quarter to two that M. Theopoulos appeared. He came in a waft of scent, a tall, broad man, with curly, negroid hair and a good-natured oily face. With him came Herr Braum.

He hesitated for a moment, and approached their table. Hélène rose to meet him, stretched out a hand, and dragged him down into the seat beside her. 'Dear Elias,' she said. 'I had thought that you were not coming to-night, and I was sad. Permit that I introduce M'sieur Ouarren, who has been entertaining us so well.'

The Minister's eyes flickered to the bottles, critically, and then away. 'I am enchanted,' he said thickly. 'It is a pleasure to meet M'sieur Ouarren.'

'On the contrary,' said Warren, 'and beyond doubt, the pleasure is entirely mine. M'sieur will do me the honour to drink a glass of wine?'

Herr Braum sank down into a seat by Virginio, ill at ease. Hélène poured a glass of champagne for the Minister, kissed the lip of the glass, and handed it to him to drink.

Warren caught the waiter's eye. 'Cigars,' he said. 'Havanas, of the best.'

The Minister settled into his chair, one arm around Hélène. 'You have visited in Visgrad before?' he asked Warren.

'Twice before—in connection with the Visgrad waterworks. I had some part in that business.'

'Ah, the waterworks. M. Potiscu has told me.' The Minister ruminated for a moment. 'That was a very good business,' he said at last, reflectively.

'If all my business could be of equal benefit to the Laevatian people,' said Warren, 'I should indeed be pleased.'

The band beat to a heavy rhythm, the dancers moved upon the floor, the cigar smoke curled about them, thickening the air. Twice Theopoulos took Hélène down to dance upon the floor, but returned each time to the cigars and French champagne. From time to time one or other of the party left to do a turn of cabaret, and returned.

The evening was drawing on. The air grew thicker, heavier; small beads of perspiration appeared upon the heavy countenance. Warren turned to the Minister.

'It grows warm,' he said, 'too warm to dance. M'sieur would perhaps prefer the cards?'

The heavy face lit up. 'Assuredly. You know our game of cards?'

Warren smiled, and shook his head. 'I have been here for so short a time. One game, perhaps—when I was here before. . . . You put down three cards, so——'

'Ja—ja—ja,' said the Minister. 'And then one other, so. That is in order. That game we call Polski Bank.'

Warren nodded. 'I remember the name, now. We could play that game, if you wish?'

'With all my heart.' He fumbled in his waistcoat pocket and produced a wad of greasy notes. They cut the cards round, and Herr Braum took the first Bank.

Half an hour later they paused. The Minister had won sixty-three dinars—about six pounds; Warren had lost seventy-two; the German and Virginio were about all square. In high good-humour Theopoulos took Hélène down to dance again.

Herr Braum smiled at Warren. 'Matters have not gone well for you to-night. For a financial expert, to lose so much money!' He made a little clicking noise with his teeth.

'In finance,' said Warren, 'one does not always win from the first deal. One must have courage, and see the game through.'

'That is to say,' said the German, 'if one has the financial strength to see the game through to the end.'

Warren eyed him steadily. 'In England, we do not engage in games unless we can pay if we lose,' he said. He picked up the cards and shuffled them. 'Let us play a game until the Minister returns,' he said. 'We two will play alone—Virginio here can Bank for us. Unless, perhaps,' he added, 'your country has not the financial resources of my own?'

The German smiled. 'A war of international finance. M'sieur, let us begin.'

The Minister returned after the second hand, and took another glass of the champagne. 'M'sieur,' said Warren, 'I ask your pardon, but this game is between us two. Herr Braum has doubted my financial standing, and—in our English idiom—I go to trim the pants off him.'

Rita translated quickly, and in Rabelaisian manner. The Minister laughed, and took another cigar. 'This will be good to watch,' he said. 'Germany against England, to the death. Proceed, Messieurs.'

Virginio dealt the cards again. 'A hundred dinars,' said the German insolently, and threw a note down on the left-hand card. 'That is, if that is not too high a stake.'

Warren beckoned to the waiter. 'Bring counters,' he said. He turned to the German, laying down his note upon the centre card. 'M'sieur, I suggest that one yellow counter counts a hundred dinars, a blue one five hundred dinars, and a red one a thousand dinars.'

The German moistened his lips. 'That will be convenient.'

The Minister leaned across the table and filled another glass for himself. 'This is indeed a game.'

They played on for an hour. Slowly the place was emptying, and the band beat more slowly, the thick air grew less oppressive. Virginio sat dealing, impassive, hardly moving. Theopoulos sat with one arm around Hélène and lounging in his seat, smoking innumerable cigars. Pepita leaned both elbows on the table, watching the game intently, a glass beneath her hands. At Warren's side the pile of coloured chips grew steadily.

At last he paused. 'M'sieur,' he said, 'I am desolated, but the fortune does not seem to be with you to-night. Would you prefer that we should stop?'

'By no means,' said the German. 'We will go on.'

'For the honour of Germany,' said Warren softly. 'It is as you wish, M'sieur.' He turned to the Minister. 'I fear that this must be infinitely boring, M'sieur.'

'By no means,' said the Laevatian thickly.

Warren bowed. 'For me,' he said, looking at his watch, 'I do not agree. It is late; it is not good to be awake beyond five o'clock. Soon we must make an end; if M'sieur will agree, from now onwards we play only with the red counters.'

The German nodded shortly. Pepita laughed, tense, and a little shrill. 'I declare—the English think of nothing but their beds.'

In half an hour the pale light was visible around the edges of the curtains at the windows; the band was silent. The German got up suddenly from the table. 'I will not go further.'

Warren nodded gravely. 'As you wish, M'sieur. I am desolated that your fortune has been so unfavourable.' He turned to Virginio. 'And the count?'

The croupier figured with a paper and a pencil. 'Eighteen thousand and seven hundred dinars.' He passed the pad to Theopoulos. 'M'sieur le Ministre perhaps would verify the account?'

Theopoulos yawned, and leaned erect. 'It is in order,' he said heavily. 'Eighteen thousand and seven hundred dinars, from Herr Braum to M'sieur Ouarren. Over nineteen hundred of your English sterling. It makes a record for the Gonea.'

'I will send a draft during the day,' said the German shortly. He left them with a formal bow, and went towards the entrance, outlined in grey light.

The others followed him, and dispersed in the chilly morning streets.

Warren went back to his hotel, and slept till midday; then he got up and had a bath, dressed carefully, and went downstairs to lunch. As he passed through the hall, the porter handed him an envelope; it contained Herr Braum's cheque upon a Berlin bank.

He slept again after lunch, then walked by the river for an hour. He dined alone, and went to the Gonea about ten o'clock.

Pepita came to him. 'M'sieur is now satisfied?'

'But certainly. It was well arranged, that. For to-night, also, I desire to make the party, to play cards with M. Theopoulos.'

'I declare, M'sieur, it will be necessary to have care. It will not be wise that you should win from M. Theopoulos.'

He smiled. 'Mademoiselle, you must be still one half asleep. It is not my intention to win.'

She pouted. 'M'sieur—I do not think you are an honest man. I have sympathy for the poor Herr Braum.'

He smiled again. 'To-night, then, you may have sympathy for the poor M. Warren.'

He stopped a waiter. 'Ask M. Virginio if he will visit us, to take a glass of wine.'

He went to meet the saturnine young man as he approached. 'It was well arranged, last night,' he said. He passed an envelope to the other. 'That, I think, will find itself in order—eighteen hundred and seventy-six dinars, thirty cents.'

The other bowed. 'M'sieur is punctilious to keep a bargain.'

'It would not be possible to do business otherwise. To-night also, we will make the party—yes? This time, again, I wish to play with M. Theopoulos, and to lose money.'

'Assuredly. I do not think that Herr Braum will accompany him to-night.'

'So? For what reason?'

'One has said that Herr Braum to-day was received coldly today by the Minister. One has also said that this evening the Minister has received M. Potiscu, and that for an hour they have discussed your business, M'sieur.'

Warren nodded slowly. 'That may be.'

He went back to Pepita; presently they were joined again by Hélène, Rita, and Virginio. Presently Theopoulos arrived; he came sauntering to their table.

Warren rose to meet him. 'This is indeed a pleasure, M'sieur. Permit that I pour for you a glass of wine. Herr Braum, he is not with you to-night?'

The Minister shrugged his shoulders. 'I do not know what has become of him. Perhaps he has returned to Germany.'

'I was desolated at his bad fortune last night. I wished to offer him the return game.'

The Minister chuckled. 'I do not think, M'sieur, that he would wish to play.'

Warren looked concerned. 'Then you should play for him, M'sieur. I won a large amount of money; it is right that there should be the return game. The game of Polski Bank is governed much by chance; it is impossible that chance should run in one way all the time.'

The Minister eyed him narrowly. 'One would imagine so, M'sieur. But certainly we will play again. This time, perhaps, I trim the pants from you, is it not so?'

'I hope not, M'sieur.'

His hopes were unfulfilled. When in the cold dawn the party finally broke up, he owed the Minister two thousand and seventy-five pounds sterling.

He rose from the table. 'It is true, M'sieur,' he said a little ruefully, 'the luck does not run in the same way for two evenings running.' He produced a cheque-book. 'I can write you now my draft, M'sieur—or perhaps it would be more convenient if I obtain notes in dinars during the day?'

The Minister grasped him affectionately by the arm. 'That will be the more convenient, dear M'sieur Ouarren,' he said silkily. 'We are here in Visgrad, and an English cheque will not be so good. But do not derange yourself. In the afternoon, at about five o'clock, we meet at the Ministry to discuss the tank ships for the Oil Development?'

Warren nodded. 'That will be a suitable occasion, M'sieur. I will obtain the notes by then.'

He walked for a little in the town before returning to his hotel. A few early ox-carts went creaking through the streets; in the houses there was a faint stir of awakening life. He stood for a few moments by the bridge over the river, drawing long, deep breaths; the air was fresh after the staleness of the cabaret. It was faintly aromatic, perfumed with the dust, the wood smoke, pines, and garlic of the town.

Far to the north, he thought of Sharples, grey and desolate in the same dawn, bitterly idle.

'Well,' he said, half to himself, 'we're on the way.'

THE Consul tapped his pince-nez nervously upon the desk. 'It was good of you to come down, Mr. Warren,' he began. 'The Ambassador wanted me to have a word with you.'

'Oh, yes?'

The Consul coughed. 'The Ambassador feels very strongly that it is the duty of the English community in Visgrad to set an example of probity and correct behaviour in these Balkan states.' He coughed again. . . . 'After all, you will understand better than most of us that it is on those principles that our commercial prosperity is founded.'

'Hadn't you better tell me what you're driving at?'

'It's about those parties of yours at this night-club the Gonea, Mr. Warren. The Ambassador was not at all pleased when he heard about them.'

Warren nodded slowly. 'I'm exceedingly sorry if they don't fit in with his ideas,' he said. 'But I really don't see what it's got to do with him.'

The Consul raised his eyebrows. 'Is it correct that on successive evenings you have won, and lost, sums up to two thousand pounds a night?'

'That is so.'

'Well, Mr. Warren—as of course you know—the Ambassador is the head of the British community in this country. When a man as well-recommended as you are arrives in Visgrad and begins to gamble on that scale, and—if I may say so—in the most dubious company, it naturally engages the attention of the Embassy. And I may tell you frankly, Mr. Warren, that the Embassy don't like it.'

There was a silence in the room. 'You mean,' said Warren, 'that unless I mend my ways I shall no longer be *persona grata* at the Embassy.'

'You put it very bluntly. But—well, that is the gist of it.'

'That means, the British Government would withdraw their support. They'd tell the Laevatian Government that they'd be wiser not to deal with me?'

'I cannot recall such a case. But in the extreme, the Ambassador might decide to take that action.'

Warren smiled. 'Well,' he said, 'you can tell the Ambassador that I'm going to mend my ways. I don't think it will be necessary for me to gamble on that scale again—that's served its turn. But I tell you, I'm not going home without my order. And you know how business is done out here as well as I do.'

The Consul sighed. 'I know—and that's what makes it difficult. However, I'll tell the Ambassador what you have said, and I am sure he will be satisfied.'

For three days Warren worked for eighteen hours a day. He engaged a sitting-room as an office and obtained the services of a stenographer; he spent the business hours in conferences, principally at the Treasury. The afternoons and evenings were spent in getting out new drafts for the next day. Before going to bed he dropped in for an hour at the Gonea with Pepita; that was his sole diversion.

At the end of that time he had reached the point where he could go no further without consultation with the market in London.

He explained this to M. Potiscu at the Treasury. 'It is necessary that I return to London for a short time to explore the underwriting,' he said in French. 'Also, I will arrange for the preparation of the plans of the tank ships, for the Ministry of Marine. In fifteen days I will return again; in the meantime, the Cabinet will no doubt consider these, the Heads of our Agreement.' He indicated the papers in his hand.

M. Potiscu, small and rotund, and very Eastern, said, 'May you go in peace, with the protection of Allah.'

Warren bowed. 'I thank you infinitely. Without the work which you have done, M'sieur, and the assistance which you have given, our business could not have progressed so far.'

'You are most kind.'

Warren continued, 'I wish you to know how deeply the group that I represent appreciate your assistance, M'sieur. It has occurred to me that perhaps there is some little thing that is not easily obtained in Visgrad, some present that I could bring back with me from London that would serve to indicate our gratitude?'

M. Potiscu thought for a few moments. 'Always,' he said, 'I have desired an umbrella, with the handle all in jewels. Jewels of all colours, blue and red and white and green, and blue again. Of a green silk, and with the stick all silver. Such umbrellas cannot be obtained in Visgrad, and I have desired one very greatly.'

Warren swallowed hard. 'I am disappointed, M'sieur, that you have chosen so small a gift,' he said. 'But you may rest assured—the umbrella shall be of the best that London can produce.'

'If it is possible, then, to add one more thing,' said M. Potiscu, rather rapidly, 'you would bring from London a dozen bottles of your Worcestershire sauce. In the summer, you understand, the meat is sometimes not good.'

Warren left for London the next day. Travelling via Berlin he landed at Croydon at about nine o'clock at night, and drove up to his flat.

He went down to his office early in the morning, and spent the forenoon clearing the arrears of his routine work. For the afternoon he made an appointment with a firm of naval architects, who came to see him.

He outlined to them the business of the oil tankers. They discussed the proposition for an hour. 'Within limits,' he said, 'we can sell them what we like. But we've got to have a preliminary specification and a lot of drawings out within a fortnight, and then one of you will have to come out with me to Visgrad.'

'There's no difficulty in that.'

He eyed them for a moment. 'In the event of this business going through, I take it that your firm would be prepared to make the whole of the detail drawings and take entire responsibility for the design? I have in mind to build these vessels in a yard that has been closed down for a time. I don't want to have to set up a design department of my own.'

'You need have no fears on that score, Mr. Warren. We are very well accustomed to that class of work.'

He nodded. 'I know you are. That's why I asked you to come along.' He got up from his desk. 'All right, I'll write to you to-night confirming all this. And you will get right on with the job.'

They left him, and he turned back to the consideration of a letter on his desk. It read:

> St. Mary's Hospital,
> Sharples,
> Northumberland.

Dear Mr. Warren,

*You asked me if I could let you know if I thought
of anybody who could manage the Yard. I've been re-
luctant to make a suggestion, because of course it's not
easy for a woman to really appreciate how good a man is at
his work.*

*But I think you might investigate Mr. Grierson, who
is now an assistant manager with the Clydeside Ship and
Foundry Company. I have not seen him for about four
years. He was an apprentice in our yard, and after that
he became an assistant manager. I remember Daddy
telling me how well they all thought of him, and that
he'd end up as a director. He must be about thirty-eight
years old now. He got married seven or eight years ago,
not very long before we closed down. I remember him
chiefly because he was so tremendously energetic. Nobody
could keep up with him. He was very popular when he was
here.*

*I am coming down to London for a few days on the 17th,
and shall be staying with my aunt at 17, Chichester
Avenue, Ealing. I could see you then and tell you more
about him, if you are interested.*

> *Yours sincerely,*
> *Alice MacMahon.*

He reached out for the telephone, and put in a call to
the hospital in Sharples. It came in a few minutes; he
asked for the Almoner.

He heard her voice. 'Miss MacMahon speaking.'

'This is Henry Warren, Miss MacMahon.'

'Oh—where are you speaking from? Are you in Sharples?'

'No—I'm speaking from London. I got your letter; I'm sorry I haven't answered it before. I've been abroad.'

'On business?'

'Yes. I've been in Laevatia. Miss MacMahon, about your man Grierson. I'd like to meet him, to have a talk with him. He lives up on the Clyde somewhere, I suppose?'

'I think so.'

'Do you know his address—where I could get hold of him?'

'I can't tell you off-hand. I could find out and let you have it in to-night's post.'

'That would do fine. Send it to the office—you know my office address? Lisle Court.'

'That's the one I've got, isn't it? Where you used to work, and they forward letters for you still?'

'That's right.'

'They didn't forward mine. All right, Mr. Warren— I'll let you have that in to-night's post. Does this mean that things are getting warm?'

He laughed. 'They're getting so damned hot I'm pretty sure to burn my fingers. You said in your letter you'll be down in London next week. Will you come and lunch with me?'

'I'd love to, Mr. Warren.'

'What about Tuesday?'

'That would do all right.'

'Good. Tuesday, at one o'clock—at the Savoy? I'll meet you at the entrance to the grill room.'

'I'll be there.'

She laid down the receiver; Mr. Williams looked at her inquiringly. 'Was yon Mr. Henry Warren?'

She nodded. 'Our own out-of-work clerk. I'm going to have lunch with him at the Savoy.'

He said, 'Mm. And when you've filled him with intoxicating liquor, ye can wheedle out of him the way we can save another half of one per cent upon the overdraft.' He mused a little. 'I should have kenned he was a banker, all the time. Nobody else would know them tricks.'

In the morning Warren went down to talk to Mr. Heinroth. He proposed to him the flotation of an issue of preference shares in the Laevatian Oil Development, a company in which the whole of the ordinary shares would be held by the Laevatian Government.

Mr. Heinroth gave him a cigar, and heard him attentively to the end. 'You'd never put it over with a name like that,' he said. 'Wants to be something short and snappy —something that the country clergymen can remember. I should call it Laevol Limited, or something like that.'

Warren eyed him for a moment. 'I don't look at it like that,' he said. 'I don't put it forward in the trustee class, but it's better than that. I've been out there for the last fortnight, and in my opinion it's sound. In any case, I'm making myself responsible for twenty-five per cent of the underwriting.'

There was a silence. Mr. Heinroth looked at him attentively. 'You are?'

There was another silence. 'It might be possible to get the market round to it,' said Mr. Heinroth at last. 'The first reaction is bound to be unfavourable, of course. When we had that loan fiasco the year before last I thought that everything Laevatian was dead for the next ten years. They're bound to bring that up, you know.'

Warren nodded. 'At the same time, it's potentially

148

a rich country.' Mr. Heinroth nodded slowly. 'Provided that the proposition's good business. I don't see why that loan should interfere with it.'

'There would have to be collateral security for the dividend, of course—and absolutely unimpeachable.'

'Naturally. I've got the profit on the State Railway for that. For the last ten years it's been well in excess of the sum required to guarantee this dividend.'

'That sounds all right. But—I don't know . . .'

They discussed it together for another hour. At last Warren got up to take his leave. 'Think it over,' he said, 'and give me a ring in a couple of days. I'd like to have your support in this, because I think it may be the means of opening up development in general down there.'

Mr. Heinroth nodded wisely. 'That's probably due. Well, I'll go round my corner of the market and see what the reaction is, and you go round yours. And then we'll have another talk.'

Mr. Heinroth slept on it, and then put it to Mr. Todd and Mr. Castroni over the luncheon table. 'If it was anybody else but Warren,' he said frankly, 'I'd have nothing to do with it. After that loan was repudiated, I swore I would never touch Laevatia again. But with Warren behind it—well, it makes a difference.'

Mr. Castroni sipped his coffee. 'In the last ten years I've been in most of Warren's things,' he said. 'When I've used my judgment and stayed out, I've been sorry.'

'I know,' said Mr. Heinroth. 'I feel rather like that too.'

'The country's just about due to be opened up,' said Mr. Todd. 'You've got to remember he did a good job with the waterworks out there. He knows what he's up to, all right. Speaking for myself, I'd go with him.'

'Maslin said much the same,' said Mr. Heinroth. 'But I thought I'd like to know what you two thought about it.'

That evening Warren dined alone at his club. In the smoking-room after dinner he saw Lord Cheriton sitting by himself; he strolled over and dropped into a chair beside him.

'Evening,' said the young man. 'I haven't seen you here for some time. Been away?'

Warren nodded. He selected a cigar carefully and poured out his coffee. 'I got laid up soon after you had dinner at my place that night,' he said. 'Had to have an operation. Since then I've been abroad.'

'Are things getting any better, do you think?'

Warren shrugged his shoulders. 'The reactions from this gold business have done a bit of good,' he said. 'You can't say how long it's going to last. I don't see any sign of a general improvement yet.'

'Pity.'

Warren glanced at him. 'Why?'

'I want a job.'

'You're not the only one.' They smoked in silence for a little. Then Warren said:

'Chucking up the Army?'

The young man nodded.

'What are you doing that for?'

'I want to do a spot of work before I get too old. I don't mean selling motor-cars, or flying aeroplanes. A real job that one can get one's teeth into. There's nothing like that for me in the Army.'

'No, I suppose not.'

After a time Warren spoke again. 'I was in Northumberland a little time ago—in Sharples. They told me at the local hospital about your mother—what a lot she does for them.'

The young man nodded. 'That's not far from my home, of course—we own a lot of land around there. That place Sharples is in a terrible mess.'

Warren nodded.

The young man turned a little in his chair. 'Mind you, it hasn't been like that always. I remember it when I was a boy—in the War—when it was the devil of a place. Full of work, and the river full of ships. They built a lot of destroyers there, for the Admiralty. Foreign Governments, too. There were seven Barlow destroyers at the Battle of Jutland.'

'So I heard,' said Warren.

Cheriton glanced at him curiously. 'What took you to Sharples?'

Warren did not answer for a minute. Then he said 'I was looking at the shipyard.'

'Were you, by Jove. Are you going to do anything with it?'

'I don't know. If anyone wants a packet of grief, he can start building ships in a yard that's been empty for five years.'

The other thought about it for a minute. 'I suppose you're right. At the same time, that's the sort of job I'd like to be in on.'

'You would?'

'Well, of course—that was always our family business, you know.' Warren nodded slowly, remembering. 'Not Sharples, of course—Sunderland. My father sold out from the Sunderland yard in 1907 and after that he never touched shipbuilding again. But that was where my grandfather made his money.'

They smoked in silence for a little time. 'I don't know if anything will come of this thing in Sharples or not,' said Warren. 'In any case, don't talk about it.

But if it should get along I'll remember what you've said. That is, if you're really going to chuck the Army.'

'I sent in my papers last month.' The young man turned to him. 'I'd like nothing better than to get dug in to that, if I'd be any good to you.'

Warren eyed him for a moment. 'I'll let you know within a month if there's anything developing up there or not,' he said.

A week later he was waiting in the lounge of the Savoy grill room for Miss MacMahon. She came to him punctually, dressed quietly in grey. He guided her to a table. 'Did you come up from Ealing?' he inquired.

She nodded. 'By the District Railway. I've been shopping all the morning.'

He ordered lunch. 'You said you'd been in Laevatia,' she reminded him. 'Was that on business?'

He nodded. 'I was in Visgrad for a fortnight.'

'I've never been in the Balkans. Are the people nice out there?'

He shrugged his shoulders. 'A man like me, going on business, never meets the real people. If I had to judge the Visgrad people by the ones I've met I'd say they were a lot of sewer rats, but that may not be fair.'

'Did you go out on shipping business?'

'Not primarily. That may arise out of it.'

She eyed him steadily. 'Do you think there's any chance for us up there?'

'I honestly don't know. But I promise you this—I'm doing my best.'

Her eyes softened. 'I knew you'd be doing that.'

Lunch came to them. 'I saw your man Grierson on Monday,' he said presently.

She laid her fork down. 'Where did you see him?'

'In Glasgow.'

'Did you go up there specially for that?'

'Yes.'

'What did you think of him?'

'I liked him very well. He'll come to us when we want him.'

'You mean—to Barlows?'

He nodded.

'But isn't he in a good job now?'

'He'll be in a better one if we start up again.'

'He wouldn't be so secure.'

'I'm not so sure of that.' He smiled, thinking of the finances of the Clydeside Ship and Foundry Company. 'But anyway, he'll take the risk of that—upon the terms I offered him. I believe he really wants to get back to Sharples.'

'They all do that, Mr. Warren. You'll have no difficulty to get them back again, once the Yard starts up. Sharples was a jolly little town before—before this happened to us. Everybody liked Sharples.'

He glanced at her curiously, smiling a little. 'I suppose it was always full of smoke and steam, and raining all the time?'

'It wasn't,' she said defensively. 'And, anyway, the towns up there are all like that. But Sharples was a nice size, and people were happy there.'

He said, 'I know.'

They continued with their lunch, chatting of other things. With the coffee, she said:

'I've been thinking a lot since last we met, about what you told me of the difficulty of getting anyone to order the first ship.' He was silent. 'Do you see your way to get over that now?'

He smiled. 'I suppose I must, musn't I? Otherwise I wouldn't have gone to see Grierson.'

She coloured. 'I'm so sorry,' she said, a little stiffly. 'I suppose that's confidential.'

He smiled. 'Discreditable things are usually confidential,' he said. 'I thought everybody knew that.'

She stared at him. 'What do you mean?'

He met her eyes. 'Do you think I'm an honest man?'

'Of course I do.'

'Well, I'm not. Nor is anybody else who gets business out of Laevatia.'

He turned, and called the waiter for the bill. 'If you've got time this afternoon, I'd like you to come with me. I've got to do some shopping.'

He paid the bill, and they went out into the clamour of the Strand. He hailed a taxi.

'Where are we going to?' she asked.

He smiled. 'Old Bond Street,' he said to the driver. 'Conolly's—the jewellers, you know. On the right-hand side.'

They got into the cab. The girl turned to him. 'What are we going there for?'

'To buy an umbrella,' he said shortly. She looked at him curiously, but did not ask any more questions.

He took her into the shop. The manager came forward to meet them, bowing a little. 'Everything is quite in order now. Mr. Warren,' he said quietly. 'I think you will be satisfied this time.'

Warren nodded. 'May I see it?'

The manager spoke quickly to an assistant, who vanished into the back regions. The girl turned to Warren. 'This isn't an umbrella shop,' she said. 'What is this all about?'

The assistant returned, bearing with him a red leather case some three feet long. He handed it to the manager, who laid it on a table in a shaft of sunlight. He opened it.

The sun threw dazzling reflections from the jewels on the handle, the silver stick; the pale green silk lay there translucent, shimmering. The girl caught her breath. 'But what a wonderful thing!' she exclaimed. 'It *is* an umbrella, isn't it?'

'Certainly, Madam,' said the manager gravely. He lifted it from the case, undid the silk retaining band with delicate care, and opened it. Warren took it from him and examined it critically.

'That's all right now,' he said. 'I'll take it away with me. You cleared the cheque?'

The manager bowed. 'Everything is quite in order, Mr. Warren.' He took it from him, and began to fold it. 'It is a beautiful piece of work, in its own style. The Maharajah of Bitapore was visiting our workrooms yesterday, and admired it very greatly. He wished to buy it, but I had to tell him that it was already sold. It is for an Oriental gentleman, I suppose?'

Warren nodded. 'That is so.'

The umbrella was laid back on its bed of cream-coloured kid, and the lid closed down. The assistant hailed a taxi, and the case was carried out and installed ceremoniously with them in the cab. Warren gave the address of his flat.

'Is that where you live?' asked the girl.

He nodded. 'If you don't mind coming along, I'll take this thing up there.'

In the flat he laid it on the table of his sitting-room. The girl fingered the case. 'May I see it again?'

'Of course.'

She lifted it from the case and opened it again; the jewels gleamed brightly in the sunlight. 'It really is a beautiful thing,' she said at last. 'Who is it for?'

'It's for the Treasurer of Laevatia. We should call

F

him the Chancellor of the Exchequer. Opposite number to Mr. Neville Chamberlain.'

She stood for a moment. 'Do you mean you're giving it to him as a present?'

'That's right. Quite a nice one, isn't it?'

'It must have cost an awful lot of money.'

'About three hundred pounds.'

'Is it because he's helping you to get an order for the ships?'

'Yes. It's a bribe.'

She looked uncomfortable. 'I've heard about this sort of thing, of course. Do you have to do a lot of it in your business?'

'I've never done it before.'

She stared at him in wonder. 'Are you having to bribe anyone else?'

He smiled. 'One or two. But we don't use the word bribe, much. We say, satisfy them.'

'What else have you had to give?'

'Let's see. So far it's about four thousand pounds in cash, this umbrella, and a case of Worcester sauce.'

She laid the umbrella down, and turned towards the window. 'You don't like doing this business, Mr. Warren, do you?'

'No,' he said simply. 'I don't.'

'It doesn't fit in with your reputation, either.'

'What do you know about that?'

She smiled. 'We asked the auditors, Mr. Williams and I. And they found out from London, and told us who you were.'

He stared at her. 'You mean you got a confidential report on me?'

She nodded. 'It didn't say anything about bribing the Chancellor of the Exchequer.'

'I should hope it didn't.'

She eyed him for a moment. 'Why are you doing all this, Mr. Warren?'

'Because I want to see Sharples get cracking again.'

There was a silence.

'I asked you to come and see this thing this afternoon,' he said, 'because I wanted you to understand. It's not going to be very easy to get Sharples going. I'd go so far as to say it can't be done by ordinary business—I told you that from the first.'

'I know,' she said quietly.

'It can't be done in kid gloves. Nobody's going to get that Yard working again and keep his hands clean.'

There was a long silence after he said that. The girl moved over to the window and stood looking out upon the traffic of the street below, the sunlit pavements. Warren remained standing by the table; he picked up the umbrella and rolled it, and put it carefully in its case.

'That's not very nice,' she said at last.

'No. But it's true.'

She turned towards the door. 'I must be going on. It's been terribly good of you to give me lunch, and tell me what you have, Mr. Warren.'

'That's nothing,' he said gravely. 'But—be discreet for a bit longer. I'll tell you when you may begin to talk about it in Sharples.'

She nodded. 'I understand.' She turned to him, and held out her hand. 'Good-bye. And all the luck in the world.'

He took her hand. 'Good-bye,' he said, and stood for a few moments after she had gone. Then he went down to the office.

Heinroth rang him up on the next day. 'I've been going round about,' he said. 'That Laevatian Government thing of yours. It's not an easy proposition—as, of course, you know. But there's a certain amount of interest, after all. If you like, I'll come along to you and we can have a talk.'

'How much can your lot write?' asked Warren directly.

'Well, that's what I wanted to talk about. I should think another twenty-five per cent.'

Warren nodded. 'Come right along. With what I've got we're practically home upon the underwriting then.'

He rang off and sat for a time in thought. Morgan, his secretary, slipped in.

'The solicitors rang up while you were away,' he said. 'They rang again this morning—yes, Page and Mayne. They wanted to serve some papers. I said that you would get in touch with them.'

'Lord, yes,' said Warren. 'I'll do that at once.' He had forgotten all about his divorce.

CHAPTER IX

THREE days later, his underwriting tentatively arranged, Warren left for Visgrad via Berlin by air. In that three days he had registered the Hawside Ship and Engineering Company Ltd., with a nominal capital of one hundred pounds and seven clerks as its subscribers. His own name did not appear.

He reached Visgrad late one evening, dined at his hotel, and went out to the Gonea.

Pepita greeted him effusively. 'M'sieur, you are returned! I declare, I am very content. It has been dull here in the evenings since M'sieur went back to London. Only a fat Austrian, who made a proposal so rude—you understand, M'sieur, quite intolerable. I have hit him on the face, and broken his spectacles.'

'That must have been amusing, Mademoiselle.'

She gave him one of her brilliant smiles. 'He was so angry. He has made complaint to the management, but I have told them—' she leaned forward volubly—'I have told them—I am artiste—I do not sleep with the clientèle. It is not in my contract, that.'

He nodded. 'Quite right. It would not be dignified for an artiste to be like a common girl.'

She smiled again. 'M'sieur, you understand so well. I declare, I am very content that you have returned. And, M'sieur, I have received a letter from Sulina, from the Sister of the Annunciation. She has said that my little one has been enchanted with her presents, and with the perambulator. All day she has promenaded in the garden of the convent, M'sieur, to play that she was nurse—you understand? And, M'sieur, the Sister has said that it has been necessary that the perambulator should be at the side of her bed so that she would sleep content. It was well thought of, that, M'sieur.'

Warren said, 'I am glad that I have been able to give so much happiness, Mademoiselle.'

She nodded. 'It was well thought of, and very kind. M'sieur, we have worked to remind M. Theopoulos and M. Potiscu of your business—Hélène, Virginio, and myself. It has not been allowed to rest because you have been in London. 'M'sieur will be satisfied with the progress.' She hailed a waiter.

'Virginio—ask him if he will come to M'sieur.'

Virginio came to them, and bowed from the waist.

'*Enchanté,*' he said.

Warren bowed. 'A great pleasure. Permit me to offer you a glass of wine.'

The dancer slipped into a seat. 'Pepita will have told you that our business has progressed, M'sieur,' he said. 'The good Hélène has arranged with M. Theopoulos that the Heads of your Agreement were presented to the Cabinet eight days ago, and M. Potiscu has spoken for the Treasury.'

Warren asked, 'The Cabinet has approved?'

'I declare, M'sieur,' said Pepita, 'it would have made a situation quite insupportable if they had not approved. I have said to all the world—here, you understand, M'sieur, in the Gonea—I have said to Rita, and to Maria, and to Bertha the friend of M. Lutonski, and to Lorissa, and to Jeanne—I have said to all the artistes who are accustomed to the company of a Minister, you understand, M'sieur—I have said that it is necessary that the Cabinet should approve the business. You will understand, I have told them of your great kindness to my little one and all the world has agreed—quite of one mind, M'sieur—it has been necessary that the Cabinet should approve.'

Virginio said, 'The Ministers have agreed the Heads of the Agreement, as presented by the Commission, M'sieur. All is now in order for the final documents to be prepared, granting to M'sieur the right to make the issue on those terms for three months. It will be necessary, however, for the constitution of the Board to be further discussed.'

Warren eyed him curiously. 'You have good information of the business.'

The other bowed slightly. 'M'sieur need have no fear. It is quite accurate.'

Warren stayed with them for an hour, then left before the Ministers arrived and went to his hotel.

Next morning he went down to the Treasury, a long parcel tucked beneath his arm.

He laid it on the table in the office of the Treasurer. 'I have consulted with my colleagues,' he said to M. Potiscu after the preliminary courtesies. 'They were quite desolated that you had asked so small a present. To them, and also to myself, it has not seemed fitting that a man of such influence should receive a present only of an umbrella.'

M. Potiscu smiled, and made a deprecating gesture, his eyes fixed upon the case in childlike eagerness.

Warren continued, 'But since that was your wish, M'sieur, we have resolved that the umbrella should be of the very best that London could produce. Never in the world, M'sieur, has there been such an umbrella before.'

He opened the case; the Chancellor of the Exchequer beamed with delight and reached for the handle.

'No Indian Rajah,' said Warren, embarking on a flight of fancy, 'has ever had an umbrella such as this one. It is the finest that has ever been produced. It cost,' he said, instinctively doubling up, 'no less than six hundred pounds.'

The effect was all that he had hoped for. The Minister exclaimed with delight at the price, opened the umbrella, examined it, held it above his head, glancing furtively at the mirror.

'It is too kind,' he said. 'And the Worcestershire sauce also?'

'But certainly,' said Warren. 'I have had that sent direct to the residence of M'sieur from my hotel.'

It was some time before he could get him down to business.

He left the Treasury an hour later; M. Potiscu was accommodating but inattentive and Warren judged it better to leave him to the enjoyment of his present. He went over to the English Club, and up into the smoking-room for a pink gin.

He found the Air Attaché there, with the Consul and an Under-Secretary. They greeted him affably and stood him a drink. 'How's London?'

'Raining,' said Warren. 'Here's luck.'

The Consul leaned towards him. 'I understand your matter went before the Cabinet the other night,' he said. 'I hope it is progressing well?'

Warren nodded. 'I was very pleased to see how well it had been going in my absence. I had expected that it would have been at a standstill.'

'I think, Mr. Warren,' said the Consul weightily, 'you may have to thank His Excellency for that. I believe that he has expressed to M. Deleben that your proposals were viewed favourably by His Majesty's Government.'

Warren nodded. 'I am sure that must have had a great influence on the matter,' he said gravely.

The open window of the first-floor smoking-room led on to a balcony overlooking the Litescu. The Air Attaché, lounging by the window looking down into the street, stiffened to attention.

'Good God!' he said. 'Come and take a load of this.'

The others got up and looked out. Down the rotten pavement on the other side of the street strutted M. Potiscu, the umbrella held above his head as a sunshade. The sun shone brilliantly upon the pale green silk, the silver stick, and shot bright coloured beams in all directions from the handle. A small admiring crowd was following him.

'It's old Potiscu,' said the Air Attaché.

'Whatever is that thing he's got?' asked the Under-Secretary.

'It's an umbrella. With a silver stick. And just look at the handle.'

They looked in silence as the Treasurer passed by, a very happy man.

'Where do you think he got that from?'

'Blowed if I know. Looks as if it cost somebody a packet.'

'You mean, somebody's slipped it him?'

'I wouldn't be surprised. Who's trying to get something out of him these days?'

Warren moved hastily towards the door. 'I must be getting on. See you in the bar to-night?' He left the club.

The Air Attaché looked after him, and laughed. 'Did he slip that across?'

The Consùl looked up, startled. 'Oh—I hope not, very much. His Excellency would be very much upset if that were so.'

'Never mind,' said the Under-Secretary diplomatically. 'Perhaps it isn't.'

The next fortnight passed in a welter of business. Warren was joined at his hotel by two members of the firm of naval architects; they turned a sitting-room into a drawing office to cater for the modifications to the oil tankers required by M. Theopoulos. In addition to that side of the business, there was the legal side. After long consultation with the Commercial Secretary, Warren picked a small Armenian Jew to be his legal adviser. Mr. Pennington was careful to point out that he was not an honest man, but opined that he was probably more honest than the rest. Warren reinforced him with a solicitor from London.

Most evenings he went into the Gonea and spent an hour with Pepita. He played Polski Bank with M. Theopoulos on two or three occasions, losing about forty pounds each time; the Laevatian was unable to repeat his first epic coup.

He took Pepita out again one Sunday into the high mountains, driven by a Greek. They drove all day among the pine-woods and the flowers, relaxed and content. Once Warren said:

'You have saved one half of the hundred and fifty thousand francs which is your aim, Mademoiselle—is is not so?'

She nodded energetically. 'It is now a little more than one half. It is now possible for me to save more quickly— you understand, M'sieur—one becomes known to the clientèle.'

'When you have reached a hundred and fifty thousand francs, you will retire from dancing, Mademoiselle?'

'But certainly. It is not pleasant, this life of moving

164

always to a new place, M'sieur. That makes itself plain.'

'What will you do?'

'I shall go back to Corsica, to Sulina. It is my own place, that.'

'Is Sulina a big town?'

She shook her head. 'No M'sieur—not a big town. It is in the south, a town, you understand, where the houses are not separate—compact, standing as a block upon the hillside two kilos from the sea, in the olive woods.'

'Will you find much there to occupy you, Mademoiselle?'

She shrugged her shoulders. 'I declare, M'sieur, I do not care to be occupied all day. My little one is there, and there will be an occupation for me, is it not so? The Sisters of the Annunciation take care of my little one, and that is good, you understand, M'sieur, but it will be better that I shall take care of her for myself.'

Warren nodded.

'Perhaps,' she went on, 'I shall teach the young girls how to dance.' She laughed suddenly. 'Perhaps,' she said, 'I shall marry, and then I shall grow fat.' She made an expressive motion with her hands to indicate an ample bust.

'Perhaps,' said Warren, 'I shall come one day to Sulina to see how fat you have become, and to see your little one. And to drink champagne with you again.'

She laughed. 'But, M'sieur, we have no champagne in Sulina—not even Greek champagne. We have only our own wine, which is pink in colour, and very sour. You would not like it, M'sieur, I assure you.'

He smiled. 'That we will see.'

Her face fell, and she grew serious. 'It will be necessary for us to wait for some years, first,' she said. 'It is insupportable, that, M'sieur, to have to wait so long.'

He patted her hand. 'One must have courage, Mademoiselle,' he said.

She smiled. 'That is necessary. And it is necessary also to take exercise, that one may not grow fat too soon. Let us stop the car, M'sieur, and walk a little in the woods.

He took her back to Visgrad in the afternoon, in time for her repose before the opening of the cabaret.

The business was drawing towards its climax. The Agreement was in draft form in two languages, giving to Warren the right to form the company upon certain terms, defined in the Agreement, for a period of three months. The order for the ships was incorporated in an appendix to the Agreement, as one of the terms agreed. This document went into draft in seven successive stages, bandied from lawyers to Government and back again to lawyers. It progressed, however, as well as could be expected.

'Glad I'm not that fellow Warren,' said the Air Attaché. 'Works from nine in the morning till ten at night, and then goes out to roister with Theopoulos and Potiscu. A great life for them as likes that sort of thing.'

Quite suddenly, it was finished. Warren sat back in his chair one evening, and stared at the little Jew. 'I'll take that amendment,' he said. 'It doesn't mean anything, anyway.'

He stared at the little man. 'That's the end, then,' he said wonderingly. 'You can go ahead and get that engrossed for signature now.'

'Okay, boss,' said the Armenian.

Warren went down next morning to see M. Potiscu. 'The Agreement is now being engrossed,' he said. 'If it is suitable to you and to M. Theopoulos, we could meet to-morrow afternoon at the British Consulate to sign the documents.'

The little rotund man before him bowed. 'I will speak with M. Theopoulos.'

'I should be infinitely obliged.'

A look of cunning crept into the stolid little face before him. 'God,' thought Warren, 'what's coming now?'

'You will return at once to London, after the signing?' asked the Laevatian.

'But certainly. Is it that I can do you any service there?'

The Treasurer bowed. 'I am infinitely obliged, M'sieur. It is the umbrella, that your group were so kind as to send for me. I have considered the matter, and I find it is not quite what I require.'

Warren gazed at him dumbly.

'Perhaps, M'sieur, you would be so good as to return it to the shop, and give me the six hundred pounds instead?'

Warren pulled himself together. This was the culmination of the business; he knew it, and the Laevatian knew it. A false move now would throw the business back for many months.

He bowed. 'M'sieur,' he said, 'it would give me the greatest pleasure. I will arrange with the bank, and to-morrow evening meet you with the notes in the Gonea.'

The little man beamed oilily. 'You are so kind. And the umbrella?'

'Perhaps you would be so good as to have it sent to my hotel, M'sieur?'

He never saw it again. M. Potiscu said that somebody in the hotel must have stolen it. It was a pity.

Next day, with some ceremony, the documents received their signatures in the office of the Consul, being signed on British territory.

'His Excellency will be very pleased that this is

satisfactorily arranged?' remarked the Consul, after it was over and the Ministers had gone. 'We like to do everything we can to help on British trade.'

'Perhaps you would tell His Excellency,' said Warren gravely, 'that without his help I could not have concluded the deal. I am very deeply grateful for all his assistance.'

He may have been. But he went back to his hotel and booked a passage on the morning service to Berlin, and then did his packing. He tore up a great amount of paper, drafts of various agreements, and burned the pieces in the grate. Then he went down and dined alone, and went out to the Gonea.

That evening he played Polski Bank again for the last time with Theopoulos, and, assisted by Virginio, lost twenty pounds to keep him sweet for the future. In a dark corner he gave six hundred pounds in dinars to Potiscu. In another dark corner he gave two pounds to Virginio, commission on Theopoulos. Quite openly he gave a bracelet to Hélène worth about twenty pounds.

The grey dawn was showing round the edges of the curtains before he had an opportunity to speak to Pepita alone.

'Mademoiselle,' he said, 'this is the end. I go back to my own country in an hour or two, and I do not expect to return for many months—perhaps, if all goes well, for years.'

She nodded. 'For me, also, there will be a change. To-day I have received from Smyrna the offer of an appointment—a good offer, M'sieur, that one must not refuse. You understand, I have been twice in Smyrna before, and now I am artiste known to the clientèle. One can demand a good engagement, so.'

'Do you like Smyrna, Mademoiselle?'

She shrugged her shoulders. 'It is as good as Visgrad. It is not gay like Athens, or even Istanbul, but the engagement is a good one, and one will save money.'

He eyed her for a moment. 'Mademoiselle,' he said, 'without your aid I could not have succeeded in my business. I should have departed for England, if you had not introduced me to Theopoulos.'

She laughed merrily. 'The English, they get sleepy too soon. It is droll, that.' She laid her hand upon his own. 'M'sieur, I am glad that you have been successful in your business. I declare, I am happy that I have been able to keep you from your bed that night, and to help the meeting with the Minister. M'sieur, you were kind to my little one, and that sort of kindness one does not forget.'

He smiled. 'Mademoiselle, I know that you seek no reward for what you did. Nevertheless, without your aid the business could not have been done.' He produced an envelope from his breast pocket. 'Mademoiselle, in a big business, such as the one that I have now concluded here, it is possible to pay commission for the help that is received. One more drop to the bucket will not greatly matter, when the scale of the business is considered.'

He handed her the envelope. 'You should take this to the Credit Lyonnais in the Litescu,' he said. 'They will arrange for the money to be paid in Corsica without difficulty of the exchange.'

She dropped her eyes. 'M'sieur, you are too kind. It was not for this that I have tried to help you.'

'I know that, Mademoiselle,' he said.

She tucked the envelope unopened into her bag. 'We will dance once more, M'sieur?' she said.

That afternoon she left the little hotel where she lived, and went stalking through the town in a blaze of passion. She was a shade too elegantly dressed, as ever; she tripped along on her high, patent-leather heels, her face aflame.

She turned into the French bank in the Litescu. She stormed up to the counter, and flung a slip of paper at the clerk.

'This draft—it is not good?' she inquired scornfully. 'One makes a mock of me? Ah—I declare, it is insupportable, that!'

Nonchalantly, the clerk picked up the slip of paper and unfolded it; impassively he studied it. 'One moment, Mademoiselle,' he said, and retired to the back regions.

She was a little damped by his indifference. 'I declare —I will not wait to be insulted once again,' she exclaimed. 'It is not right that one should treat me so.'

In the bank nobody paid the slightest attention to her outburst. She remained by the counter, tapping one foot irritably upon the floor.

The clerk returned.

'You deceive yourself, Mademoiselle,' he said courteously. 'This is a cheque of the English financier, M'sieur Ouarren, value seventy-five thousand francs, French. We have special instructions to receive this cheque. It is in order, perfectly.'

She gripped the counter, and stood staring at the cheque, fascinated. 'Ten thousand pardons,' she said at last, in a low tone. 'I thought that one had mocked himself of me.'

Slowly she raised her head, and stood there staring down the marble hall towards the door, wide open in the sun. Outside, across the dusty street, there was a gap between the houses; she could see the hill behind the town, rising in folds to the high mountains, blue-grey with olive woods. There would be little farms up there with cobbled paths and small, walled pastures: there would be terraced gardens for the vines and for the flowers, the roses, the carnations, and mimosa.

It would be like that in Sulina.

CHAPTER X

A FORTNIGHT later, Mr. Donald Grierson came to Sharples.

He had spent the previous day in London with Warren. He was a red-haired, burly man of good north-country stock, about forty years of age, energetic and outspoken.

'Oh, aye,' he said, 'they let me go all right. The Clydeside aren't that full of work. Mind, they wanted to know what I was going to, but I didn't let on.'

Warren asked: 'Have you been in Sharples recently?'

Grierson shook his head. 'I was there four years back. Not since. They tell me things is very bad in Sharples.'

Warren nodded. 'Now, let me show you what I've done so far.'

Grierson laid his hand upon a heavy roll. 'These are the plans?'

They worked on steadily all through the day. At the end of it Grierson faced him across the table.

'Well, Mr. Warren,' he said thoughtfully, 'I'd like you to know how it all strikes me before I go up North on to the job, the way we'll understand each other from the start.'

He drew through a dead pipe between his teeth. 'The architects are good, and the designs are good. You've been well advised there. And the price you've got—well, in the Clydeside to-day, we'd reckon that a fair price, that you'd not lose much on, any road. You've done a good job getting those ships at that price, Mr. Warren.'

He smiled broadly. 'I'd like to know how it was done.'

He continued, 'And your progress payments scheme is none so bad, though I'd rather have seen a bit more on the materials. You need have no fear about the ships themselves—they'll be good, sound ships before ever they leave the yard. But whether we'll build them at a profit . . . that I very much doubt.'

Warren nodded slowly.

'In my opinion, Mr. Warren,' said the manager evenly, 'you'd better budget for a fifty-thousand loss on the three ships.'

'So much as that?'

'I think so, Mr. Warren. Mind you, don't think I'm setting up an alibi right from the start, but look at it fair. Four hundred and twenty thousand pounds of work, at what in normal times we'd reckon a cut price, although it's none so bad these days. And starting from a yard that's dead, stone dead and derelict. It's not reasonable to expect a profit, Mr. Warren. We're going to lose money at the start, and I'd say that it would be the thick end of that sum before we're cracking as a proper yard again.'

Warren smiled slowly. 'Well, go to it,' he replied. 'Make it as little as you can.'

The manager got to his feet. 'You can depend upon it that we'll do that,' he said. 'And now, with your leave, I'll go and get a bite of something to eat, and then I'll get along to King's Cross. Time I was on the job.'

He got to Sharples early the next day, and walked down from the station to the 'Bull's Head', carrying his bag. Once or twice he saw a man he recognised and gave a friendly nod; his heart sank at the aspect of the town. There was no life, no spirit in the place; it was with a serious face that he rang the bell of the hotel.

A slatternly girl came and unbolted the door. 'Mr. Hancock home?' he asked.

'Aye,' she said, 'he's within. Will ye step inside?'

The landlord came lumbering into the hall.

'Eh, Mr. Hancock, you remember me? I want a room for a few nights till I can get fixed up—I'm working here from now on.'

The landlord greeted him warmly. 'Sit ye down, an' let me draw ye a can o' bitter, an' tell me what brings ye back to Sharples,' he exclaimed. 'Sit ye right down.'

'I'd rather have a mug of tea, if it's the same to you.'

In half an hour he had learned a great deal about Sharples, and it was with a more thoughtful face than ever that he walked down to the Yard. He routed out the watchman, Robbins, from his hut. 'You remember me?' he said. 'Grierson, my name. I remember you when I was working here—in the stores, weren't you? I mind your face. I'm the new manager. You've had a letter?'

'Oh, aye,' the old man quavered. 'A letter come yesterday. I told the missus, I said, I couldn't make head nor tail of it, I said.'

Grierson eyed him critically and his heart sank again; even the watchman was too old to be of any real service. He was starting from absolutely nothing.

'Well,' he said quietly, 'I'm manager here from now on, Robbins. Get the offices opened up this afternoon and get a room cleaned up for me. I'll go in Mr. Drew's old room for the time being.'

He took the old man's keys and started on a tour of inspection of the Yard, note-book in hand. It took him two hours and a half; at the end of that time he had been in every store and shed, and had filled three pages of his book.

Then he went down to the Labour Exchange.

Within a quarter of an hour the town was in a ferment.

The news spread from the door, carried on running feet, that Mr. Grierson was within, him as was under Mr. Drew, and they were taking on a ganger and ten men for labouring down at the Yard. By the time it had run through the town as far as Pilgrim Street it was to the effect that Barlows had got a good order for ships, Mr. Drew and Mr. Grierson were in the town, and fifty men were needed at the Labour Exchange at once. By the time it got to the top of the town it seemed that two hundred skilled men were required, specially platers.

The town became revitalised that afternoon, awoke to running life. Men struggled into jackets, crammed their caps upon their heads and went swarming down the hill to the Exchange; wives routed out the stay-at-homes, the pessimists, and sent them packing off to join the throng. Outside the doors of the Exchange the crowd swelled to over a thousand men, filling the street, and waiting patiently for news.

Grierson, coming out of the side door after an hour's conference with the manager of the Exchange, was surrounded and besieged by questions. He hesitated for a moment, then fought his way to the main steps of the Exchange.

On the steps he stood above them, visible to everyone. 'Now, see here, lads,' he said. 'I've come back here as manager of Barlows Yard, only it's not Barlows any longer. It's been taken over as a new Company. Don't ask me what we're going to build, because I don't rightly know myself, and if I did I wouldn't be able to tell you.'

A voice cried out anxiously, 'Will ye be needing

platers, mister?' The speaker was jostled into silence by his mates.

The manager laughed, and some of the men laughed with him. 'Go easy, lad,' he said. 'We got to get an order for a ship before we start and plate her. I'm hopeful we may get an order, but we haven't got one yet. Soon as we do, we'll be needing platers, fitters, riveters, joiners—all sorts. At present I've taken on ten men for cleaning up the Yard and getting straight, and there'll be no more needed for a while. It'll be no good anyone coming to the gate or writing letters to the Company, because I'm taking on through the Exchange. That's fair to everyone. Now, get along back home to your teas and don't come pestering me, 'cos I know nothing more than what I've told you.'

He came down from the steps, pushed his way through them, and went back to the Yard. The men stood about in little groups for an hour or more, slowly dispersing to their homes.

The news got to the hospital as soon as anywhere. It came, no doubt, from the out-patients; it went flowing through the cold stone corridors into the wards. In the children's ward it came from a nurse to Sister, who passed it on to Miss MacMahon.

'Nurse says there's something happening in the town,' said Sister. 'Something about Barlows starting up again.'

At the words something seemed to turn over inside the Almoner; she straightened up above the cot and stared at the sister. 'That—that's splendid news,' she said uncertainly. To the sister's astonishment, she was blushing. 'Do you know any more?'

The nurse said, 'They were saying down in out-patients something about a Mr. Grierson being in charge. Some name like that.'

'Would that be Billy Grierson that was?' inquired the sister thoughtfully. 'I wonder if there's any truth in it?'

Miss MacMahon left the children's ward and went down to the office. She found Mr. Williams there alone. 'They're saying in the wards that the Yard's starting up again,' she exclaimed. 'Is it true?'

He laid down his pen. 'Aye,' he said cautiously, 'I did hear something about it. They're saying Mr. Grierson's back, and taken on ten men down at the Yard.'

She said, 'It's wonderful!'

He eyed her dourly. 'This'll be something of your Mr. Warren and his wurrk, nae doubt?' He noted her flushed face and bright eyes.

'It might be. But he never told me it would be so soon.'

'Ah, weel,' said the Secretary, 'maybe ye'll get him better trained one day.'

Next day the work of cleaning up the Yard began. Grierson, deep in work of every sort, found time to keep an eye on his ten labourers, and what he saw displeased him very much. In the late afternoon he called the ganger to him.

'Ye'll have to get your men working better than this, or ye're no ganger for me,' he said brusquely, but not unkindly. 'Lord love you, man, there's not a day's work done among the lot of them!'

The man agreed. 'It's no a good day's work. I'm feared they're terrible soft, but they're wanting to please you. Go easy with them for a week, Mr. Grierson, and ye'll see a big difference.'

'I'll be needing to,' said Grierson grimly.

The man hesitated. 'I was wondering, Mr. Grierson, if ye'd consider paying by the day, the first week or two, and not wait till the week-end, the way they'd get a better dinner, this first week.'

The manager thought quickly. Precedent was everything in a shipyard; he could let himself in for endless trouble if he made a false move at the start. But the request was reasonable—the men could not do heavy work on a starvation diet. 'I'll no do that,' he said. 'This first week, I'll give each man two bob a day out of my own pocket, as a gift—not wages. And I'll look to you to see it's spent on food—not beer.' His eye strayed across the Yard. 'Now, get along and jerk 'em up a bit. Look at that big chap—there, wheeling that barrow-load of stuff. What's his name?'

'McCoy, sir.'

'God love us, man, he might be going to his own funeral.'

He turned back to his office, disheartened. He had not reckoned in his costs that he would have to feed his men up before setting them to work.

Two days later he wrote his views to Warren in London.

As regards the labour here (he wrote), *the position is very bad, and we should realise it. I have ten men clearing up the yard and putting the slips in order, as stated in my last letter, but not one of these is fit for a proper day's work. They are very soft, and there is no strength in them. I have laid off two and replaced them, but the new ones are as bad. These are labourers, of course, but I think we shall find the tradesmen will be just the same; I do not think there is a man in the town that is fit for a real day's work.*

I am now getting very worried about the fifty thousand pounds loss that I told you when I was in London. Unless we can get some decent labour to work with, that figure will be very much increased. I would like to talk this over with you before you definitely decide to put the order with this yard, as I do not want you to feel that I have been leading you astray.

Warren received this letter in his office the next day. He read it twice with a grim face, then put it in a drawer of his desk. One didn't want to have that sort of letter floating round the office before a public issue.

He reached out to the telephone, and put in a call to the Yard. Five minutes later he was speaking to Grierson. 'I'll get down to Newcastle on Friday night, late. Can you arrange to pick me up at the hotel on Saturday morning, and drive me out to Sharples?'

'I'll call for you myself, in my own car, Mr. Warren. I'll be right glad to have a crack with you about the Yard.'

Warren laid down the receiver, and sat for a few minutes deep in thought. Then he reached out for a sheet of private notepaper and wrote:

Dear Miss MacMahom,
I shall be in Sharples on Saturday morning, at the yard. Would you care to lunch with me? I don't know where one does lunch in Sharples, or if you would be free to lunch in Newcastle, but if you would give me a ring at the yard we might be able to fix something up.
Yours sincerely,
Henry Warren.

He posted this, and turned again to the set-up of Laevol Ltd. The sticking point in that lay in the collateral security for dividend; without such a security the Company would be purely speculative and quite unlikely to secure support. Even the most hardened speculator

179

would fight shy of a gamble in Laevatia, preferring to do his gambling against unloaded dice.

The collateral security that he had got upon the profits of the State Railway removed the issue from the speculative class and put it, if not in among the trustee stock, at any rate into the realms of serious business. He had negotiated an agreement, signed and sealed in Visgrad, between Laevol Ltd. and the Laevatian Government pledging the profit of the railway to support the Laevol dividend, but this agreement, between a Government-controlled company and the Government, had not of course been signed on British territory, and was subject to the laws of Laevatia. And, as Warren very well knew, the laws of Laevatia were laws unto themselves.

It would look all right in the prospectus, of course; he was not worried about that. The dangers that he knew existed lay concealed too deep in the legal system of Laevatia for any solicitor connected with the issue in London to be likely to unearth them. It probably would be all right, in fact, so long as all went according to plan.

Anyway, there was nothing to be done about it now. The whole thing was a pretty rocky deal that would be carried on in his name alone, and he would have to see it through.

He turned again to the wording of the prospectus. He worked on that all day with the solicitors, had it printed over-night and circulated to the underwriters, and spent the next day deep in conference with them. Plumberg came back to talk to him again of silver, and Heinroth's cousin, over from Paris with a Finn, demanded his attention.

For three days he did not leave the office before nine at night.

He freed himself on Friday afternoon, and caught the train to Newcastle. He slept at the hotel, indifferently, and greeted his manager after an early breakfast. Together they drove out upon the Sharples road.

'I'm right glad you've been able to get down,' said Grierson. 'It's proper that you should see for yourself the way things stand.'

They reached the Yard and went into the office. For some time Grierson outlined the work that he was doing in the Yard in preparation for the order; then he came to his main point.

'It's the men I'm worried about, Mr. Warren. I can see my way in everything but that.'

Warren nodded. 'I know,' he said. 'I got your letter. Tell me what the trouble is, exactly.'

'They've got no stamina, Mr. Warren. I never saw such. It's on account of Sharples being a small town, I think. Most places, on the Clyde or that, a man would maybe get a spell of work now and again in one yard or the other; he wouldn't be out of work continuous, if you take my meaning. But here, there's been no other yard to go to. All these men here have been out of work five and a half years, and they've not got the strength. I tell you, Mr. Warren, we're going to have a job to get the work from them that you've a right to expect.'

Warren got up and went to the window; the manager came and stood beside him. 'Look at that chap there now, handling that baulk of stuff. Did you ever see aught like it?'

They stood for a few minutes looking out into the Yard. Then Warren turned back to the room.

'I've known of this,' he said, 'before you told me.' He looked the other in the eyes. 'At the same time, I mean to get things started here again.'

He dropped into a chair by the table. 'Tell me this. Suppose we go ahead now and build these ships, and more ships after them. Maybe we'll lose a lot of money.'

'You will that.'

'In two years from the start, how will we be then? The men will have had two years of steady work, regular food and beer. Will we still be working at a disadvantage then, compared with other yards?'

The manager thought for a long time before answering. 'No,' he said at last, 'I'd not say that we will. Two years is long enough for a man to get back his skill and strength, if he's ever going to. Mind, there's some forty-five or fifty years old, that'll never come back to work again, after five years' idleness. But in two years' time I think we could compete in price, Mr. Warren. After all, it's a handy size, this Yard and it'd not take a great deal of work to meet our overhead.

'But it'll be two years of bloody grief,' he said.

Warren nodded. 'Still, I think we'll go ahead. You should have your order by the end of the month, and be able to get started ordering materials. We'll want sufficient capital to see us through, but I'll look after that.'

The manager smiled. 'It's as you say. Mind, you'll have a bonny little business if you can carry it through. Sharples folk were aye good folk to work before the slump came, and this Yard showed a profit every year.

'Soon as we get on to our feet,' he said, 'we want to try and get back on to Admiralty work again. That's where the Yard used to make its profit. There was seven Barlow destroyers at the Battle of Jutland, Mr. Warren. Did ye ever hear that?'

They went out, and spent some time in going round the Yard. Warren noticed a considerable difference since he had last seen it: the piles of scrap were cleared away, the fence had been repaired, the berths were orderly.

'You're getting it in shape, all right,' he said.

'Aye,' said the manager, 'but there's a lot to do yet before we can start an' build.'

He glanced across the Yard, critically. Beside the hydraulic guillotine he saw a woman coming towards them, picking her way delicately through the Yard. 'Yon's Miss MacMahon,' he said, 'her that's working at the hospital. Her father was solicitor to Barlows.'

Warren nodded. 'I think she's come for me.'

They walked to meet her; she greeted them both equally. To Grierson she said, 'That man Harrington's got a poisoned hand. It'll be some time before he works again.'

The manager turned aside. 'He was only on for three days,' he said resentfully. 'They're ower delicate, these folks.'

'Give them a chance,' she said. 'They're bursting with anxiety to get to work.'

'Aye, an' then when you set them to work they go off sick. I know they're willing, Miss MacMahon, but you can't build ships with nothing but good wishes.'

'They'll harden up.'

'Aye,' he said, 'we must do the best we can with the material we've got.'

She turned to Warren. 'I've got lunch for you in my room up at the hospital,' she said. 'Is that all right? There's really nowhere else that you could go, except the "Bull's Head", and that's not much.'

He smiled. 'That's very kind of you,' he said. He turned again to Grierson, and had a final word or two with him, then left the Yard with the girl and went walking up towards the hospital.

'You can't imagine what this little bit of work that's going on here now has meant,' she told him. 'It's psychological. Everybody's talking now about the Yard, and what the chances are of work again. It's helped the place enormously.'

He wrinkled his brows. 'Just by giving them something to look forward to?'

She nodded. 'It's been terrible this year,' she said gravely. 'You know how it is when someone's desperately ill—for days they may keep cheerful, hanging on. And then, one day, they let go, just don't care any more, and you know they're sinking then, that they'll never get back.' She turned to him. 'That's what it's been like in Sharples all this year, Mr. Warren. They've been— sinking.

'I honestly believe,' she said, 'that if you'd come along this time next year you wouldn't have been able to do anything at all in Sharples.'

'We've got a bad enough job now,' he said grimly.

They went into the hospital. In the front hall they passed the Matron, round and rubicund. She smiled at them, and Warren stopped and spoke to her.

She beamed. 'Your lunch is ready,' she said to them. 'I've just been along, and it's quite ready for you when you want it.'

'That's very kind of you,' he said. 'I didn't mean to give you the trouble.'

'Hoots, Mr. Warren, that's no trouble. You're welcome to it, any time that you're in Sharples. I've been thinking, the hotel accommodation's none so good in Sharples just now. I can alway fit you up with a bed here, if at any time you want to stay the night.'

'You'll have to pay for that,' said the Almoner. 'That's my end of the business.'

'Any time you like,' said the Matron. 'Just let us have a card.'

She left them, and they went on down the passage to the Almoner's room, where lunch was spread upon the table by the fire. A ward maid waited on them.

'How long have you been back from Visgrad?' asked the girl.

'Getting on for a month. I was out there for about a fortnight after we had lunch together.'

She smiled. 'Did you take out the umbrella with you?'

He nodded.

'And it worked?'

'I got what I wanted—the right to float the business on the London market.'

She wrinkled her brows. 'Does that mean orders for ships?'

'Broadly speaking, it does. If that issue goes all right, and I have no doubt that it will, it means that the Company, Laevol Ltd., will have to order tankers.'

'Will they be ordered from us, here?'

'I've arranged for that.'

She stared into the fire. 'It's wonderful,' she said quietly. 'The change that it will mean—to everything. I can't get used to the idea.'

He smiled. 'That isn't quite the end of the story. The next thing is, we've got to get some capital for the Yard to work with, to finance the order and for new equipment and machinery. That means another issue.'

She wrinkled her brows again. 'You mean, because of the order from Laevol, you'll be able to get in more money to capitalise the Yard?'

'That's it, broadly.'

They went on with their lunch, talking of Sharples, of the Yard, and of the hospital. And presently she said:

'About this new company, Laevol Ltd., Mr. Warren. I'd like to take up some shares in it, if I may. I had a legacy the other day, so I've got a little money to invest now.'

He did not answer for a minute. Then he said, 'How much did you think of putting into it?'

'About five hundred pounds.' She hesitated, and then said, 'Could you arrange that for me?'

He shook his head, smiling. 'No, I couldn't.'

'But why not?'

He eyed her for a moment. 'I wouldn't play about with foreign industrials, if I were you,' he said. 'Leave that to the people who make a study of that sort of thing —the big corporations and insurance companies.'

She met his eyes. 'But you're offering the shares to people like me, aren't you?'

'That's a matter of form,' he said easily. 'There's only one way to make a public issue, and that's to offer it to the public. But the bulk of this issue will be taken up by the investment corporations.'

She said, 'I see.'

'I think you might split your five hundred into two lots,' he remarked. 'If you'll let me look into it when I get back to town, I can let you have details of a couple of sound investments that will give you a safe dividend, and a slow capital appreciation. Then you could tell your bank to buy the shares—or, if you like, I'll handle it for you.'

She turned and faced him. 'You mustn't take that trouble, Mr. Warren,' she said evenly. 'I haven't got any money to invest, really. I only asked you that because I wanted to know what you really thought of Laevol Ltd.'

There was a little silence.

'Well,' he said heavily. 'You know that now.'

'Let's have our coffee by the fire,' she said gently. 'The maid can clear the table then.' She made him sit in the arm-chair, and poured out coffee for him.

'I'm sorry I did that,' she said at last, and smiled at him. 'It was mean. But since we had that talk in London, in your rooms, I've known that things weren't right, I felt then that you hated the whole thing. You do, don't you?'

He sat there in the chair before the fire, and sipped his coffee. 'It's autumn now,' he said at last. 'I told you in the spring that I would get this place going again, that day we went to see the mine. And I'm doing it. You don't imagine I hate doing that, do you?'

'No,' she said wonderingly, 'I don't.'

He went on, half to himself, 'In my sort of business it's not very easy to see clearly what one's working for. A young man works to make money, or to get married.' He raised his head. 'You know that I'm divorcing my wife?'

'Yes,' she said quietly, 'I know that.'

'Well. One gets to a stage, later on in life, when the things one used to work for don't quite fit. I've got all the money I could ever want to use. And it's when you get to my age that you begin to wonder what in hell you go on working for. What you expect to get out of it.'

There was a silence. She did not interrupt and presently he went on.

'One can't just give up working, and do nothing. And so one's got to find a motive, an excuse for going on doing the job one knows. I had time to think about all this when I was here in hospital. I was right away from it then, able to see my job from the outside. And it seemed to me then, as it does now, that there's only one thing really worth working for in the City. That's to create work.

G

'I don't know if you've ever thought about machines,' he said. 'Every machine that's put into a factory displaces labour. That's a very old story, of course. The man who's put to work the machine isn't any better off than he was before; the three men that are thrown out of a job are very much worse off. But the cure isn't Socialism—or if it is, I'm too much of a capitalist myself to see it. The cure is for somebody to buckle to and make a job for the three men.

'I believe that that's the thing most worth doing in this modern world,' he said quietly. 'To create jobs that men can work at, and be proud of, and make money by their work. There's no dignity, no decency, or health to-day for men that haven't got a job. All other things depend on work to-day: without work men are utterly undone.'

He had been speaking so softly that she had to strain to hear what he was saying; now he was silent for a very long time. At last he raised his head.

'You asked me about Laevol. Laevol's a rotten company. But you know that already.'

She stirred in her chair. 'How is it rotten?'

'It's like an apple with a worm in it. It looks all right outside. If the worm's got into the core, you may be able to eat the whole apple and never know it's there. Alternatively, you may find half of him after the first bite.'

She smiled faintly. 'I see. You mean it's not a very reliable company?'

'That is so. But nobody knows just what's wrong with it but me.'

'And you can't put it right?'

He shook his head. 'It's all set now. I've got all the underwriting contracts in. You'll see the prospectus

188

advertised next Friday, in the papers; it goes to the public on Tuesday following. The issue's going to be a great success.'

'What happens after that?'

He lit a cigarette. 'After that? The first thing Laevol does is to place its order for the ships, three oil tankers. The Hawside Ship and Engineering Company take that order—and glad to get it.'

She exclaimed, 'Hawside? Did you call the Company after our little river here, the Haws?'

He nodded. 'As good a name as any other. I never put much weight on names, myself.'

She wrinkled her brows. 'Is that the Company that's going to work here, then?'

He nodded, blowing out a cloud of smoke. 'The Hawside Company was registered some weeks ago. I sold the Yard to them the other day—on paper. You might say that the Hawside Company is here already.'

She stared at him wonderingly. 'But—but what does the Company consist of?'

He smiled. 'Seven clerks, with a one pound share each. My own accountant is the secretary; the shareholders haven't elected a Board yet. It's got a capital of one hundred pounds, but that's not all paid up, of course.'

'Is that the Company that's going to build the ships?'

He nodded. 'That's right. It's going to suffer a sea change next week—into something rich and strange, as you might say. It's going to print itself a lot more shares. And it's going to acquire a Board. I'm going to be chairman.'

'And what happens then?'

'Then it's ready to take the Laevol order for the oil tankers—four hundred and fifty thousand pounds' worth of work. It won't have any money to build them with, of course, so it goes to the public with its new shares, and makes an issue for five hundred thousand pounds. Then it gets down to work and builds the ships.'

She eyed him steadily. 'Is a company of that sort going to be all right?'

He passed his hand across his eyes, a little wearily. 'It's going to be as right as I can make it. I can't say more than that. It will have money, and an order to work at, good premises, a good secretary, and Mr. Grierson. I'm going to be chairman myself, to stand by the Company for the first year or two. If I bring that to Sharples, I'll have done the best I can to get things started here again.'

She laid her hand impulsively upon his arm. 'Don't think I'm criticising what you've done.'

'You'd have a right to,' he replied. 'It's not a very bright set-up, and I'm not proud of it. But to get anything at all to start up in the middle of a slump like this is difficult. I've done the best I can. You'll get some work in Sharples—for a time, at any rate.'

'The Hawside Company hasn't got a worm?'

He smiled and shook his head. 'You needn't worry about that. When that gets going it depends upon itself alone. It may lose money at the start; I think it will. But there'll be no trickery in it that you need fear, no conjuring with cards, or umbrellas.'

She turned and faced him. 'And this is really going to happen? We're going to have a company established here with four hundred and fifty thousand pounds' worth of work, and a capital of five hundred thousand?'

He nodded. 'You can count on that within two months from now. After that, we've got to tackle the rolling-mills and see if we can get them started up again.'

She eyed him steadily. 'You've done a very splendid thing,' she said. 'I knew that somebody would come to help us. It must give you a great feeling of satisfaction to have done all this.'

He smiled. 'I suppose it ought to,' he said quietly. 'I've been too tired to think about it much.'

THE Laevol issue, on the whole, was well received. The *Financial Argus* described it as 'an interesting issue, designed to develop the great natural resources of the Balkans, launched under the most favourable auspices.' The *Daily Toiler* referred to it as 'financial chicanery; sponsored by the Government in a futile attempt to bolster up an outworn Capitalist régime in Laevatia.' In Warren's view the quite unfounded reference to the Government in the latter excerpt was as great an asset to the issue as the restrained benediction of the *Argus*; in any event, the issue was over-subscribed three times.

'Get going on this right away,' said Warren to Morgan. 'I want an analysis of the applications by Friday; I've fixed the allotment committee for Monday morning. See if you can think of some formula to squeeze out the little chaps.'

His secretary glanced at him curiously. 'I'll do my best to get out something, sir. You would like to eliminate the small investor, so far as possible?'

Warren nodded. 'Get them right out of it.'

They were got out of it, by more or less questionable devices, and to their own exceeding discontent. A number of letters reached the Company voicing their grievance, amongst them six pages from Canon Ward-Stephenson of The Nook, Shoreham-on-Sea. It appeared that the Canon had applied for six hundred one pound shares, and had been allotted sixty. He threatened legal action. The threat being accepted, he approached

Mr. Castroni, with whom he had a slight acquaintance, for his intervention in the matter. Mr. Castroni rang up Mr. Warren.

'Of course,' said Warren easily. 'I felt myself that the allotment committee were perhaps a little hard on the smaller subscribers. If he's really very anxious, I daresay I could get him five-hundred privately—at par.'

'That's very good of you,' said Mr. Castroni. 'He's a cantankerous old man, and we don't want any bother.'

Warren rang off, and sat for a minute marvelling at the simple cupidity of the religious orders. Then he turned to the consideration of the Hawside Ship and Engineering Company Ltd.

The increase of the capital was in the hands of his solicitors; within the next few days he had to form his Board. He reached out for the telephone, and asked Lord Cheriton to lunch with him.

Over the cheese he said, 'I've got a job for you,' and told him of the Hawside Ship and Engineering Company. 'I'm going to take the chair; I'd like it if you'd come upon the Board.'

The young man flushed with pleasure. 'I'd like nothing better, as you know. But I'd want to work at any business I go into—not just attend a meeting once a month.'

Warren nodded. 'That's what I want you for. I can't be up in Sharples all the time myself; I've got to keep things spinning round down here. I want you to be vice-chairman and work in the business.'

The other frowned. 'I don't want to be a passenger. And there's one small point you seem to have forgotten; I don't know anything about building ships.'

'I know. But I've got to have someone there that I can trust, who can make a team out of the staff I'm going to take on. And with your position in the county, the Company will have prestige that it will need, in the difficult years at first.'

The other grinned. 'Pull my weight as a figurehead until I've learned to talk sense about the business? All right, I'm on. I never thought I'd earn my living as a guinea-pig.' He paused. 'But who *is* going to build the ships? We'd better get in somebody, one man at any rate, who knows something about the job. Just for the sake of appearances, what? I mean, the public will expect it.'

Warren laughed, and told him about Grierson. 'Then I've got a really good man, Jenkins, for a secretary,' he said. 'Grierson has his staff pretty well planned. It's all further advanced than you think.'

He considered for a minute. 'I'm going to put Grierson on the Board,' he said, 'as managing director—as soon as I'm sure of him. In six months' time, perhaps. It's a pity we can't do it now, but I wouldn't take the chance until we know him better. That means going to the public without much technical strength on the Board . . . make the underwriting difficult. We'll have to meet that point.'

Cheriton said, 'I could put it up to old Sir David Hogan.'

Warren mused. 'He's a very good name—the public would like that. But he was a shipowner, wasn't he? Not a builder?'

'I believe he'd jump at it, all the same.'

'I daresay. How old is he?'

'Seventy-three. But he's still hale and hearty. He'd like it from the point of view of getting something done for Sharples.'

'It's a good idea, that,' said Warren. 'Let me think about it for a day.'

Two days later, his Board complete, Warren set about his underwriting contracts. Heinroth wagged his head. 'I can't tell what to make of you, Warren,' he said. 'It's second sight, or something. I thought that last Laevatian thing of yours would leave us all stuck in the soup, and it was taken up three times. But still, old boy—a shipyard, in these days! I wouldn't pick that for a winner, on my own.'

'Do as you like,' said Warren equably. 'I'm in it up to the neck, myself—and not for a squashed sausage, either.'

Mr. Heinroth eyed him narrowly. 'You think we're on the turn, I suppose.'

'Stick to the business in hand,' said Warren. 'Do you want any of this thing?'

'I'll take a walk around,' said Mr. Heinroth. 'Give you a tinkle later on this afternoon.'

He took his walk around, to Mr. Castroni and to Mr. Todd. 'I've given up using my own judgment,' said Mr. Todd resignedly. 'I'll take twenty-five thousand, if that's what you're doing. I believe that Laevol thing went off on Warren's name alone, you know.'

'This one'll do the same,' said Mr. Castroni. 'I never mind much what the issue is, so long as it's handled right. And that man's never made a bloomer yet.'

Mr. Heinroth gave his tinkle, satisfactorily. Other people did the same, in three days the underwriting was satisfactorily arranged.

Warren rang up Grierson in Sharples. 'We're all set now,' he said. 'You'd better come up here to-morrow, and stay while we make the contract with Laevol.'

They laboured for a week upon the various contracts necessary before the Hawside Ship and Engineering Company went to the public for subscription. The Grierson went back to the Yard, with Jenkins the new secretary.

He called his nucleus of foremen together in his office.

'Well, lads,' he said. 'We've got three ships to build—oil tankers of ten thousand tons. You know what that means to Sharples, and you can thank Mr. Warren for it, and nobody else. Just you remember that. And another thing. There's work for eighteen months in these three ships, but if they are not built at a profit there's an end of it, because the Yard'll be bust again. Just keep that in your nappers. If we want more work after this lot's over, we've got to get these ships out cheap.'

The foreman riveter said, 'That's a bloody fact.' The others grunted inarticulately.

One said, 'Will we be able to tell this in the town now, Mr. Grierson?'

He nodded. 'Aye, the cat's out of the bag now. Materials are all on order, and plates due here next week. There's a plan of the ships that you can see on Mr. Sanders' board up in the drawing office. Now get along with you, and start to reckon what you'll want. Be back here for a meeting at three o'clock.'

'We'll dae our best, Mr. Grierson,' said one awkwardly. 'Eh, but it's a grand oppaortoonity for the toon.'

They filed out of the office.

That week appendicitis removed Miss Sale, Warren's personal stenographer, from his business. In the final drafting of the prospectus of the Hawside Ship and Engineering Company he was compelled to use a new, exotic acquisition of the firm, Miss ffolliot-Johnson. He did not know where Miss ffolliot-Johnson had come from; within a couple of hours he was past caring where she went.

He rang the buzzer for Morgan. 'You'd better fire that girl,' he said sharply. 'I don't want to see her here again—she's no damn good to us. She can't write English, she can't spell, she can't type, and she stinks like a drain. Get her out of the place at once.'

It was, of course, unfortunate that the door was open, and every word he said could be heard in the main office.

With that contretempts, the prospectus was drafted to his satisfaction, and the satisfaction of the underwriters. Knowing the moods of the investing public, he paid special attention to the paragraph about prospective profits. He wrote:

'The orders which are now in hand are taken at a price which should be profitable, after allowing an ample margin for contingencies. These orders will not be completed in the first financial year. It is anticipated that the profit on the completed work in the second year will be sufficient to permit a dividend appropriate to the two years of working.'

Morgan read this with an impassive face. 'A little definite, sir, is it not?'

Warren shrugged his shoulders. 'We shan't get underwriting for it otherwise. I don't think there's anything wrong with that. You've got to commit yourself these days, if an industrial issue is to be put over at all.'

The secretary said no more.

Cheriton passed it without comment. Sir David Hogan passed it with the observation, in writing, 'As regards the profits, one can only trust to the technical staff. I understand that you have checked their estimates in detail, and as no one can do more I am content to let the prospectus go forward in its present form. Indeed, I think it is a very good one, and I see no reason why we should not make this Company a great success.'

Warren sat for a long time motionless, this letter in his hand. Before him on his desk lay the acceptance notes of underwriting, neat in a file. He now had only to send the prospectus to the printers, and set in hand the distribution to the banks and stockbrokers.

He buzzed for Morgan. 'I'm going out,' he said. 'I'll be back after lunch.'

He felt the need of exercise to clear his mind. He took a taxi to the Horse Guards Parade, dismissed it, and began to walk along beside the lake. Half consciously, he was looking for a sign.

It was a raw November day. Upon the bridge that spans the lake a few children with their nursemaids were feeding the ducks with bread, children of means, warmly attired in new, clean overcoats and little scarves, flushed with excitement; such children as he might have had himself. He passed them and went on, across the Mall and on through the Green Park towards Hyde Park Corner, walking with nervous haste, uneasy and irresolute. He crossed the Corner and went through the gates into Hyde Park, and walked for a time westwards towards the Serpentine.

And presently, a little tired and footsore in his City shoes, he dropped down on to a park seat, facing the lake. At the other end of the seat there was a man, shabby and motionless, without an overcoat.

Warren sat for a time, staring out over the lake. Half consciously he took out his cigarette case and lit a cigarette with his lighter. He exhaled a long blue cloud, soothing his worried nerves.

He became aware that the man at the far end of the seat was watching him hungrily. He offered his case.

'Cigarette?'

'Don't mind if I do,' said the man awkwardly. Warren leaned across and lit it for him; as he did so, for a moment he studied the lean, sensitive face, the capable, sinewy

198

hands, the rotten boots. They smoked in silence for a time.

'Out of a job?' asked Warren.

The other nodded without speaking.

'Long?'

'Eleven months.'

'What's your job?'

'Cabinet maker. I was in the furniture trade.'

'Bad luck.'

The man said very quietly, 'All very well, to say bad luck. But you've got a home, and that. It's seven months now since I saw my wife. I wish that I was dead.'

He got up and walked away.

Warren sat for a time, and watched him till he disappeared. Then he flung his cigarette into the lake, walked down towards the Albert Hall, and took a taxi to the City.

'You can get these printed right away,' he said to Morgan. 'The issue is on Tuesday week.'

This time the issue was more doubtfully received. The *Argus* said, 'Whether the present can be regarded as a fit time for a shipyard issue must remain a matter for debate, as must the prospects of the company in spite of the prospectus statements. The names upon the Board are good, however, and with the initial orders in hand the company may well be carried to success.'

The *Daily Toiler* struck a different note. 'While we cannot but deplore the system of finance which governs industry in the country, we welcome the establishment of more employment on the north-east coast. This issue will bring much relief to Sharples, and for that reason we recommend it to our readers.'

Which, as Mr. Heinroth ruefully observed, was not a great relief to him.

Mr. Grierson received a copy of the prospectus in his office in the Yard the day before the issue, and read it with attention. Before he had finished, Jennings had come into his room.

'You're reading our prospectus?'

The manager sucked at his pipe. 'Aye,' he said slowly. 'I was just reading the bit about the profits that we're going to make.'

They stared at it in silence for a time.

'It's not right,' said the manager at last. 'I've told him different all along, that we should make a loss.'

The secretary sighed. 'Yes. Of course, he wouldn't get his money if he told the public that.'

'I don't like it,' said Grierson. 'I don't like it at all.'

The secretary shrugged his shoulders. 'It's too late now to make a song about it. Better to let it go. He may have something in his mind that we don't know about.'

'Aye,' said the manager, 'it may be so. But I wish I could know what it was. It'd save me a good few sleepless nights.'

Canon Ward-Stephenson received a copy—Mr. Castroni saw to that—and applied again for his six hundred shares. He had some faith in that particular multiple, founded upon a tangle of beliefs about the Trinity and the known luck of the figure three.

Miss MacMahon got hold of the prospectus with some difficulty, and put in for a hundred pounds.

Miss ffolliot-Johnson also got hold of a copy, but did not apply for any shares. Instead, she took it to a bedroom in the boarding-house in Kensington that she lived in, and read it with some care. Then she got up and took from her handkerchief drawer a letter, written by Grierson, that she had removed from a drawer in the desk of her late employer. She compared the two documents carefully, with tightened lips.

Then she put them away together.

The issues of shares in the Hawside Ship and Engineering Company was about twenty per cent oversubscribed.

CHAPTER XII

In the next month Sharples stirred and woke to life. It was difficult to tell the moment of awakening. More labourers were taken on each day. A few riggers were started, and a couple of crane hands. The boiler and the power house squads were taken on, and reported gloomily about their Augean stable. One day a ganger and a plate-laying squad appeared upon the railway siding leading to the Yard, tapping the rails and grumbling at the lack of wedges in the chairs, taken for firewood long before. A few days later a tank engine puffed along the line with five bogie waggons laden with steel plate, and three days after that the rattling clamour of a pneumatic riveter burst from the yards.

The women crowded to their doors, and stood listening entranced to the sweet symphony. 'That's a riveter, that is,' they said. 'Just fancy . . .'

The man driving the rivets in the keel plate dropped the tool thankfully when the whistle blew for dinner, and surveyed the burst and bleeding blisters on his palms. 'Christ,' he said to his holder-up, 'this is a bloody caper, no mistake.'

Grierson, critically examining the work, heard the remark and saw the hands. 'Get along to the first aid and get that dressed before you go to dinner,' he said resignedly. 'Then go and draw a pair of gloves before you start again.'

He went quickly to the storekeeper. 'Nip up into the town and get a dozen pairs of hedgers' gloves,' he said.

'I want them for the riveters, until their hands get hard.'
Working to build a ship in kid gloves, he thought,
bitterly. But what else could one do?

Under his tireless drive, however, the work progressed. By the end of the month he had a hundred
men employed, still largely on preparatory work. In
addition, he had made a good start with his organisation;
buying, progress, and rate-fixing were all established as
a nucleus, and his stores were falling into line.

'It's only that everyone's so willing makes it possible
at all,' he said to Cheriton one evening. 'When I go
round and see those men in gloves it makes me want
to cry.'

'It's only for a time,' said Cheriton. 'They're getting
hardened up already.'

'Aye. That first chap's left his off, I'm glad to see.'

On Christmas Eve, when the Yard closed for the
holiday, the numbers of employed had gone up to a
hundred and seventy-nine weekly wage earners. The
small, returning ripple of prosperity had not passed unnoticed in the district; a shop, long closed, reopened to
sell meat pies, cooked meats, black puddings and other
delicacies. It did a good trade over Christmas. Small
articles began to be sold at the door for the first time for
many years; a man who gleaned a sack of holly in the
country lanes disposed of it within an hour, a penny for
a spray. A hot roast chestnut barrow came upon the
streets, and did good trade.

A dairyman, apologising for a shortage at the hospital
about this time, observed that he was selling three times
what he had six months before; he didn't know where
to turn for milk, really and truly. Mr. Williams repri-
manded him severely and sent him away.

'It's quite true, what he said, you know,' observed

the Almoner. 'There's more milk being bought now in the town than ever before.'

Mr. Williams grunted. 'Aye,' he said. 'Soon as they get a little money they go and spend it.'

'On their children.'

'Aye. But they spend it, instead of saving for the next time.'

'I wouldn't quibble about what they spend on milk,' said Miss MacMahon. 'I suppose you can tell how prosperous a town is by the amount it spends on milk. Mr. Warren ought to know about that; he deals with commodities.'

She told him about it next time he came to lunch with her. He came to Sharples once a week, arriving upon Friday afternoon, staying the night with Cheriton, lunching with her on Saturday at the hospital, and going back to London on an evening train. He missed one Saturday; when next he came she thought him looking worn and ill. He told her he had had a touch of influenza.

'You're looking rotten,' she remarked. 'Come up to the fire and get warm. How long have you been out of bed?'

'About two days,' he said.

She eyed him for a minute. 'You ought to take a holiday. Didn't your doctor tell you that?'

'I didn't have one. All I had was a sort of feverish cold.'

'You're going to have one now.' She lifted the telephone receiver and spoke into it. 'Would you ask Dr. Davies if he would be good enough to come along to my room when he's done his lunch?' She laid the receiver down.

He frowned. 'That isn't necessary in the least.'

She laid her hand upon his arm. 'Don't be cross. I'd

like it if you'd let him look you over. He's house phy-sician here, quite good at his job. He'll make you up a tonic to take back with you.'

He laughed. 'Serves me right for putting my nose inside a hospital.'

Davies, a serious-minded, sandy-haired young man, took him to an adjoining room and stethoscoped him thoroughly. 'You had this operation here, last March, didn't you?' he enquired. 'And you've had no rest since then. You went straight out of here and went to work at once.'

Warren pulled on his coat. 'Very silly of me, I suppose.'

The young doctor smiled faintly. 'Not altogether the best thing you could have done.'

He laid his stethoscope upon the table. 'I should take a good long holiday now, if I were you. Go somewhere where it's warm—the south of France, perhaps—and don't take things too energetically. In a month you'll be a different man.'

Warren shook his head. 'I can't do that. I've got to keep things going.'

They discussed the matter for a little. 'Well,' said Davies at last. 'I'll make you up a tonic. But really, you should take it easier, you know.'

The financier smiled. 'You might as well tell a chap who's out of work to drink three pints of milk a day.'

The young man flushed. 'I'm here to tell people what they ought to do. I can't see that they do it, either with you or anybody else.'

Warren nodded. 'That's right—I'm sorry I said that about the milk. But I can't get a holiday just yet.'

He went back to London on the evening train, carry-ing with him in his bag a large bottle of medicine, like any out-patient. Miss MacMahon walked with him to the station and saw him off.

'Mind you take that tonic,' she reminded him. 'It cost a lot of money, and we didn't give it you for fun.'

He smiled. 'It's good of you to look after me like this,' he said quietly.

'Why, no,' she said. 'It's good of you to look after us.'

The train carried him away towards Newcastle, and she turned back to the hospital. In the corridor, outside the Common Room, she stopped Davies.

'What did you think of Mr. Warren?'

The sandy-haired young man considered seriously for a minute. 'There's nothing organically wrong, you understand. He's very much run down. A certain amount of nervous indigestion, and that sort of thing. I got the impression that he was working far harder than he ought to, probably worrying about his work. But I imagine that's his normal life.'

The Almoner bit her lip. 'That's half the trouble.'

During the early months of the New Year employment in the Yard increased enormously. By the end of January about four hundred and eighty men were working on the tankers; in the next month the figure rose to over seven hundred, and to a thousand by the end of March. With this increase in employment in the town, shops of all sorts began to come to life again; exteriors were repainted, giving Palmer Street a less desolate appearance, windows became filled with the new stock. A new shop opened to sell bicycles and motor bicycles; the increase of the traffic in the streets became most noticeable.

In April the Yard got another order, for a cargo steamer of three thousand tons.

It came through Sir David Hogan, who induced an

impecunious shipowner associate to speculate on the future to the extent of ordering a replacement to his fleet. The deal was placed with the Yard through Warren Sons and Mortimer; the price was cut to bed-rock for the sake of the order.

'Lord love us,' said Grierson. 'We'll have to call this one the *Misery*. At that price she'll be nothing but grief to us.'

Jennings turned over the pages of the contract. 'It says here she's to be called the *Argosy*. Twelve-inch lettering bow and stern.'

'*Argosy* nothing. She'll be the Misery to us.'

'She'll give us continuity of work,' said Warren. 'Time enough to worry about prices when we've got our reputation back as builders of good ships. Till then we've got to take what we can get, and like it.'

He took his tale to Miss MacMahon, and told her all about it. 'It's wonderful,' she exclaimed. 'You must be terribly proud to have done this. Because this is a real order, isn't it? I mean, there isn't a worm in this apple?'

Warren smiled. 'No—this one is comparatively sound.'

She considered for a minute. 'There's one point that I don't quite see,' she said. 'Why did your firm have to come into it at all? Why wasn't the order placed straight with the Yard?'

He smiled, a little cynically. 'Shipbuilding finance,' he said. 'It sounds better put that way. Ordinary people call it hire purchase.'

'Oh . . .'

'In times like these,' he explained, 'the shipowner has all his money locked up in his ships. He may want another ship, but he hasn't got the cash to pay for it. The shipbuilder, on the other hand, hasn't got the money to build it.'

'But that's absurd,' she said. 'You can't get anywhere, if that's the way of it.'

He smiled. 'Oh, yes, you can. They both come running to the bank to borrow money.'

There was a momentary silence.

'I see,' she said. 'So Sharples can't quite get along without you, even yet.'

'Not quite,' he said. 'But every order that we get brings the Yard nearer to standing on its own feet. That's why I'm so pleased we've got this little ship to build. It means that owners will consider us again.'

She eyed him steadily. 'So far as I can see, it means that one bank is considering us all the time.'

'That may be. But I couldn't have gone against the owner, if he'd had no confidence that Sharples could turn out a decent ship.'

She turned towards the window. 'Sharples is getting like it used to be,' she said. She stared out into the street. 'Last year, on a Saturday night about this time, there wouldn't have been a soul about. Just—desolate. And now, look at them.'

He came and stood beside her. The street was thronged with women shopping with their men, laden with baskets and with paper bags, shabby and ragged, but alive and vital in the light of the street-lamps. A few cars, tradesmen's vans, stood in the road; there were many bicycles.

'It's different, isn't it?' she said. 'They're talking about getting the trams running.'

'It's certainly a change.' He smiled. 'Another sign of progress. I didn't know you had an evening paper here.'

She nodded. 'Did you see the boy?'

'Down there, coming towards us.'

She peered down the street. 'It's only on Saturdays that we get that. Because of the football news. It comes from Newcastle.'

They stood and watched the crowd as the boy came towards them. For a minute he was hidden from their sight. Then the crowd parted and he was quite near to them; his placard was displayed before their eyes.

It said: 'REVOLUTION IN LAEVATIA'.

'Oh—look,' said the girl. 'Does that mean anything?'

She glanced up quickly at Warren; his face was very hard. 'It's a bad one, that,' he said quietly. 'Let me go and get a paper.'

He came back in a minute with the paper in his hand, and spread it out upon her table. Together they read down the short account in silence.

'Well,' he said. 'It couldn't have been worse.'

She laid her hand upon his arm. 'I'm terribly sorry. Did you know any of these people who were shot? Deleben, the Prime Minister—did you know him?'

He nodded. 'He wasn't a bad chap.' He paused. 'The other one—Theopoulos—the one who was shot in the cabaret. He was the one I did the business with.'

There was a long silence. The girl looked up at him at last, powerless to help. 'This is a very bad one,' he repeated. 'I don't know what this is going to mean.'

She turned again to the paper. 'I don't understand about these parties. The People's Party were in power, were they?'

He nodded. 'They were the conservatives. The Government were pretty stable under them. But this other lot—the Social Reform Party—they're just the mob. And look who's leading them!'

She stared at it, uncomprehending. 'Potiscu? Did you know him?'

He laughed shortly. 'He's the one who got the umbrella.'

He stared at the account again. 'Looting—and burning—murdering in cabarets—soldiers shooting down their officers in cafés. . . . God knows what this will mean to us, up here.'

She stared up at him, open-eyed. 'I hadn't thought of that.'

He smiled. 'Don't worry—it'll pan out all right. But I must get along to London right away.'

He caught the night train down from Newcastle, and was in London in the early hours of Sunday morning. He went straight to his flat and read the morning papers carefully; the situation was as bad as it could be. He spent an hour at the Laevatian Embassy, but got little comfort there; in the afternoon he attended an emergency conference at the London offices of Laevol Ltd. He came away from that with little new information, but with one certainty: the preference dividend due in May and secured upon the profits of the State Railway, would not be paid.

'There can't be any profit on the railway after this,' remarked the secretary. 'Look at the Decree—free transport of all food materials and free travelling for all manual workers. There cannot possibly be any profit after that to pay our dividend. And anyway, they'll probably rescind the Agreement now—it's subject to Laevatian law, that one.'

Warren's lips narrowed to a line. 'It's bad,' he said.

'It's bad, all right,' remarked the secretary, a little hostile. 'This should have been foreseen.'

In the City the next morning, the Laevatian news was treated with concerned derision, as a joke in rather poor taste. During the day the Laevol shares fell catastrophically from twenty-two shillings to fourteen and six; next day they were marked down to about nine shillings, where they hovered for a week or two. A feeling of hostility was evident; the *Argus*, relating the news, took the occasion to comment acidly upon the 'flotation of a certain company, which would now seem to be a subject for investigation.'

Mr. Todd, who held few of the Laevol shares, took the matter philosophically. 'Write 'em off the books,' he said, 'They'll never be worth anything now.'

Mr. Castroni was not amused. 'My godfathers,' he said. 'To hear you talk! I put the best clients that I've got into this thing, and look at it now! Thirty thousand pounds of my clients' money gone already, and the rest not worth a sausage. Look at that!'

'Moral—use your own judgment, and not other people's,' said Mr. Todd.

Mr. Castroni ground his cigarette out in the tray. 'This thing's a bloody racket,' he said bitterly, 'and I've let Warren suck me in. I've been a fool, and now I've got to pay for it. I felt that there was something crooked in it when he gave the Laevol order to his other company, that Hawside thing. That paper's right—there's something here wants digging into, and I'm going to do it.'

Mr. Todd gazed at him in wonder. 'You won't find anything that you can lay a finger on,' he said. 'Look at the issues that they've been behind.'

'That may be,' said Mr. Castroni. 'If there's nothing in it but a run of bad luck, I shall be glad. But with the letters I've been getting from my clients . . .'

He broke off. 'There's a retired canon down at Shoreham,' he said bitterly. 'One of the best I've got. And now, he rings me up to tell me that I've swindled him. Me! I've come to the conclusion that he has been swindled, but it's not by me.'

His researches led him in the end to Warren's office. Warren received him courteously.

'I agree,' he said, after the first discussion, 'that the Company has had a setback. I am concerned about it, because in some degree I feel it as a reflection on my House. Our issues do not usually have setbacks of this sort. But then, a revolution is itself unusual.'

Mr. Castroni eyed him for a minute. 'You had a bit of bad luck there. Now, I've been studying the Agreement with the then Government of Laevatia. It was rather an unusual proviso that the contract for the ships be placed through your House, rather than at public tender?'

Warren shrugged his shoulders. 'That was a part of the deal. It was disclosed in the prospectus that you underwrote. Are you objecting to it now?'

Mr. Castroni swallowed something. 'I was merely remarking on the matter. Apart from that, the security for the dividend has fallen down. I didn't understand that that was subject to Laevatian law.'

'You should read the prospectus. But, in any case, an agreement between a foreign company and its own Government isn't usually ruled by British law.'

He got up from his desk. 'I see that you are feeling badly about Laevol,' he said quietly, 'and I am sorry for that. But, as I say, we didn't cater for a revolution in the country.'

Mr. Castroni rose to go. 'I'm not only feeling badly,' he said evenly. 'I'm feeling that I've been had for a mug, but I can't prove it yet.'

In spite of her inability to write English, to spell, and to type, and in spite of a certain physical disability,

Miss ffolliot-Johnson had quite enough intelligence to follow the affairs of Laevol with interest. She was accustomed to spend occasional week-ends with her uncle down at Shoreham, but it was sheer coincidence that brought the canon to her uncle's house to tea one Saturday.

Canon Ward-Stephenson was still full of his great trouble. 'I am not a habitual dealer on the Stock Exchange,' he informed his host, '—far from it. We clergy have little money to indulge such tastes. But quite recently I was persuaded by my broker—persuaded, I may say, against my better judgment—to invest a very considerable sum, a very considerable sum indeed, in a new issue, Laevol Ltd.'

Miss ffolliot-Johnson stiffened to attention.

'And what is the result? It appears to me—I may, of course, be in error—that all decency and honest dealing, all proper rectitude, have vanished from the City since the War. No, I do not think I am in error. I do not think that is an over-statement. The issue has hardly been upon the market for three months, and look at the shares now! I see that they are quoted at eight shillings and threepence for the one-pound shares, and are quite unlikely to declare the dividend which was supposed to have been guaranteed. To put the matter plainly, I have been swindled out of a great many hundreds of pounds.'

His host made sympathetic noises. 'These bucket shops,' he said. 'I don't know why they allow them to continue.'

'But this was not a bucket shop,' exclaimed the canon. 'The Company was launched by a firm of bankers, Warren Sons and Mortimer, who were supposed to be above reproach. I satisfied myself upon that point most

213

particularly. No, the fact of the matter is that there is an infection of dishonest dealing which has crept into the City since the War, even into concerns that seem to be of good repute.'

Miss ffolliot-Johnson laughed shortly. 'You wouldn't call Warren Sons and Mortimer a firm of good repute,' she said shortly. 'I mean, one has to be careful what company one gets into, even if one is only a secretary, don't you think?' She gazed appealingly at the canon. 'I left as soon as I found out what sort of people they were running it.'

Her uncle explained. 'My niece was employed by Warren Sons and Mortimer for a short time. They seem to be a very bad crowd.'

The girl nodded. 'I never was in such a horrid office,' she said mincingly. 'I mean, it was just horrid. It's not very nice to be where people are being swindled all day long, is it? The stories I could tell!'

Without a great deal of difficulty she was induced to tell them.

'And then there was the Hawside Ship and Engineering Company,' she said. 'That was just awful, that was. Robbing the public, that's what I call it.'

The canon's heart turned over. He had about five hundred pounds invested in that company. He frowned. 'What was the trouble there?' he asked.

The girl laughed shortly. 'All of it was trouble, if you ask me. Mr. Warren had this shipyard that he'd bought by mistake or something, and he had it on his hands and it was just a dead loss to him, if you see what I mean. So he faked up this order from the Laevol Company, taking it out of one pocket and putting it into the other, that's what I call it. And then he was able to make a big issue to the public, because of that. And then he sold the shipyard, which wasn't worth anything at all, to the Hawside Company, and got it off his hands. You wouldn't hardly credit what fools people are with their money.'

The canon winced.

'I don't see that there's much harm in that,' said her uncle mildly. 'The shipyard may do very well, if it's got orders.'

'That's what it said in the prospectus,' said the girl. 'But that's all lies, just to take people in and make them put up their money.'

Canon Ward-Stephenson eyed her steadily. 'Why do you say that?'

'I know it's all lies,' she said defiantly. 'His manager wrote to him to say that they were going to make a loss of over fifty thousand pounds, and Mr. Warren put it in the prospectus that they were going to make a profit.'

Her uncle looked at her incredulously. 'But that's not right,' he said. 'You can go to prison for that.'

She tossed her head. 'That's where he ought to be, that Mr. Warren.'

'Are you sure that you aren't making a mistake?' enquired the canon.

Miss ffolliot-Johnson was offended. 'If you don't believe me, I could show you the letter.'

'What letter?' asked the canon.

She was a little confused. 'Such a funny thing,' she said. 'When I left, I found some letters in my attaché case, because I did work for the firm out of hours, sometimes. And there was that one from the manager that said about the loss.' She glanced at the canon sideways.

'I should be very interested to see it,' he remarked.

She tossed her head. 'I don't mind showing it to you.'

Three days later Mr. Heinroth sat in quiet thought

in his office for ten minutes, undisturbed. At the end of it he lifted the telephone upon his desk and rang up Warren.

'Morning, old boy,' he said. 'Give me a quarter of an hour if I come round at once?'

'What's it about?'

'Tell you when I see you. That all right? All right, old boy, I'll come right over.'

Warren laid down the receiver. There was too much 'old boy' about that conversation to be altogether healthy. He had worked with Heinroth ever since the War, and knew his moods.

Mr. Heinroth came into his office and accepted a cigarette. 'First, about this Laevol order for the ships,' he said. 'Is it true that they've stopped progress payments to the Hawside Company?'

Warren passed a hand over his eyes. 'Not quite. As you know, the Government has placed restrictions upon the export of credits from the country. The usual thing—there must be reciprocity.'

Heinroth smiled. 'You'll have to take your progress payments in olive oil and dates?'

'Broadly speaking—that is how it stands at the moment. It's a breach of contract with the Hawside Company, of course.'

'That won't help you pay your wages. Unless, of course, you can pay those in olive oil and dates.'

'It's not so bad as that. The Company could finish off these tankers on its capital, if no more payments were forthcoming of any sort.'

'It's not so good, old boy.'

'I quite agree. But revolutions never are so good.'

Mr. Heinroth got up from his chair, and crossed over to the window. He stood there with his back to the room, looking down upon the little City court that gave on to Cornhill, a few square yards of meagre grass and stunted laurel.

'There's going to be a row about the Hawside Company, Warren,' he said, without turning round.

'Who's making it?'

'Castroni.'

He turned back into the room. 'There's real trouble there,' he said. 'We've worked together now for fifteen years, and I thought I'd come along and let you know. I had Castroni in my office half an hour ago. He's got a letter that a man called Grierson—your manager, I think—wrote to you before the issue, about a fifty thousand loss.'

Warren bent down, opened a drawer of his desk, and searched carefully through some papers. 'Yes,' he said quietly, 'he's probably got that. What's he going to do with it?'

The Jew hesitated. 'He's gone down to the City Police with it,' he said gently. 'It's not Castroni really —it's some client of his that pushed him into this. But I thought I'd come along and let you know.'

There was a silence for a minute. Then Warren said, 'It's good of you to have come round, Heinroth.' He smiled, with a sardonic humour. 'Perhaps one day I'll be able to do as much for you.'

The other laughed. 'Not me, old boy—I've got my fingers crossed. I keep them that way all the time.'

He went away, and Warren sat back in his chair for a few minutes, considering the matter. Then he buzzed for Morgan.

'I'm going up to Sharples at once,' he said. 'On the noon train. Ring up Lord Cheriton at the Yard, and tell him that I'm coming up, and that I'd like to dine with him to-night. Say I've got something urgent to discuss. Ring Plumberg and say that I can't see him this afternoon. Put off Delaney. If anybody calls while I'm away, you can say where I am and I'll be back on Thursday morning.'

That night he dined with young Lord Cheriton, alone with his wife at their country house at Garton, ten miles west of Sharples. When Lady Cheriton had left them with the coffee and cigars he broached the subject that he had come north about.

'There's trouble about the Company, down in the City, Cheriton,' he said.

His host did not seem very much put out. 'Have another glass of port,' he said. He shoved the decanter across the table. 'Is it over the prospectus?'

Warren raised his eyebrows. 'How did you know?'

The young man laughed. 'It was a pretty hot document. Jennings took me through it sentence by sentence, especially the bit about the profit we were going to make.'

'That's the bit that's making all the trouble. I suppose you know by now that we'll be making a colossal loss on these three ships?'

The young man shrugged his shoulders. 'I told Jennings that that seems to me to be beside the point. The real thing is—can we get the Company through and make it into a success? We decided we were going to start this thing and get some work back here again. Having decided to do that, we've got to see it through. As I told them all up here, you'd never have got the money if you'd told the public what the real position was.'

'We're a precious pair,' said Warren very quietly. 'Couple of bloody share-pushers, if you ask me.'

'That's right,' said Cheriton. 'I don't want you to think that I came into this thing with my eyes shut. I took a good deal of advice, as a matter of fact. It seemed to me to be a good thing to do. I'm sorry if we're going to burn our fingers now—that's just too bad. But I'm not sorry that we started up this thing in Sharples.'

He turned to Warren. 'What is this trouble all about?'

Warren told him, omitting the City Police.

They smoked in silence for a time.

'Are all of us in this?' asked Cheriton. 'We all signed the prospectus.'

Warren shook his head. 'We haven't got to be. You and Hogan have got to keep out of it—leave the dirt to me. I've been in the City all my life, and I know how to handle it.'

Cheriton frowned. 'I don't much like the sound of that.'

Warren smiled. 'I don't give a damn whether you like it or not,' he said. 'I'm chairman of the Company, and I'm telling you what I want done.'

He paused. 'You two have got to keep out of it. There's a bad row coming up, but if we're all mixed up in it the Company will bust, and that's not what we set out to achieve. Now, it's quite possible that I may have to resign from the Board over this. If that happens, you've got to take the chair yourself.'

The young man stirred uneasily. 'I can't do that. I haven't got enough experience.'

'You've got old Hogan behind you. He's too old to put into the chair, but he'll back you for all he's worth. Next, you've got to make Grierson managing director. He didn't have anything to do with the prospectus, and that will please the shareholders.'

The other nodded. 'That's a good move. I've been meaning to suggest that for some time.'

'If there's a row, and I retire, you'll have to call an extraordinary general meeting of the Company to make these changes. Have that in the Yard—the registered offices of the Company. It's three hundred miles from London, and you won't get many shareholders will come that far to make a row. I'll see that you get proxies enough to carry any motion that you want. Fix things so that the shareholders who do turn up have a look round the Yard before the meeting, and they'll come in all enthusiastic. And then, away you go with a new lease of life.'

The young man looked troubled. 'I see it can be managed,' he replied. 'At the same time, I hope very much that you aren't going to retire.'

'I hope so, too. I started this thing, and I want to see it through. At the same time, we've got to think first of the Company. If the hunt is really up, and I'm afraid it is, you may be better off without me. But we'll have to see how it goes on.'

'There's one good thing,' said Cheriton. 'I think we can get all the work we want to keep the Yard alive. Old Hogan's found another shipowner—wants two small colliers.'

Warren grunted. 'You'd better stick out for a better price, from now on.'

Next day he went down to the Yard with Cheriton. The three large berths were occupied by frames and steelwork growing into oil tankers; on the first of these the framework was completed, and the plating well ahead. In one of the two smaller berths the keel plate of the little tramp had been laid down, and frames were laid out on the ground beside.

'It's coming on,' said Warren to Grierson. 'Beginning to see something now.'

'Oh, aye. And the men are working better, too.'

'How many have you got employed?'

'Something over fourteen hundred. I'll find out for you, and let you know. But we'll be needing a lot more, now we're coming on to the plating. That releases a lot of work, you understand.'

'How many will you have employed by August?'

'The inside of two thousand five hundred,' said the manager, after a minute's thought. 'Two three to two five.'

'And launch the first one at the end of October?'

'Aye—we'll not be far off that.'

Warren stared up at the framing, towering high above his head. 'It's so—immense . . .' he said slowly. 'I've never watched ships being built before. I'd not know how to start about a job like this.'

Grierson chuckled. 'Start where you started this one, Mr. Warren,' he remarked. 'Down in an office in the City.'

Warren smiled. 'I meant the building of them.'

'Oh, aye, it's not that difficult. You keep on adding bit to bit, you understand, and they get done before you know.'

Warren spent the morning wandering around the Yard. He was amazed again at what he had created. He watched the growing ships, the working men; it was incredible to him that he had started all this industry. He could not make himself believe that he was part of the organisation; he saw himself as a spectator to a great work being done by someone else.

He left that Yard at lunch time with regret, and went up to the hospital to lunch with the Almoner. She was waiting for him in her little room, the table laid for lunch, the room alight with daffodils.

'It seems all wrong for you to be up here in the middle of the week,' she said. 'It makes me feel tomorrow will be Sunday.'

She paused. 'It doesn't mean trouble, does it?'

He smiled at her. 'Not more than I can manage.'

'How did the Laevol thing go off?'

'Oh, that's all right.'

She said no more, but busied herself in giving him his lunch. She talked to him of Sharples, of the Yard and of the hospital; she told him there was talk of a new cinema.

'Another thing,' she said. 'There aren't so many patients coming to the hospital. I was going over the returns with Mr. Williams, and comparing them with last year. Out-patients are down a lot. In-patients as well, but not so much.'

'You'll be losing your job if this goes on.'

'I don't know that I'd mind so much about that now.'

He nodded slowly. 'It makes a difference, now the place is getting on its feet. I feel the same.'

She looked up, startled. 'You do?'

He did not answer her question, but began to talk about the Council, and the administration of the town. But with the coffee he turned again to her.

'I'm going back on the four-thirty,' he said. 'Before I go, I'm going to take a walk up on to the hill—towards the mine. Would you care to come up there this afternoon?'

'What for?'

He smiled. 'I want to see the place as a whole, before I go back.'

She thought about it for a moment. 'I'd like to.'

In the warm afternoon they walked together up the

hill out of the town. At the top, they paused beside a gate.

'This is the place I wanted to come to,' he said. 'We came here once before.'

She nodded. 'You told me you were going to put the town to work again. And now you've done it. Are you satisfied?'

He stared out over the town. A wreath of smoke hung over it, dimming the outlines of the river. 'It's not finished yet,' he said. 'We've only made a start. I'd like to see the rolling-mills get started up, even if we had to leave the mine. But I think it will come now; if the Yard gets a decent run of work the rest will come back.'

He turned to her. 'I may be retiring from the Board,' he said.

She was amazed. 'But—you can't do that . . .' she said. 'I mean—you are the Company. You started it for us.'

He nodded. 'That's so. But there are two sorts of people in the company world—the starters and the runners. The people who can start things up aren't usually the best at running them—you want a different sort of mind for that. I've been a starter all my life— I never was a runner. But all my Board are runners— Cheriton, Hogan and Grierson. They're all good runners. Your Company would be quite safe with them.'

'But—why should you retire?'

'I've done my job,' he said simply, 'and I'm tired. I want to have a rest.'

She laid her hand upon his arm. 'You ought to take a holiday.'

'I may be going to retire from business altogether,' he said. 'I don't know that I shall ever work again.'

There was a momentary silence, and then he said,

'When my wife left me, I had to look around for something big to get stuck into—in the way of work. I found this Sharples thing to work at. It's been the hardest thing I've ever had to tackle, and the best worth doing. But now, my job is coming to an end; Sharples is going now. There'll be difficulties ahead, of course, but not more than the Yard can overcome. There's not the need for me here now. I might look out for something else to start, but I don't think I shall.'

'You must take a long rest,' she said. 'Travel for a time —forget about your work.'

He smiled. 'It's not much fun doing that alone. Would you come with me?'

There was a pause; the wind sighed in the hedges, over the blackened town. 'If you wanted me to,' she said quietly.

He shook his head. 'There's a couple of months to go before my decree gets made absolute,' he said. 'We'll wait and see what happens in the meantime.'

She raised her eyes to his. 'I know that you're expecting trouble of some sort,' she said. 'I don't know what it is, and you don't want to tell me. But I want you to know this. I'm here, if you want me, and I'll always be here if you want me. That—that's what I wanted you to know.'

He smiled down at her. 'I've known that long enough. If it hadn't been for that I should have chucked this Sharples business long ago.'

She dropped her eyes. 'I'm not sure that I quite know what you mean.'

'I mean just this,' he said. 'You had faith in the town, that it could pull itself up out of the mess if once it got a chance. And I had faith in you.'

He stared out over the river and the Yard. 'That's what brought work back here again,' he said.

224

He turned to her, and took her hand in his. 'We'll be able to do great things together,' he said quietly. 'I might put off retiring, after all.'

She stood there looking up at him, her hand held in his own. 'You've got your own romantic style,' she said softly. 'I like it, Henry, because it's you—the real you. I wouldn't feel it was the real you if you were making love to me, in all your trouble. I'd feel that you were acting. But when we get in smoother water, I'll expect a bit more than talk about your companies.'

He stroked the hand that he still held in his own. 'A house in Oxfordshire,' he said. 'In the country somewhere, by a river. Where one could do some fishing, of the quieter sort. Would that be what you'd like?'

She nodded without speaking.

And presently she stirred. 'It's nearly four,' she said. 'I know you want to catch that train, and I won't keep you maundering with me. But Henry—remember this. I'm always here.'

'I know, my dear,' he said. 'It's that that makes this bloody thing worth while.'

He went back with her to the town, and caught his train to London. He took a taxi to his flat and slept uneasily; in the morning he went down to his office.

Morgan came in to him shortly after he arrived. 'A Superintendent Bullen of the City Police was here late yesterday afternoon,' he said. 'I told him that you would be in in the morning.'

There was a momentary silence.

'All right,' said Warren evenly. 'I'll give him a ring.'

The secretary retired. Warren got up from his desk, walked to the window, and stood for a few minutes looking down on the familiar little court. Then he turned back to the telephone.

'Superintendent Bullen?' he enquired. 'This is Henry Warren speaking—Warren Sons and Mortimer.'

He listened for a moment. 'You'd better come along here right away.'

In a few minutes two quietly dressed City gentlemen were with him in the room.

'I shall have to ask you to come down the street with me to my office, Mr. Warren,' said the Superintendent. 'I have a warrant here for your arrest, on charges in connection with the Hawside Ship and Engineering Company Ltd.'

CHAPTER XIII

ALLARDYCE, his solicitor, was distressed and shocked. He came hurrying to the Guildhall, to the visiting-room where Warren was waiting for him. A policeman was seated in the room.

Warren rose from behind the long table that divided the room. 'Sorry to have brought you to a place like this,' he said.

The solicitor sank into a chair on the other side of the table. 'I cannot tell you how sorry I was to get your message. Still—I understand that our time is limited. I have found out that you appear before the magistrates to-morrow morning—yes, of course, you know that. The police will ask for a remand. I shall apply for bail, of course.'

'You won't get it,' said Warren.

'I think we may. I shall plead that in a case of this sort the defence cannot be handled adequately except in your own office. The complexity of the matter. The mass of documents that have to be examined.'

Warren smiled. 'There isn't going to be a defence,' he said.

Allardyce eyed him seriously. 'Do you mean you want to plead guilty?'

'That's right.'

The solicitor was silent. 'I find that very difficult to believe,' he said at last. 'If facts are as stated in the charge, there must be some good reason for those facts. Your business isn't a bucket shop. You had no reason to want to make money in that way—and in point of fact, I understand that you made practically nothing out of the issue.'

Warren nodded. 'All the same,' he said, 'there will be no defence.'

'Why not?'

'For several reasons. Firstly, because I did it.'

The solicitor raised his hand, and shot a quick glance at the policeman.

'I very much appreciate your wish to get me out of this,' said Warren. 'But frankly, Allardyce, that isn't practical. There's a confidential letter of mine that they've got hold of which blows the gaff properly. I'm sorry, but there it is. It's a waste of my money and the Crown's money to contest a case like this.'

I think,' said the solicitor, 'that you should make an effort.'

'I don't,' said Warren.

After a pause he said, 'You'd better understand my point of view. We couldn't win this case, but even if we did, I'm finished in the City after this. That's the first point—whether we plead guilty or not guilty, I'm retiring from the City.'

'I see that,' said Allardyce thoughtfully.

'The next thing is, I'm very much concerned about the Hawside Company. I took all of this risk upon myself to get that shipyard started up, and if it comes to grief I shall have done it all for nothing. My arrest won't have done them any good. Still, they'll get over that, I think—so long as it doesn't drag on for too long. But the quicker it's over, and the less dirty linen washed in public, the better chance that Company will have.'

'Is your interest in the Company so valuable as that?'

Warren shook his head. 'I haven't got much in it.

About three thousand pounds or so. But I should be very sorry to see it go under now. Given a decent chance, I think it can get through.'

The solicitor gazed at him curiously. 'It seems to mean a great deal to you. But surely, a company that has no soul to be damned, nor backside to be kicked, hardly deserves so much consideration.'

'Our time is getting short,' said Warren. 'That is my line, and that is what I'm going to do. How long do you think I'll get?'

The solicitor laughed nervously. 'I really don't know. Eighteen months?'

Warren shook his head. 'I think a good bit more than that.'

He appeared next morning in the police court, neatly dressed and listening to the proceedings with detached gravity. The charges were read over in the court:

'. . . for that he, Henry Warren, on the twelfth day of November, 1934, being a director of a public company called the Hawside Ship and Engineering Company did circulate a certain written statement which was false in certain material particulars, to wit, in that it was therein falsely stated that certain orders undertaken by the company should prove to be profitable, he the said Henry Warren well knowing the said statement to be false; with intent to induce divers persons unknown to become shareholders in the said public company, contrary to Section 84 of the Larceny Act, 1861.'

For good measure, he was also charged with fraudently converting moneys belonging to the company for his own use.

The police asked for a remand, which was granted. Allardyce asked for bail, which was refused. Warren went to Brixton in the Black Maria, after formalities in court which had lasted barely for ten minutes.

'Let me get on with it,' he said to Allardyce that afternoon. 'You can plead not guilty to that second charge, of fraudulent conversion. But there's nothing in that—they'll cut it out before the trial.'

'You're still sure that you want to plead guilty on the first charge?'

'Absolutely. All you've got to do is to get it through as quickly and as quietly as possible.'

The solicitor sighed. 'If that's really the line you want to take, I'll do my best for you.'

'There's one thing more. Tell Morgan to come down and see me here to-morrow. There's a good bit of business to be cleared up before I go into retirement.'

'I suppose so. What are you going to do with Warren Sons and Mortimer?'

'That's what I am wondering myself.'

He settled down in Brixton not uncomfortably. His room was bare, but that worried him very little, nor did the close restraint distress him. He discovered that the first and most important element of comfort is an easy mind; freedom from worry and responsibility, he found, formed a considerable palliative to his imprisonment. He had no regrets about the issue of his false prospectus, no great sense of guilt. Instead he had a feeling of achievement and of work well done. Within a very few days of his incarceration he found that he could lie contented on his bed for a great part of the day, quietly contemplating what he had done, what lay before him.

'You'd hardly believe it,' said Morgan to his wife one

night, 'but I believe he's happier in prison than he was when he was out.'

'That may well be, with the sort of wife he had.'

'That may be something to do with it. But he hasn't seen her for a year or so. The decree will be made absolute next month.'

'Is he quite right in his head?'

'I think so. But you know how irritable he used to be? Well, you'd think it would be worse than ever now. Not a bit of it. I've never known him so good-humoured.'

His wife smiled. 'Maybe he's got another girl,' she said.

'If that's it, she may have to wait some time,' said Morgan.

In Sharples the news was greeted with dismay. Warren had never taken any public part in the affairs of the town, had never made a speech or attended any sort of public function. Only a few people in the town knew him by sight. In spite of this, perhaps, because of this, he had become a legend in the place, a myth, a fairy tale. For the last six months every child in the town had known the story of the stranger, the poor tramp who had been operated on up in the hospital, who, turning to fairy banker, in gratitude had started up the shipyard for them once again and set them working on three oil tankers, with money coming in regular. Every mother told that story to her children; in the secretive, dumb hearts of the adolescents it burned like a flame. In the pubs towards closing time the men, alcoholically senti-mental, would lift their cans to 'Mister Bloody Warren', and turn again to their darts.

And now their Mr. Warren was in clink. It was a shocking thing, incredible. The solid earth beneath their feet seemed to tremble and to slip away; before them loomed the abyss of unemployment once again.

The Almoner heard it first from Mr. Williams. He was working at his ledgers as she came into the office; he stopped, and raised his head.

'Did ye hear the news?' he asked, uncertainly.

She shook her head. 'What's that?'

He hesitated. 'They're saying your Mr. Warren's in a bit of trouble,' he said diffidently.

She said, 'Where?'

'I'm hoping maybe that it's wrong,' he said gently. 'But they're saying that he's been arrested, in London, for fraudulent conversion and a charge of falsifying a prospectus.'

She did not speak.

'I think is must be all of a mistake,' he said, after a moment.

She shook her head. 'I don't think so. I think it may be true.'

She turned to him. 'Where did you get this from?'

'I was on the telephone down to the Yard, speaking to Jennings. He told me that the news had just come through.'

'He knew that this was coming,' she said in a low tone. 'All the time when he was up here last, he must have known of this.'

She raised her head. 'Let me know anything else you hear.' She left him, and went up to her room.

She sat for half an hour upon her bed, staring before her, motionless. Then she got up, took out a writing pad, and settled down to put her thoughts into a letter.

I don't know what the trouble is exactly, yet, [she wrote]. *Probably if I did I shouldn't understand it, because I suppose it's all company and business stuff. All I know is what everybody else in Sharples knows; that over two thousand families are now in work and happy, who last year were sinking, down and out, and utterly wretched. I know that that is what you set out to do, and whatever else may happen now, I think you must be very proud and happy to have done so much for us. And as for me, I'm very proud that I've had the experience of seeing such a wonderful thing done, even at such a cost. You told me from the first that nothing could be done for us by honest means. I can't be sorry for the decision that you took, and I don't suppose you are. But I am most deeply sorry that you didn't have the luck to get away with it.*

I suppose that you are going to be tried upon these charges. I can't believe it will go wrong for you; I shall be praying all the luck in the world for you on that day, and everyone up here will be doing the same. But if things should go badly, then I want you to know that I'm with you one hundred per cent. I've lost the sense of difference between the right thing and the wrong thing long ago where Sharples was concerned. I only know one thing for certain; that what you did for us up here was right. My dear, I'm terribly proud of you.

Warren received this letter in Brixton Prison. He answered it a couple of days later.

My dear,

I want to thank you for your letter, and I want to tell you myself, rather than you should see it in the papers, that I'm going to prison. In business there isn't a shadow of excuse for what I did. I am certainly guilty on the first charge, and I should only waste the time and money of the court by pleading otherwise. And so, I am afraid that it may be some time before we meet again.

My main concern now is to see that the Company gets through. I think it will do so, given reasonable luck in trade revival in the country, and that now seems to be well on the way. I have seen Cheriton and Hogan in that last few days and told them what I think they ought to do, and now it is largely out of my hands. This time in Brixton on remand is valuable to me because I can write letters relatively freely, and I am making what arrangements are in my power so to arrange my own business that it can be called upon to support your company in Sharples with financial help, if needs be, while I am in prison. Later on the letter position will get more difficult—one in three months seems to be the ration— and so I must do all my business now.

And lastly, about ourselves. In a few weeks' time my decree will be made absolute. If I had got away with it in this affair, I should have asked you to marry me as soon as that happened. I believe you know that. Because I'm now in quod, I'm not going to insult your intelligence by pretending that I'm just a very good friend. I'm not. When I get out of this I shall probably ask you to marry me because I think we could be wonderfully happy together—and you'll probably refuse me for my prison record. That's all I'm going to say about that, but now you know what's coming to you.

Be tranquil. It isn't coming for some time.

Warren was tried at the Old Bailey, about a month after his arrest. Because of his plea of guilty to the first charge the proceedings were short, almost a formality. No evidence was offered by the Crown upon the second charge, and acquittal on this charge was ordered by the judge. The first charge was proved upon the plea of guilty.

The judge, magnificent in scarlet and ermine, said:
'You have pleaded guilty to the charge of issuing a

234

prospectus statement of the Hawside Ship and Engineering Company, well knowing that statement to be false in its material particulars, with the intention of defrauding the public. That charge has now been proved against you. It has been suggested upon your behalf that I should treat this as a first offence. I cannot take that course. A heartless and wicked fraud has been practised upon the public, which must bring a great deal of distress to many people; in my view that offence is aggravated by the position which you have held hitherto. I find that the charge has been proved against you, I find that fraud was committed deliberately for your own ends, and I sentence you to three years' penal servitude.'

Warren was ushered from the dock, and the judge turned to the next case.

He served his sentence in Parkhurst Prison, in the Isle of Wight. He was taken there by two prison officers three days after the trial, admitted to the prison, and put into a cell.

He was uncomfortable at first, with all the strangeness of a new boy at school. He found Parkhurst to be not unlike his public school in many ways, and very similar indeed to the new boy. There was the same awkward search for information about times of work and exercise and meals, about rights and privileges.

Another similarity that made him feel at home in the first days was to the Army. He had served for the first six months of the War as a private soldier, a gunner in the Royal Field Artillery; rough food and clothing were no novelty to him. He did not like them, but they held no terrors for him; they were not strange, unknown things. And in another way, they brought with them an association that was not unwelcome to him.

This association was a memory of a very restful time.

235

Looking back upon his life since he had left his public school, the five years before the War, the War itself, and the time subsequent, one period stood out in memory as utterly different from the rest. During the time when he had been a private soldier he had held no responsibility for anything at all. That made that six months totally different from the rest of his working life. It had been a pleasant time, a very restful time, when nothing had been expected of him but that he should keep his body and his equipment clean and in good condition. Beyond that, he was not responsible for anything at all, not even for securing his own food or his own bed. All that was done for him. He held that six months in his memory as a time of great mental rest, a peace that he had never known before or since.

In Parkhurst Prison he found these circumstances to be largely reproduced, but modified in ways that made them appropriate to his age. The immensely strenuous physical labour of the Army was replaced by a working day of five hours in the shoe shop, learning to build army boots, and by an hour's parade a day in the prison exercise yard. The rest of the twenty-four hours were spent in his cell, with no responsibilities at all.

It lies in the nature of a man to make himself a home, and Warren grew very fond of his cell. It was a small room, but big enough for him, with walls half painted, half whitewashed, and kept at a comfortable temperature by a hot-water radiator. The heavily barred window looked to the east over the Cowes-Newport road and the valley of the Medina to the higher land by Wootton; being upon the top floor of his hall he could see most of the east end of the Island. He soon found that the prison discipline wisely connives at the possession of small, innocent articles, and in the eighth month of his sentence he obtained possession of a small telescope constructed out of cardboard tubes. From that time on the scrutiny of the wide, varied countryside became an abiding interest to him; for the first time in his life he had leisure to enjoy and savour to the full the simple pleasure of watching other people go about their work.

He was allowed two books a week from the prison library. In the first week of his sentence he read both books through in one day, devouring them with the swift efficiency that he gave to all his business matters. He finished that day with the restless, nervous fatigue that he had come to regard as part of a normal life—and was out of literature for the rest of the week. On the third day he read half of one of the books through again, and was surprised to notice that there was something to be gained by doing so.

By the third month he was taking his books slowly, as a connoisseur, thinking about them and extracting the last ounce from each. Never before had he had leisure to do that with any book, and he found a new pleasure in reading in this way.

For the first time in his life, too, he had long hours for reflection. He soon found that it was possible to sleep more than twelve hours a day, and he did so for months on end; in spite of that, there were many hours in each day when he had no occupation but to reflect. His reflections were not troublesome to him. He would have to serve two years and three months if he obtained full remission of sentence for good conduct; he had arranged a calendar among the studs on the door of his cell on which he could cross off the days in pencil. He was forty-four years old. It was a pity to lose two years and three months of your life at that age, but it was not an impossibly long time, and he was not distressed by the idea. His sentence had not involved the loss of any money to him personally, and he would still have ample for his needs when he came out of prison. He would never be able to go back to the City. He did not particularly want to do so. But he would have to find some other occupation for his still abundant energy, and it was on that problem that his reflections principally concentrated.

With his restless, vivid imagination that had started so many enterprises in the past, this soon developed into an absorbing occupation. With a pencil on a sheet of paper he planned for himself a contemplation, a comprehensive mental survey which would cover the entire field of possible occupations for his later years. He planned his survey in main sections of industries and occupations, with subsections geographical. Thus on a morning, turning to his page, he would discover that his programme was to consider the timber industry on the west coast of Canada. That day the active brain was dragging out of pigeon-holes in that dim filing-room we call the memory all that he had ever heard about that industry, the economics, processes, personalities, geography, scenery, potentialities. All day he lay upon his bed, sifting and sorting his material, occupied and amused.

He was, in fact, engaged in living a life of pure contemplation in conditions that were comfortable and yet sufficiently ascetic. His position was entirely comparable to that of a novice in a monastery. The same detachment from the turmoil of the outside world, the same ascetic life, the same long hours of contemplation rule the novice and the prisoner, and Warren found in prison a great part of the peace that a more devout man might find within a monastery.

And with this peace, cause or effect, came sleep. The

238

nervous strain of twenty years came soaking out of him in month after month of quiet, dreamless sleep. He slept, and slept, and slept.

A convict in prison is allowed a visit from a friend or relative after the first four months of his sentence, thereafter every three months; in long sentences the visits grow more frequent as the years go on. The visit lasts for half an hour. Warren's first visit, after four months, was by Lord Cheriton.

They met in one of the visiting-rooms down by the gate.

'We've not got very long,' said Cheriton. 'I came down because I knew that you'd like to hear how things are going on in Sharples, and because I want your advice before our next Board meeting.'

'How did your Extraordinary General Meeting go off?'

'Never a hitch. Only about seven turned up, and those principally because they wanted to see the Yard at work. We elected Grierson to the Board, you know.'

Warren nodded. 'That was the right thing to do.'

'I think so. Now for the orders in hand. The Laevol orders are much more secure now than when you saw them last—the Delaware Oil Corporation have come in on that, you know. The progress payments are practically up-to-date, and I think those ships will be all right. But if they aren't, the North Borneos are in the market for two tankers. Hogan reckons he could shift two of them there, if needs be. But I think they'll be all right with Laevol.'

'Watch out for trickery on the last payment,' said Warren. 'Take nothing but real money.'

Cheriton nodded. 'After the tankers, we've got three small tramps, and one vessel of eight thousand tons—

for Carew and Mason. She's at a fair price—the others aren't so good. But the real thing is, we've got a good chance of a look-in on the Admiralty side.'

'Rearmament?'

'That's right. I went with Hogan to the Admiralty the other day for a formal conference on our capacity. They've got us earmarked for a couple of destroyers, if things get too bad politically and they have to accelerate the programme.'

'That's very good, if it comes off.'

'I don't suppose it will. Now, that's about all of my news. We've got two thousand eight hundred men employed, and that's about our full capacity, unless we went on night shift and that's not practical upon commercial work.'

He paused. 'Now, what I want from you is this, Warren. Have you got any view about our first year's balance sheet?'

'Plenty,' said Warren.

He leaned his arms upon the table. 'You must make this first year's accounts as bad as ever they can be,' he said. 'You've got a marvellous opportunity to do so now, one that you'll never have again. You must examine every contract that you've got, with Jennings, and Grierson must tell the auditors that every contract will be carried out at a loss. He'll probably be right, of course—but he must pile it on. You've got to make reserves this year against every possible contingency, probable or improbable.'

'I see.'

'You must show in this year all the losses that you're going to make next year, and the year after. If you can swing the figure of this year's loss up to a hundred thousand pounds—that's grand. If you can get the auditors to make it a hundred and fifty thousand—so much the better.'

Cheriton shook his head. 'I don't think we could get it up to that.'

'Get it as high as you can. In your chairman's speech, just say that full reserves have been made in this year's accounts for contracts negotiated by the late chairman. That's literally all you need to say by way of explanation.'

'I don't exactly like the thought of that.'

'I do. Man alive, you've got a chance here to make the Yard secure for the next ten years if you can play your hand the way it should be played. Pile everything into this year's loss, including a lot that really ought not to be there. If you do that, next year you'll be bound to show a profit, and the year after, if you've done it properly this year. Then, as soon as you're showing profits and a decent show of orders in hand, get rid of this year's losses by writing down your capital, pay a dividend, and make another issue to replace the capital.'

'I see what you mean,' said Cheriton at last. 'I'll have to think it over. But we've got nobody upon the Board, now that you're shut up here, to help us in that sort of business.'

Warren smiled. 'That's probably a good thing, in itself. It's possible to be too clever in that way.' He thought for a minute. 'Still, I'm sure that what I've told you is your proper course. Look, go and have a talk with Heinroth. Tell him that you've seen me, and tell him that I've suggested this. Get his advice. He's very close in with the market, and he underwrote the issue, so he'll want to see it go. He's a good chap, too. Tell him I want his help in this thing as a personal matter. Take his advice.'

Cheriton nodded. 'He's a Jew, I suppose?'

'He is,' said Warren firmly, 'and a damn good chap. I did a lot with Heinroth, and he never let me down.'

Cheriton went away, and Warren settled down again to his quiet life. In a short letter, a fortnight later, Cheriton told Warren that they had discussed the Company with Heinroth, and that they were proceeding cautiously upon the lines that Warren had suggested.

He got another letter, a week after that, from Miss MacMahon. 'I don't know,' she wrote diffidently, 'if you would like me to come and see you. I'll understand you if you feel you'd rather not. But Lord Cheriton told me that he's been to see you, and I understand that you are allowed a visitor every three months. I have to come to London early in the New Year, and I could come on down from there. Get a message to me before then to let me know if you'd like me to come down; you know I'd come a great deal farther than that. But I know you can't write very often, so I shan't expect to hear from you before Christmas.'

He had an opportunity that month to include a message to her in a letter written to Cheriton by special permission, on matters connected with the Company. He wrote, 'Tell Miss MacMahon I agree with her proposal in regard to the man that she wrote to me about, and I should be glad if she would carry on upon the lines that she suggests.'

She came to him on a raw, windy day in January, when he had served seven months of his sentence. She got up from the table as he came into the visiting-room.

'I shouldn't have known you,' she exclaimed. 'You're looking so well. Henry—whatever have they done to you? You're looking ten years younger.'

He smiled at her. 'I'm sorry, my dear. That wasn't what was meant to happen to me here.'

'But it has!' She stepped back merrily, and looked at him. 'It's quite absurd. You've put on weight, haven't you?'

He nodded. 'About a stone. I'm up to twelve stone now.'

'You should be more than that.' She came and sat down with him at the table, the warder discreetly in the background. 'You know, Henry, I was afraid you might be terribly run down. I sort of dreaded what you might be like. One thinks about such horrible things—prison, you know. When one doesn't know about it.'

'I know,' he said. 'It's very sweet of you to come.'

'I had to, if you'd let me. And now I find you simply bursting with health like this. My dear, I'm terribly glad. Tell me, do you find the time pass very slowly?'

He shook his head. 'I did for the first week. But now—I don't know. It just slips away.'

She settled down to tell him all about Sharples and such items of the business of the shipyard as she knew. He learned that the town was growing almost normal; new shops had been opened, Woolworths had returned, and the trams were running once again. There was a lot of talk that Lord Cheriton was trying to open up the rolling-mills again. Attendances at out-patients were very much down on last year. The first of the oil tankers had been launched shortly before Christmas, and was now finishing at the quayside. There was a lot of talk in the town that they might have to build destroyers for the Admiralty.

The half-hour allowed them for the visit, stretched by the warder in charge to forty minutes, was over before she had been able to tell him half of all her news; Warren went back to his cell, cheerful and content. Equally happily she walked back along the Cowes road to Newport station, to begin upon her long journey back to Sharples.

She came to him again in April, and in July, and every three months for the remainder of his sentence. In the intervals she wrote to him each week, long, informative letters designed to keep him in touch with the world of his business interests, to supply him with the information in the newspapers that were withheld from him. She got into touch with Morgan, still secretary of Warren Sons and Mortimer, and learned from him weekly what his chief would like to know. Besides her own news, and the news of Sharples, her letters told him about commodity prices, the Gold Standard, and the rates on Treasury Bills. He learned about the French Budget from her and about the changes in the Government in Greece, and he was continuously informed about the principal movements of the stock market.

In November 1937 Warren was released, and walked out of the prison a free man.

He had told nobody the exact day of his release; he did not know it himself until a few days previously. He went by bus to Cowes, and thence by boat and train to Southampton and London. There he reported to the Criminal Record Officer at Scotland Yard, and went to a hotel.

Next day, he travelled up to Sharples by night. He breakfasted in Newcastle, and took the local train to Sharples. A talkative gentleman, stout and rubicund, got into the carriage with him, observed that it was a fine morning, and extracted from him the information that he was going to Sharples.

'Eh, Sharples,' he said, wheezing a little. 'Wonderful the way that Sharples has come on. Time was—not so long ago, either—there wasn't a man in work in Sharples. And that's a fact I'm telling you.'

Warren nodded. 'I heard it had a bad time in the slump.'

'Aye. And then there was that financial swindle some years back. One of those fly-by-night City financiers—chairman of the shipyard, too—he got them in a proper mess. Got three years for it, he did, and serve him dam' well right. But since that time they've gone ahead, and they've been full of work this long time past. Building destroyers for the Admiralty now, so they tell me.'

'It's good to see the work come back again,' said Warren mildly.

'Aye. Barlows the shipyard was, before they changed the name. There was seven Barlow destroyers at the Battle of Jutland—did ye ever hear that?'

Warren got out of the train at Sharples, and went walking through the streets towards the Yard. The town was utterly different from his memory of it; in two and a half years it had changed almost beyond all recognition. The streets were full of cars, delivery vans, vehicles of all sorts; the pavements thronged with house-wives shopping with their baskets. The desolate air of cleanliness had altogether gone; the sky was grimed with chimney smoke. The children playing in the little streets looked more robust and better clothed, with colour in their cheeks. At every corner there appeared to be a new shop front, trams and buses clanged and screamed along the streets, and around the doors of the re-opened Woolworths perambulators were clustered thickly. He passed a new, large super-cinema.

The clamour of the shipyard beat upon his ears a quarter of a mile away, the surge and ebb of the clatter of the pneumatic riveters. As he approached the gate he saw the half-built ships looming up behind the wall; there was one, half plated on the slips, that was obviously a warship of some sort. He approached the gate slowly, almost diffidently. So much had happened here; it was so different from when he last had seen it. He had the feeling of an interloper in the place.

Upon the blackened, ten-foot wall not many yards from the gate there was a sign that he did not remember. Hesitating for a moment to go in, he went across to look at it. It was a bronze plaque, about three feet square, apparently a memorial of some sort, dignified and restrained. As he approached he saw it bore, embossed in low relief, the sculptured head and shoulders of a man, in profile. He read the words below.

HENRY WARREN

1934

HE GAVE US WORK

He stood there staring at it for a few minutes, smiling a little; illogically moisture welled into his eyes. A few children, playing some complicated game chalked out upon the pavement, stopped to notice the stranger.

'Mary,' said Ellen Anderson in a hoarse whisper. 'Ma-ree! Coom over here. I got somethin' I want to tell you.'

'That bloke there,' she whispered. 'It's the man in the picture.'

' 'Tisn't.'

' 'Course it is.'

'I bet you 'tisn't.'

'I bet *you*.'

'All right. Now you got to go and ask him.'

246

Ellen wriggled nervously. '*You* ask him.'

'*You* got to ask him. You bet it was.'

'All right. I *will* ask him.' Warren became aware of a very dirty little girl pulling at his sleeve.

'Please, mister,' she whispered nervously. 'Are you the man in the picsher?'

Warren smiled. 'That's right,' he said. 'I'm the man in the picture.'

The little girl left him, sped across the road, and into the kitchen of a little house. 'Coom over here and look, Mummy—quick!' she gasped. 'I seen the man in the picsher!'

Warren turned into the Yard, and went down to the office.

In the African bush, and in towns like Sharples, news travels very fast. Warren was hardly at the office building before a dozen women were clustered at the gate, peering at him down the entrance road. He had hardly got to Cheriton's office before the men upon the ships knew all about it. A chattering and gossiping ran down the streets from house to house; women threw their shawls over their heads, went to the door and out into the street—to see what was happening. Within the Yard the men upon the ground sidled towards the offices; the men upon the ships, seeing the flow, knocked off their work and paused to watch. The word went round from mouth to mouth that Mr. Warren had come back.

Dennison, the foreman plater, stopped a thin trickle of men leaving the job. 'God love us, men,' he cried, 'are ye all daft? It's twenty minutes yet to go before dinner. Get back on to the job.'

'They're saying Mr. Warren's in the offices.'

'What's that to you? Get back along, and go on working till it's time for dinner.'

247

'Hoots,' said one. 'If it wasn't for Mr. Warren there wouldn't be no dinner.'

There was a laugh. The stream of men towards the offices grew larger, uncontrollable. In a moment men were streaming off the ships, the foremen pleading with them desperately. Only the fitters in the engine-room of one destroyer stayed at work; their foreman had been middleweight boxing champion in the Navy.

The men surged round the offices. They surged into the time office led by Jock McCoy, a charge hand labourer. The desk clerk rose like a flushed partridge.

'You're not allowed in here,' he cried.

The navvy thrust his way across the room. 'Git oot o' the way, ye wee daft fule,' he said. 'There ane thing only in this place will tell the toon that Mr. Warren's back, an' that thing's gaen' to wurk. An' if ye dinna like it, ye can stop yer bluidy earoles.'

The hooter wailed in short, staccato bursts. It blew long blasts, short blasts, continuous blasts, intermittent blasts as various hands tried the experience of pulling at the cord. It brought the women to the doors, the shopkeepers out into the streets, enquiring what the noise was all about. It brought a stream of women and children down towards the gates. It brought the farm hands, far beyond the town, to a standstill beside their byres; in the little harbour at the entrance to the river it brought the fishermen together, wondering what the row was all about. It brought the stoker in the shipyard from his boilers in a frenzy, agonised that he was losing all his steam.

It brought the Sisters in the hospital to the entrance of their wards. It brought the porter flying to the Almoner's little office off the Secretary's room.

She started in her chair. 'But it can't be . . .' she

exclaimed. 'He wasn't coming here till some time next week!'

She sat hesitant, irresolute, listening to the mad cacophony of the hooter. Out of her window she saw people in the street, all streaming down towards the yard.

Mr. Williams came into his office, a sheaf of invoices in hand. He sat down at his table, opened a ledger. Presently he raised his head and looked at her.

'They're saying that your Mr. Warren's in the town,' he said mildly. 'Are ye no' going down to meet him?'

Then she, too, left her desk, and ran with the rest.

THE END